ENTANGLED
A MAGGIE FINN NOVEL

ENTANGLED
A MAGGIE FINN NOVEL

BY
KATHLEEN COSGROVE

ENTANGLED

Copyright © 2015 Kathleen Cosgrove

All rights reserved. No part of this book may be reproduced, duplicated, copied, or transmitted in any form or by any means without the express written consent and permission of the author.

This is a work of fiction. The names, characters, places, and incidents are fictitious or are used fictitiously. Any resemblance to any person or persons, living or dead, is purely coincidental.

ISBN: 1512332542
ISBN-13: 978-1512332544

Published by Kathleen Cosgrove

Cover Art by Charlie Wetherington
Interior by D. Alan Lewis

ACKNOWLEDGEMENTS

To the members of The Nashville Writer's Meetup Group / Mystery, Suspense, Thriller, Writers. Thank you for your help making this a better story than I could have written without you.

Special thanks to Lily Wilson and Bob Mangeot, brilliant writers each, for caring enough to make me a better writer.

To Author D. Alan Lewis for his technical help in turning my document into a book.

To Tom Coyne, Associate Medical Examiner in District 21 Florida, for generously sharing his expertise.

To Pam Bellotti, marine biologist, for her technical advice.

To Gary "Lash" Lashbrook for his insight into Vietnam veterans and PTSD, and for his service to our country.

DEDICATION

This is for my mother Chris and sister Pat who taught me how to keep on laughing through the scary parts, and for my brother Dave for always having my back.

ENTANGLED

ONE

The instructions the boat captain gave me for the use of the knife were vague, but I felt better having it in case I needed to cut myself free were I to be pulled through the Gulf of Mexico by my catch, a la Captain Ahab.

Deep-sea fishing can be fun as long as someone else baits the line, holds the pole for you until you get a bite and then hauls in the catch when your arms get tired. Thus was the experience for the four bikini clad co-eds who had also booked this charter.

I, on the other hand, have not worn a bikini since Jimmy Carter was nailing solar panels onto the roof of the White House. Today I was sporting a *Ben and Jerry's* ball cap, an oversized Yankees jersey that once belonged to my ex-husband and seven or eight layers of sunscreen.

Captain Billy, of *Billy's Big Boats,* was regaling the young ladies with his tale of once captaining the actor who played the blind guy in *Star Trek* when something nearly jerked me out of my chair. In truth I was strapped in, but the belt nearly sawed me in half.

"Billy?" I yelled to him. "Something's pulling here!"

Billy glanced over disinterestedly and said, "Good, good job Maggie, hold the line."

My feet could get no traction sliding in seawater and fish scales on a boat that was only slightly more seaworthy than a '58 Buick sealed with duct tape.

"Billy? I might need a hand here."

Billy did not hear me over the giggling, his own as well as the girls'.

The pull on my arms and hands was becoming painful but I was not about to let go, my pride wouldn't allow it. Those girls were young and beautiful and—young but I was the one that was going to haul in a, I don't know, a tuna or a giant squid.

I was like Spencer Tracy in *The Old Man and the Sea*. I began speaking to it using a Cuban accent.

"Fish, I love you and respect you very much but I will kill you dead before this day ends."

Sweat poured into my eyes and onto my sunglasses giving everything a blurry, distant look so I could not see if the fish was jumping, swimming away or charging me.

"Fish, you are a brave and worthy adversary but I am afraid that, on this day, you must die in order to fulfill my need to be avenged. Also, you will be a glorious meal to the many tourists who dine this night at The Gulfside Grill."

Just as my hands were losing their grip, *Billy's Big Boat* leaned hard to the port side as my catch stopped there, anchoring us. Two of the young ladies fell conveniently onto Billy who also fell, not so conveniently, into the bucket of chum.

The girls, now covered in minnows and shrimp, began to scream. Billy, scrambling to his feet, tripping over buckets and skidding in water was stringing curses together so creatively that, under different circumstances, I would have applauded. Then he and his crewmen attached the line to a mechanized pulley and drew up the catch. It turned out to be, not as I had suspected a gigantic fish, but a net filled with several medium-sized fish and three average-sized dead guys.

After some debate and even more gagging it was decided to cut the net and throw most of the dead sea-life over board. The bloated and horrifically disfigured bodies were then arranged, side-by-side, in the aft end of the boat.

Captain Billy called the marine police and one of his men sedated our hysterical debutants with Rum and Diet Coke. Someone found a pirate flag under a seat cushion and laid it across the men's faces but their distorted bodies were still visible to anyone brave enough to look. I tried, in the interest of journalism, because I was, in fact, a journalist to inspect them a bit closer. I especially wanted a better look at what appeared to be a whistle around the neck of one of the corpses. I knelt closer to look at it and at the same time inhaled the accompanying putrid odor. My next plan of action was to lean over the railing and recycle my lunch.

The bikini girls and the crew hovered so far to the front of the boat I thought we might take on water so I volunteered to go to the back and add my weight to that of the three guys on deck with their eyeballs missing.

On dry land, answering questions from one of the uniformed officers I said, "So, a triple murder, bet that's a call you don't get too often."

I had no idea if the men were murdered or merely drowned but I was baiting him, so to speak.

"Huh? What?" he asked, looking forlornly at his fellow officers who were assigned the task of questioning the girls from the boat who had been much too busy shrieking and saying, "Oh my God," to be bothered pulling t-shirts over their skimpy tops. The regularly scheduled late afternoon storm clouds were moving in from the west and the gusting wind that preceded them gave the women an even sexier, hair-blown look. It had all the makings of a Playboy photo shoot but with corpses.

He ignored my question and asked, "Why were you on the boat today?"

"I did a trade-off with Billy."

He raised an eyebrow, and before the smirk could fully form on his lips I said, "Don't *even* go there. We traded for ad space on my website."

I had no desire to speak to this man another minute. I wanted to talk to my only friend on the Fort Myers police force, Rose.

Rose Shelton is the new prodigy at the department. Her marksmanship skills are legendary; she's smart, ambitious and fun. She also happens to be one of the most beautiful women I know, an amalgam of Diana Ross and Jennifer Lopez with a Whoppi Goldberg attitude.

"Is Officer Shelton coming?" I asked. "I'd like to talk to her if she's here. No offense but we're friends."

"That figures," he said without looking up.

He wrote something on his notepad and I stood on my toes and craned my neck in an effort to read it.

"No, Shelton's working another case," he said, turning the pad away. "Did you know the deceased?"

"I'm the one that hooked them and reeled them in but other than that, no."

His expression became not so much one of admiration at my amazing dead-body retrieval skills, but more of an astonished one like I had sprouted antlers.

"Yes, yes, I know," I said. "I'm not sure I believe it myself and I was there. So, are we done? Because if we are I'd like to go speak to those gentlemen over there."

He nodded and I proceeded to where they were loading the bodies.

A woman I noticed as head of forensics was near the coroner's van. I almost didn't recognize her in the white coverall suit that made her look as though she were transporting plutonium.

"Hello," I called to her, in my practiced, non-intimidating yet firm voice.

She turned and said, "Oh, it's you, that figures."

"Hi Miranda, nice to see you too," I said. "Why are you, you know, doing this?" I turned my head into the back of the van.

Miranda was my version of an archenemy, but I needed her so I didn't take her attitude personally. I pretended she was merely socially awkward. I smiled broadly to help her feel less so.

"Don't touch anything," she said. "You're not supposed to be here anyway."

"A little late for that, I'm the one that reeled them in."

She raised her right eyebrow, that being a skill, by the way, I'd never been able to master.

"Ok, so, I had some help reeling them in, but it was me that hooked them and helped open the ne…"

She interrupted, "Yeah, why'd you do that? I thought you were experienced enough by now to know better than to tamper with evidence."

I could see sweat pouring from under her cap and running onto her paper mask; she looked hot and miserable. I gave her some slack.

"They were bodies. I mean, they, well, maybe I could have—I don't know—I had to…"

"What, you thought you could do a little C.P.R. maybe? Because it seems to me that a smart *blogger* like you would have sense enough to, I don't know, figure out when a body's been floating in the ocean for a few days."

She was right, I knew better.

I had firsthand experience investigating some fairly nasty criminals when I arrived in Florida a little more than a year ago. Now I write a crime-scene blog and sell ad space for it. It pays nearly nothing, but sometimes I can trade for stuff like this trip today. A police scanner that I found used on Craigslist, a Vespa, internet access, and the willingness, a calling even, to be annoying were all I needed to start my own little career in journalism. This was the *being annoying* part.

"So," I said, "they've been dead a few days? They've been in the water that whole time? Did you notice their eyeballs were missing? Do fish go for the eyeballs first?

She walked away, but I stayed on her like a border collie.

"How come forensics is messing with the bodies before the autopsy? You'll be able to tell if they died from drowning right? I mean, I was reading on my phone that if there's no water in the pleural cavity then they were dead before they went into the water, right? Oh and what was that whistle thing?"

She stopped, turned to look at me as if I had confessed to the Lindbergh kidnapping and said, "I'm sure you didn't take anything from any of the bodies. Even *you're* not that stupid."

"A, I'm not stupid, thank you. And B, of course I didn't take anything. Why, what's missing and how would you even know if something was missing, except, you know, their eyeballs?"

She turned and walked back to the group of men in coroner gear, and when I tried to follow she said, "That's as far as you go *Mizz* Finn. If you've given your statement already, you can leave the area."

"It's ok," I called to her retreating form. "I know these social interactions make you uncomfortable."

TWO

The neighbor's cat greeted me at my door.

"Sorry," I told the creature as it purred at my ankles, "I know I smell like a walking tin of sardines, but I've got nothing for you."

I grabbed a lavender scented fabric softener-sheet from the laundry room and held it under my nose. The five o'clock news was coming on soon, so my shower would have to wait a few minutes.

A drowning at a park was the lead story, then the weather report, and then a commercial. I used the time to pull off my clothes and throw a towel around me before the ad for Weight Watchers was over. I looked down at my half-naked body with its extra ten pounds and reminded myself the TV was not judging me. In the middle of rubbing my hair with another dryer sheet, they at last began their report on the three dead guys.

"Police have not yet identified the bodies of three men who were found today entangled in a large fishing net in the Gulf of Mexico about three miles from the coast of Fort Myers Beach. Mrs. Margaret Finn of Bonita Springs discovered the bodies, but has no alleged ties to any of the deceased. Although the official cause of death has not yet been determined, the police are not ruling out homicide. If you have any information regarding this case, you are asked to contact The Fort Myers Police Department at the number you see on your screen."

There was footage of Billy's boat, the police talking to the bikini girls, and what looked like my backside as I bent over to put some things in my bag while the voice-over narrated, *"Next up, a WINK news special report, is your toilet paper killing you? Brett Davies gives us an in-depth report on what deadly chemicals are used..."*

Hitting the power button on the remote, I said to the blank screen, "Nice segue guys."

After showering and washing my hair I realized I still smelled of chum and dead bodies, so I went back and showered again.

I stuffed more dryer sheets in the pockets of my robe, and then sat at my desk to begin the day's blog entry.

Blog Sunday, June 16

Guess who hauled in her own crime scene from the depths of the Gulf of Mexico today? That's right, yours truly netted a catch of three dead bodies this afternoon while deep-sea fishing with Billy DeVito of Billy's Big Boats. So far, the police have not identified who they are, or how they died, but none of them had eyeballs. Do fish do that to bodies? Anyone with knowledge of that? The men were wearing wet suits and tanks. According to sources on the scene, their bodies appear to have been in the water for a couple of days at least. Without going into gruesome details I can tell you that it was pretty hard to make out much about their age or race. The wet suits and diving gear found with them looked generic, but I'm not an expert. One of the men had a chain with a whistle looking thing attached to it, around his neck. The net holding them, according to Billy, looked like a drift net, which he says is illegal. Anyone want to comment here on drift nets? There were lots of dead fish in there with them as well as a few dead sea-turtles. A sad and grotesque death for all. Keep checking in for more details as I get them. Comments please from anyone with information to add.

As always, please shop with our sponsors.
We're all here to be clear
Magpie

I tweeted the link for the blog, and posted to Facebook as well. I figured I'd probably get a few comments soon since it was Sunday evening, a good time for people to be home messing about on their computers, and trying to hold off Monday as if it were Godzilla rising from the Sea of Japan. I like Mondays myself. You can get stuff done, like go to police stations and coroner's offices without someone buzzing you through the front door. I find that terribly annoying, mostly since no one wants to buzz me in. They are the people stuck with the weekend shift and having to deal with me, in their minds, is piling on.

The stuff people choose to comment on in blogs is random in the extreme. Some merely write to say I'm pretty or ugly, some write to tell me they hate me, some have self-serving agendas to spew, but then sometimes I get comments that are relevant or helpful, amazing even, or at least well thought out. It's why I keep doing it; that, and being an investigative reporter was the dream I never fulfilled. It also supplements my real job. I do freelance copy editing for website companies. The pay is lousy but I work my own hours. The local paper does not like me at all, and the police find me a nuisance, but I'm pleasant and bring them pizza so they tolerate me.

I let the blog simmer out there in the interwebs while I fixed dinner and watched TV. I fried up some eggs after debating with myself what constituted a reasonable life span from *sell by* date to *eat by* date. My side dish of pretzels sat near me while I watched a documentary on the history of pie. I really wanted pie and looked in my refrigerator in case there was some in the back I had forgotten. Since I couldn't remember purchasing a pie in years, not surprisingly there was not one there.

I was feeling sorry for myself and my lack of coconut cream when I opened my laptop and refreshed the blog. I rubbed my eyes and did a double take, leaning close to the screen to make sure I was seeing it correctly. There were over a hundred comments on my post already. That's not *all* that unusual for my posts once they've sat there a few days, but this happened in a little under an hour.

"Drift nets are, and should be, illegal. If those guys were using driftnets then they deserved to die. If they died because they got caught in them, then that's poetic justice at its finest." Signed: gemeniguy

"Gemeniguy, first of all, that's not how you spell Gemini. Secondly, are you really saying that lives of those trying to make a living are literally worth less than the lives of fish?" Signed: grannybgoode

"Hey Granny, drift nets are illegal, you do the crime, you do the time and I can spell my name however the f'n hell I want to." Signed: gemeniguy

"Anyone can spell anything anyway they want, but don't be surprised when people take you for an illiterate, callous jerk." Signed grannybgoode

"Hey, gman1, I agree with you man, too many people out there over-fishing man. Grannyb, those guys had it coming. The gman is solid man." Signed thedude

"Holy shit dude, don't you know the difference between a gman and gemini?"
Signed numberonebeatlefan

"I thought this thread was supposed to be about the dead guys, not an f'in spelling bee. Go troll another blog, all of you. Signed justinsdaddy

And so it went for about twenty more comments with a couple of other people jumping into the fight before it got back to topic.

Most comments centered on illegal fishing. There were some theories about pirates, or killer dolphins, but most people fixed on the nets. Apparently large drift nets are illegal, but smaller ones are not. Everyone agreed I needed to more specific about the details of the net. They also wanted me to be more specific about the gruesome details.

The consensus seemed to be, that someone probably killed these guys for illegal fishing. This sounded extreme, but I had limited knowledge of the fishing industry and for all I knew it could be covered up in mob activity. There could be some big *fish cartels* with rival gangs taking over each other's watery territories. The more I thought of this, the more excited I got. This was going to be huge and I was in the center, as in, the safe center, in my house, on my computer.

Some people sleep with a gun in their bedside table; I sleep with a phone under my pillow. I'm nearly blind without my contacts, so the likelihood that I would wake and shoot my coat-stand rather than an intruder is about 100%. The worse thing I could do with my phone while nearsighted, would be to dial a wrong number. Or, in the case of this particular early morning, accidentally dial a friend.

"Rose, is that you?" I grabbed the phone from under my pillow when the sound of someone calling my name woke me.

"You snore," was her response.

"You called to tell me that?" I picked up the bedside clock, held it close and squinted.

"It's 3:30," I said

'You called me," she answered.

"Oh crap, sorry," I said, laying back down, rubbing my eyes. "You were the last number I called before going to bed. My head must have hit redial."

"Yeah, I got your message. The reason I wasn't at the beach today for your latest unholy mess, was because I was working another case. I heard about yours though. That makes four bodies in one day, a record for Fort Myers since I've been on the force."

"Another dead body?" I sat up, turned on the lamp, and propped pillows behind me. "Was that the one I heard about on the news, at a park?"

"Yep, now go to bed and set your phone in another room, I thought I had a pervert calling me."

"I can't go back to sleep now," I said, fumbling for my glasses. "I want to hear about your dead body. Was it an accident, or, you know—something *not* an accident?"

"Meet me at the north-end I HOP at seven," she said, and hung up.

Points of light danced on the waters of the Caloosahatchee River giving it the appearance that the heavens had showered it with billions of diamonds. A white-hot sun illuminated the gems, while boats bobbed up and down on tiny waves dancing between the sparkles. The Edison Bridge spanned this magical view, and ended just shy of the I HOP parking lot allowing me to admire the scene a few minutes more. I wondered if it were something I would ever take for granted. I promised myself I would not.

I gave my pupils a chance to adjust to the abrupt change in lighting, then scanned the room. Rose looks more like a model than a cop, so most people think she's in costume when she's dressed in her police blues. It was easy to find the booth she was in, all I had to do was follow the stares.

Rose was halfway through her *Rooty Tooty Fresh and Fruity* when I sat and ordered my breakfast off the senior menu.

"Started without you, sorry," she said between mouthfuls of blueberry pancakes. "I have to get back down to Dan's."

"Who's Dan?" I asked, pouring my coffee.

"Dolphin Dan, Dan,"

"It was Dan's place? The news made it sound like a real park."

"It *is* a real park, have you been out there lately?" she asked.

"No," I said. "He traded with me for ad space on my blog more than a year ago. It was supposed to be a *swim with the dolphins* thing. He only had one dolphin though, and all *it* did was circle the perimeter of a lagoon avoiding me for thirty minutes."

Our server brought my plate of two eggs and toast.

Rose laughed, "That would have been pretty funny to see."

"Yeah, it was loads of fun. To top it off, he keeps a pet pelican and the damned thing bit me."

"Well, it's the real deal now. Big enough to have animal rights groups after him. That was the vic, by the way."

"The victim was an activist?"

"Not heavy duty, but he did consult for one of them though, *Water Warriors*, they call themselves. It's one of those radical, crazy-ass groups. We're not sure if he got a job at Dan's to spy on him, but I don't think so. I think he was working there legit."

She slurped the last bit of soda from the bottom of her glass, and made a small burp.

"Scuse me," she said, and put a fist to the center of her chest and tapped it.

"How did he die?" I asked.

"Don't know yet, body's still at the coroner. Witness said he didn't see anything. The vic just went under and never came up, well, not till he floated up. At least that's what the guy who was with him said. I don't think it's legit though. The witness sounded kind of cagey, like he was hiding something."

"You think someone killed him?" I asked, forgetting about my food.

"I didn't say that. There you go, jumping to conclusions. No one except you has mentioned murder. Don't say that again or I'll quit telling you stuff."

"Sorry," I said, refilling my coffee, "but *what* then?"

"It's just my hunch, but my hunch is better than most people's facts. I get that from my Mexican grammy. She always knew when someone was lying, but she had to spit on 'em and see which way the saliva ran. I don't have to do that, which is good, because I'd lose my badge for sure if I started spittin' on perps."

"I've been reading about deaths from drowning after what happened yesterday. Are you sure he wasn't already dead before he went into the water? You can tell that, you know. So, if someone killed him and then…"

"How do I know?" she said, letting her fork fall to her plate for dramatic emphasis. "I'm telling you what the witness said. But like

I told you, he was acting all spooked, that's why I want to talk to him again."

"Is that where you're going now, to the park? Can I come with you?"

"Yes, and hell no. This ain't bring your sidekick to work day."

"Well, maybe I'll get a job at Dan's and go undercover," I said, watching her stand up to leave.

"Oh Lord I did not hear you say that. Whatever you do, I don't wanna know about it."

"I'm doing it!" I yelled to her as she left. Then I helped myself to her leftover pancakes.

THREE

I made the conscious decision *not to* wear make-up, and even toyed with the idea of not wearing deodorant or brushing my teeth in order to repel the advances of Dolphin Dan. But since I wanted to get info from him, and perhaps even a job, I decided to meet personal hygiene half way. It wasn't that Dan found me particularly attractive, he just came on to any woman between the ages of 24 and 104.

His great-grandfather had purchased a huge tract of beachfront property situated a little north of Bonita Beach in the late 1800's. He used it, most likely, for smuggling. It was never sold and eventually Dan inherited it. After being in the family for generations, it seemed particularly odd to me that it was being developed now.

It was now home to *Dan's Dolphin Experience* and was located off Estero Boulevard only a few miles north of Bonita Beach on Big Hickory Island. That area was as pristine and native as any coastal area in Florida. Except for a couple of speed limit signs, or a car pulled far off onto the shoulder where someone had found a good spot to fish from, there was nothing to see on either side of the road but brush.

Dan's lay on a narrow parcel of land that ran parallel between the highway and the beach, and was hidden from the road by a covering of trees. I remembered driving past it several times when I had been there previously because the sign that indicated the entrance was small and nearly hidden by brush. Now, several large *Coming Soon* banners and flags with the letters DD lined the road several feet before the entrance. The paved parking lot, which only a year ago had been gravel and mud, was now manned by an attendant who tried to get me to pay five dollars to park. After some arguing and a call from that employee to Dan, I was granted a free pass and directed to Dan's office. It was no longer a gutted 1967 Volkswagen bus, but an honest-to-God real building, next to a gift shop where a young woman wearing a *Dan's Dolphins* shirt and hat was putting plastic manatees on shelves. Dan met me there.

"Maggie, really good to see you," he shook my hand. "You gonna write about this on your blog? I have a press kit to give you and everything."

"A press kit, seriously? This place has got to be way more lavish than when I was here before."

"Oh yeah, you haven't been out here for a while then. We started the renovations a year ago last spring."

"Yeah, that would have been right after I was here, maybe it was my blog that helped your business."

"Hahaha, yeah, that's funny," he said, jabbing my shoulder with his fist.

"Well, I could write about the newly upscale Dan's, but I'd have to charge you, it'd be like advertising and..."

"Oh no, I got loads of press already, and lately, not all of it good."

"I heard about what happened. I'm really sorry, that must have been awful," I said as I examined a pair of *Dolphin Dan* mermaid salt and peppershakers. I didn't let on that I had already gotten the story from Rose.

"I think the guy had a heart attack or seizure or something down in the lagoon," said Dan. "We won't know anything until the cops get back to us."

"Who was it, a friend of yours?"

"Nah, I just met him when he came to work here. He was a vet that specialized in marine mammals, moved here from California."

"How much do you know about him?"

"His name was Alden, and he was a pretty cool dude, everyone liked him, especially the dolphins. He had a way with them. You could tell it wasn't just a job for him. He really loved them."

"He wasn't alone when it happened though, at least that's what I heard, right?" I set the shakers down and picked up a rubber shark and continued. "One of the animals couldn't have, you know, well, I heard about animals sometimes turning on their trainers."

"No, no way, Kevin was with him, he's lead trainer. If anything like that happened, he'd have known."

"Where do you know *him* from?"

"He answered an ad I had for a dolphin trainer; used to work at Sea World in San Diego. Man, you'd trip-out if you saw how many people answered that ad."

"So why'd you pick him?"

"Same thing, you can tell when someone really loves the babies. Some people connect in a cosmic way, you know what I mean?" His eyes glistened and he cleared his throat. "It's a beautiful thing to witness."

"Well, it can't be great for business, and it looks like you've sunk a lot of money into the place."

"Not me, I don't have that kind of bread, no way, I've got investors."

"Investors, lucky you." I tried on a pair of sunglasses and glanced in a mirror. "Where on earth did you find seashell rimmed frames?"

"I don't know, someone else orders the stuff. I'm the big picture guy."

Dan, the big picture guy, I thought to myself, *the guy whose car tag expired sometime in the 80's.*

"Can I see the rest of the park?" I asked him, "If you're not too busy with your big picture stuff."

"Sure, I was headed out to the lagoon next, you wanna go with me?"

"Heck yeah I do."

Our walk took us down paths canopied by banyan trees that had misting fans hidden in them to cool visitors. Peacocks wandered the park, and a dozen pink flamingos perched one-legged in a small pond. Hibiscus of pink, orange, and yellow, filled the spaces between palm trees, crepe myrtle, and sea oats. It couldn't have been more magical if a storm had blown my house there.

"Holy hell, Dan!" I said. "This place is fabulous. How did you do it so quickly?"

"The investor dudes, they wanted it up and running before season and they paid shit loads to make it happen. Come on, I'll show you the dolphin cove."

Dan went from nervous, to excited, to positively giddy as we toured the place.

"I heard you have half a dozen dolphins now" I said as we walked west toward the inlet.

Steel-drum music played from speakers hidden in shrubs.

"I do, and when lagoon numero two is finished next year, I'll have six more."

"Jeeze, who are your investors, oil sheiks?"

"A group of real estate guys, no, that's not right. Maybe they're internet tycoons."

He said that last one like a question, then glanced upwards, like one of the birds would tell him the answer.

"Ummm, maybe doctors? Maybe all three, I'm not sure. Anyway, the main dude, the one with the most money of 'em all, he's got a hard on—sorry," he looked away, embarrassed. "He's really into dolphins, like a lot. He showed up here a couple of years ago and thought it had potential and *wham*, next you know, I've got me a real attraction."

"This place looks like the lagoon from Gilligan's Island!" I exclaimed when we reached the end of the path. "It looks nothing like it did when I was here before."

"Whoa, so you noticed! That's exactly what I told the landscapers. I even gave them some Gilligan DVDs. The workers were from Mexico or Afghanistan or somewhere, I don't know the money dudes sent them out. Anyways, they never saw Gilligan before, but after watching a few episodes they came out here and created this."

He stretched out his arms as he made several 360-degree turns.

Dan is about six and half feet tall, thin with long, thick gray hair styled by the wind, a face browned and wrinkled from years in the sun, and at that moment, he looked like an ancient shaman praising the sky.

"Of course," he continued, "it's sealed off from the Gulf so the kiddies don't swim away and bad stuff can't get in."

The scene took my breath away. Hundred foot tall coconut palms lined the lagoon, and a pier stretched to the center of the basin where three tiki huts sat on stilts. One hut was for outdoor dining, another looked like a gift shop and the last one, Dan explained, was for storing equipment. A waterfall partially obscured a small cave. Large, brightly colored parrots and macaws flew from tree to tree calling to each other, and I thought I had wandered into paradise.

"Dan—Dan, this is—my God, Dan this is the most beautiful thing I ever saw! You're pretty good at this big picture stuff.

We stood there a few minutes, taking it all in and I said, "Is this where it happened, where that man drowned?" I nodded toward the water.

"Yeah," he said, "hard to believe it happened, poor guy. Big Kev was working with one of the animals and didn't see anything until it was—well, until the dude was..."

He stopped speaking and stared toward the sea. I had the impression he was looking, not at it, but at something fixed in his mind.

"I don't see any dolphins," I said.

He broke from his thoughts, looked at me and smiled.

"The kiddies, they're in the pools."

"The pools?" I asked.

His grin grew even bigger and he said, "Oh man, you're gonna dig this part, come with me."

We walked back the way we had come, but took a detour down an unpaved path. He took a key card from his pocket and used it to open the door to the building. It looked like a straw hut, but was actually brick. Inside was a small desk positioned in front of surveillance monitors, and an old timey cage-type elevator. The man seated in front of the monitors stood up quickly and rigidly, like Dan was President of the United States. I half expected him to salute.

Dan's face transfigured to that of a twelve year old with a new toy.

"This is the bitchenist part of the whole place," he said.

We entered the elevator, descended a few feet, and the door opened onto a dream. The hall before us was made of glass and outside the glass—water.

"Dan, are we were in an undersea tunnel?"

"Yep."

A few large, almost featureless fish, glided past the glass slowly while fast-moving, brightly colored, smaller fish, darted quickly in and out of my line of sight. A turtle the size of a Pekinese used its fins to propel itself toward the surface. Several rays flapped slowly by and I pressed my hands to the cool glass like a child trying to beckon the life on the other side to come to me.

"We're under the lagoon," he said. "Can you believe it? Come on, it leads to the medical room."

I tore myself away, reluctantly, until I saw the newest wonder of the place. Two small houses could have occupied the space that resembled a laboratory-operating room hybrid. We passed a man in a wet suit coming out as we entered.

"You doin' ok Big Kev?" Dan asked the man.

The man responded with a shrug and left through a door at the far side of the room.

"That's Kevin, he's the one who was with—you know."

"Poor guy," I said. "Can I meet him?"

"Not today, he's still pretty raw."

"I understand," I said, and watched Big Kev walk out. I made a mental note to hunt him down as soon as his grief subsided. I figured one more day would be long enough.

"Damn!" I said, "I can't believe this place. It's huge and, and, huge! What's that?" I pointed to the tank in the center of the room.

"I call it the kiddy pool," he said and climbed up the tank's ladder. "Hello dudes and dudesses, Daddy's home."

"It doesn't even seem possible that this all could have been built so quickly," I yelled to him. "I mean, it takes a year to get a permit for a hot dog stand and you've got a freaking *city of the future* here in less than two."

He climbed down and dried his hands on his shorts.

"I'm tellin' ya', these guys have some serious dough-ray-me. You got enough green and you can have whatever you want as quick as you want it."

A young blonde woman wearing a Dolphin Dan's t-shirt entered the room from behind me, smiled, nodded at me and said to Dan, "They're doing great, just got the labs in and it's better than I expected."

She glanced at the tablet she was holding then raised her head and continued, "Except 312, her iron levels are a bit low, I'll adjust her supplement."

She left through a door opposite the one we had entered and another woman wearing similar attire followed her calling, "Hold on Haley, I'm coming with you, I want a better look at...," and the door closed behind them.

"312?" I asked.

"We haven't named them yet, one of the investor dudes wants to do that. They still have their number designations from Fish and Wildlife, but of course, we want to give them real ones."

Dan's phone rang and he dropped it, retrieved it from the wet floor, looked at the screen, and walked away from me as he spoke to the caller. When he returned, his attitude had changed from giddy to nervous and I was certain something was not kosher in Dan's world. I wasn't sure if things really were suspicious, or I only wanted them to be. I felt more than ever though, that poking around here was going to lead to something. I didn't have to spit on Dan to figure out something was wrong.

We left the elevator and stepped back into the blinding light of the cloudless Florida afternoon and I groped my bag for sunglasses and voiced my decision.

"So Dan, you're going to need a lot of staff and I'm looking for some part time work, you got anything for me?"

"Oh, is that all that this was about?"

I saw the tension leave his body like an outgoing tide.

"Uhmm," he pondered a moment. "Well—let me think. Hey, you wanna' be my guide shark?"

I looked at him. "I'm sorry, for a minute I thought you said *guide shark.*"

"I did. It's a guide that's a shark, well you dressed like a shark. You'd be great since you've been around kids and families and, well, you're the perfect, non-intimidating size."

As we talked, we traveled back to his office where he asked me to sit while he rummaged through boxes.

Dan's office was decorated in *early chaos*. If I weren't following Dan from the door to his desk, I'd have needed a bloodhound to find it. Shipping boxes, no less than three six-foot-tall cardboard cutouts of Dan himself, a plastic palm tree, and more boxes cluttered what had already been a haphazard space.

"Here you go," he said, after he found what he had been searching for.

He threw a costume on my lap.

The thing was gray and had a tail that extended from the bottom; a foot long fin hung from the back. I held it front of me like I was deciding on a dress.

"It's got a fan too, battery operated of course," he added, retrieving a device the size of a cell phone.

He showed it to me. "I never knew they had fans, but they do, groovy, huh?"

He bent over the box pulling out several more fans.

"I think there are pocket things inside the costume to hold them."

"You want me to walk around in a shark costume?" I asked, turning it around in my hands. "It seems a little heavy."

"It's six pounds altogether with the head and shoes," he read from a paper that was included with the thing.

He reached back into the box and pulled out a large, malevolently grinning shark head. I'd imagined the designer had attempted to give it a happy, smiling face, but the result was just the opposite. It looked like it was going in for a kill.

"First of all, no," I said. "And second of all, God no. Besides, you'll terrify the children with it."

"Not if *you're* in it," he pointed at me grinning ear to ear. "I can pay you twelve—er—fifteen—I mean, twenty, twenty an hour since you'll be *head shark*."

He said that last part as if he were bestowing knighthood. I had no idea why he was being so nice or why he was paying me more money than I was making at my real job. The nicer he was, the more intrigued I became, until in a moment of weakness, I agreed.

"Alrighty then," I said. "I'll be your guide shark. I'll get business cards printed, update my resume, explore career advancement opportunities—yay me."

"Awesome!" Dan punched the air above him, oblivious to my sarcastic rant. "Groovy, can you be here tomorrow morning, like maybe eightish?" he asked.

"Is this a private party or can anyone join?" said a voice from the doorway.

"Maggie, this is Bob," Dan said and pointed to the man standing at the doorway whose arms extended across the threshold like an actor making a grand entrance.

Bob grabbed my right hand in both of his and pumped like he expected me to produce water.

"Pleased to meet you Maggie, real, real pleased to meet you."

The arm pumping continued until I said, "Are you starting work here too Bob?"

He released my hand and raised his pumping arm over his head, bowed, and waved his hand with a grand flourish, like he was doing an encore.

"Blowhole Bob, here, entertainer extraordinaire at your service. I'm a regular in the standup circuit all over South Florida. I am available for kid's parties, Bar Mitzvahs, you name it and Blowhole Bob has got an act for you. I have my own costume, custom made. Here," he extended a business card to me, "I've got a website now."

He peered over my shoulder at the card he had put in my hand and pointed, "It's got pictures, testimonials, you name it, and Bob's got it."

"Maggie," Dan said, "Bob is a mascot guide too."

Bob used his thumb to point behind himself at Dan. "He makes it sound like I'm a member of the Mascot tribal council."

He followed that with a Hollywood stereotype Native-American accent.

"I guide white man to sacred shopping grounds. We trade much wampum and smoke the peace pipe."

He laughed at his own joke while I marveled at his astonishing level of crudity.

"Blowhole, eh?" I asked Bob. "Does that mean you're a whale or..."

"Dolphin, of course," he said, stepping on my sentence. "What else could be more perfect for this place, am I right?"

His grin grew so large I could count his molars.

"What are you doing here?" he asked me. "Hot dame like you, you a swimsuit model?" he winked.

I wanted to ask him if he was born in a cheap Las Vegas lounge, or if he'd ever heard real people speak to each other, but instead I said, "That's very sweet of you to say, but no, I'm a mascot guide too," and before he could once again dip from the stereotype-well I added, "I'm a shark."

"Oh, shark eh?" he asked, grinning at Dan. "That's a tough one. You gotta get a funny dance or—or—I don't know, you'll think of something. What's your name?"

"Magg..."

'No, no, your stage name. You gotta have a stage name. Everyone loves the name Blowhole Bob, the kids, their parents, hell even the old folks, it's a great one, am I right?"

"I'll give that some thought."

"Yeah, you do that."

Then he looked at Dan, "You got my schedule yet? You know how I get all booked up."

He looked at me and winked, "I got so many appointments, I gotta hire a secretary."

"Go see Frances," Dan told him, "she's got the list. I'm all tied up, dude."

"Tied up, you and shark lady here have fun with that," he smirk-laughed.

"See ya' around Sharkey. No, that's no good, see, that's why you gotta have a name."

"Like I said," I told him, "I'll work on that."

"Yeah," he said, leaving. "Everyone loves Blowhole Bob."

"Wow," I said to Dan, "Bob is really..."

"Yeah, but he's great at his job, and the fact that he's not allowed to talk in costume helps."

"I can see that. Well, should I take this with me, try it on at home?"

"Sure, great idea. If it's too big, maybe we can get it taken in, or you could stuff it with, I don't know, hay or something."

"Good idea, I'll go check the pile of surplus hay I keep in my house, should be enough."

"Well, you know what I mean."

"Yeah, it's ok, I know," I said and walked to my car, shark head under my arm.

I was going undercover as a shark at an amusement park with an old hippie and a clown for no reason other than a hunch from Rose. I knew this was weird even for me. As I drove away, a Bobby Darin song played in my head, *"Oh, the shark has, pretty teeth, dear, and he shows 'em, pearly white..."*

ENTANGLED by Kathleen Cosgrove

FOUR

Back home, I checked my blog, Facebook, and Twitter accounts. Most of the chatter had died down and no one posted anything that I considered helpful except one lady, who said I was most definitely cursed with bad Karma and she could, for a small donation, help reverse that for me. I considered that for a moment, glanced at the past due notice from Florida Power and Light, and reconsidered. My frugal lifestyle would cause Tiny Tim to look for a new home, and yet my power bill is probably close to what they pay to keep the lights on at Buckingham Palace. I thanked the *bad Karma lady* and explained I had no room in my budget this month for exorcists.

Next, I called my friend at the local paper, Dave, to ask if there was any scuttlebutt he'd picked up on the three dead guys. Dave is in charge of computers and all things technical. Dave is also ridiculously shy and introverted, and needs wine and a Xanax just to answer the phone. In an ongoing exchange for info, I've promised to try to get Dave and his garage band a gig at *The Sun God*. The band's shtick is that they dress as women to perform, and since *The Sun God* is a bar with a drag show and I've gotten to know some of the performers there, we made a deal. Dave is shy, introverted, and the last person you'd imagine getting on stage, no less in a ball gown. He hyperventilates if someone asks him to push a button for them on an elevator. But, he wants to perform and I agreed to help, so we are working to that end.

I called Dave's cell in case they can listen in on phone calls at the paper. I didn't watch those Watergate hearings for nothing.

"H-h-hello, Maggie?"

"Dave, how are you? I was hoping you might have some news on those three dead guys."

"I, I do. I can't talk right now, I'm wiping a hard drive, but when I reinstall I'll have some time. Can I call you back?"

"Absolutely, I won't move a muscle till I hear from you, but Dave, is it good?"

"Not sure, bye," he said and hung up.

I was so excited that I paced back and forth for a while, not wanting to do anything noisy in case I didn't hear my phone ring. I was unclear as to how long it took to wipe a hard drive so I stared at the phone's screen for a while. I got bored with that and checked the refrigerator in case someone broke in to my house and put a pie in there, then sat back down and opened the laptop. I read everything I could find on how bodies decompose in the water. The amount of information I found on this topic was astonishing. Page after page of results of death by drowning and the condition of the victims after various lengths of time in the water. It was positively macabre. There was even an answer to my question of whether fish ate eyeballs and yes, apparently crabs like to nibble on the face.

I was beginning my research on drift nets when I began to worry that Dave had forgotten me. I called him again. He had, indeed, forgotten me.

"Dave, how could you forget?" I asked irritably, which is the exact opposite of how you need to speak to Dave. I regained myself and said, "Sorry, you have a lot going on I know, I'm so sorry to bother you."

"Oh gee, I did forget, sorry," he said, and I was afraid he might hyperventilate.

"No, no, it's ok," I reassured him, "I even forgot myself till just now. So, whaddya' know?"

"Oh, all three of them probably died from heart attacks," he said, matter of fact-like, "Heart attacks and drowning."

"What? That can't be right." I said. "Heart attacks, all three of them?"

I was pacing, making laps around the living room.

"That is crazy!" I said wildly, "Crazy. Oh my God. They must have been poisoned or something. Is there a tox report?"

"Yes, but the lab says they were clean."

"Could that have been because they were in the water so long?"

"No idea."

"Are you sure it was the heart attack first and then drowning? I mean, maybe drowning gave them heart attacks."

"How do I know? I'm telling you what the coroner wrote and I'm guessing he knows his job, he's been doing it here since I was a kid. Besides I think he wrote that there were tears or holes in the heart muscle. Yeah, I'm pretty sure that's what it said."

"What, what, what else do you know? Do we know who they are?"

"I got nothin' on that but *someone* knows 'cause the report says they were all around the same age, they were all from San Diego, and they were all Navy guys—well, ex-Navy guys."

"Damn! Ok, do you think there is any way to forward me that email?"

"N-no way, I don't have access to do that," he said, hyperventilating again.

"It's ok, it's ok, no big deal. Do you know how Stuart got that information?"

"Yeah, I do but I better not say. I'll only say this, he has a friend at the coroner's office. Like you and me are friends."

"Ok, gotcha. Thanks Dave. If you find out anything else, will you call?"

"Sure, no problem, I think I might be ready to, you know, The Sun God, and…"

"Oh, yeah, sure, great, whenever you're ready."

I hung up and viewed the local paper online to see how they were writing this. Stuart, Dave's info source, is the local news editor. He's handsome, sexy, and eligible. If I had to guess at the number of *friends* he has that feed him information, I'd say no less than a dozen, yet I'd never seen such a thin article. No family info, no cause of death, suspected cause of death, nothing. It said they were all here in town on a fishing vacation, but no word on the boat they were supposed to have been on, what hotel they were staying in, nothing. In a day when print news was struggling, there was always the tendency to sensationalize events, to speculate on any salacious detail. Such a gruesome incident is perfect for upping readership, and the fact that the paper was doing so little on the story made me suspect someone was strong-arming them to keep the details of it out of print.

I spent hours searching for information on the missing men. I tried the San Diego newspaper's obituary section, obituaries from each major city in the U.S, and even some Navy periodicals to find news of the deaths. I came up empty. I posted on my blog and twitter feeds, of course, to see if anyone knew who rented a boat, or hotel room, or anything at all to three middle aged guys on vacation together in either Fort Myers, Naples, or Bonita Springs. That evening I got a hit I could use. A woman who worked at a restaurant named *Harpoon Harry's* in Punta Gorda, just a few miles north of Fort Myers, remembered serving some guys who matched what I was looking for. She said they dined there frequently over the past few weeks. She had gone to the police with that, but since she had no names and no other information, the cops thanked, and then ignored her.

She gave me the date of their last visit, which was five days before I'd pulled them out of the Gulf. She said they always sat for hours at a table on the patio. They frequently left papers and napkins scribbled with drawings and numbers, which she always opened on the off chance there was a cash tip accidentally wadded up in the debris; there never was.

I made a mental note to go to that restaurant the next day and talk to that server in person.

I was brushing my teeth before going to bed when my phone rang, and by the time I answered the voice at the other end was speaking, but not to me.

"No answer, but don't worry, she's cool," said Dan's voice on the phone to whoever he was with as he was hanging up.

I called back immediately, "Dan? It's Maggie. Looks like I missed a call from you."

"Hey, Maggie. Yeah, uhhh, you still comin' in the morning right? I uh—'cause I wanted to make sure you know—I think I forgot to tell you what time…"

"You told me eight, well I think that's what you said."

"Yeah, that's right, eight. Ok. Uhmm, you heard anything back on those dead guys you uh, you fished out of The Gulf?"

"No," I answered and wondered where this was coming from.

"Yeah, well, that's good—I mean, not good for the dead guys, I mean, well, at least there's no *more* dead guys,"

There were a few seconds of silence.

"Dan, you ok?"

"Oh, yeah, yeah," his voiced perked up. "I'm great. OK, see ya' in the morning," and he hung up.

"Dolphin Dan," I mumbled to myself, "and his peli*can;* he's one crazy, blah, blah man," *and in over his head too.*

FIVE

I turned my alarm off and lay in bed arguing with myself about whether or not to forget the whole thing, or at least go at it from an angle that didn't require my getting out of bed just then. My real paying job, that of copy writer for websites, allows me to stay in my bathrobe all day and only brush my hair when I expect the pizza delivery person. I had become accustomed to that over the past year, and convincing myself to get out of bed to go stand outside with a shark head over my face took a bit of doing.

The fact that I had set the coffee maker to automatically go off was the motivation I needed. The aroma called to me like a snake charmer, and before I knew it I was fully dressed, fully caffeinated and out the door. The day was gorgeous, a real picture postcard kind of morning with endless blue skies and temperatures so mild that riding my scooter into work felt like I owned the world.

That was, at least, until I met the woman who would train me in *mascot behavior*. Frances had all the warmth and charm of a hyena out of mating season. We stood outdoors near the turtle exhibit at Dan's, mascot-lady Frances and me, close to, but not quite under, the shade of an ice cream vending trolley. I had a feeling she did this on purpose. The rumors around the mascot dressing rooms was that she used to be a school cafeteria worker of some sort. Someone else thought she had been a cook in a women's prison. Wherever she came from, and I was leaning toward the prison theory, her primary job was that of ordering food for the *Dolphateria*. Since she had a sister who performed as Fairy Godmother at Disneyworld, however, she became Dolphin Dan's mascot expert.

"First, there is to be no talking. You also cannot laugh, cough, sneeze, or make any other noises with your body," Frances instructed.

I was wearing my shark attire with the exception of the head portion. My own head was exploding with stuff I wanted to say to that, but instead I politely said, "Oh, like The Queen's guards then."

"No, nothing like that," she said with a tone that would have made one of The Queen's guards bayonet her. "You are to move about in a friendly, open way. You do understand your job is that of hospitality and not security, don't you?"

I decided one word answers and head nods would be best from here on out since my attempt at witty repartee failed miserably, so I answered, "Yes."

"Now," she continued, "if a child, or an adult for that matter, tries to touch you in any place outside the touching *area*, you are to say nothing of course, but simply move your head back and forth in the universal signal of *no.*"

My decision of two seconds earlier already forgotten I said, "Just so you know, I'm not really familiar with where a shark's personal boundaries lie. Perhaps you could fill me in. Is it dorsal fin to tail, and what about my tail? Are tails in the touching zone or..."

Frances looked over my shoulder to a point behind me, rolled her eyes, and made an exaggerated sigh. Turning to look, I saw a man whose face I remembered seeing before, although I couldn't place when or where.

I turned to shake hands but could only extend a fin. "Hello," I said, "I'm Maggie, head guide shark."

"Hello," the man said, expressionlessly. He was large, and either Hispanic or darkly tanned. His face was that of a young man, but lined and weather-beaten. Dark stubble shadowed his face and wisps of damp hair poked from the sides of his ball cap.

He looked at my extended fin questioningly but made no attempt to *shake* it.

"Ah!" I said, "It's ok, I don't bite. The teeth are in my head."

He appeared confused.

"Well, my *other* head."

Shut up I told myself. *You couldn't sound more stupid if you talked backwards.*

But of course, I didn't shut up. Instead, I kept digging myself a deeper hole.

"Ok, well, I suppose it's a good thing I'm not allowed to talk, eh Florence?" I turned to my instructor who also looked annoyed. "I mean Frances, sorry."

I turned back to the man, and in doing so inadvertently knocked Frances into the ice cream cart with my tail fin. When I turned back to stop her fall, I hit the man with my dorsal fin.

"I am so sorry everyone, really, I promise to get better at this. Are you guys ok?"

They stared at me, backing away slowly.

"Ok, I'm just going to stand here and not move or talk anymore until everyone goes away."

The man opened his mouth to say something, but Frances cut him off.

"We're busy here, if you'll excuse us."

I watched him walk away and it dawned on me who he was. It was Kevin, or as Dan called him Big Kev, the guy who was at the lagoon when the veterinarian died. I worried now that he'd never confide in me after watching me stumble around like a clown.

After a moment, I heard a clearly irritated Frances cough, then announce she had pressing matters at the *Dolphateria* and I was free to go.

Happy I had the foresight to bring a change of clothes for lunch, I stuffed the rank smelling ones I had worn under my costume into a gym bag and stowed them in a locker Frances had assigned me in the staff lounge. A toilet flushed, and Bob, the dolphin mascot, walked up behind me just as I was fishing the car keys from my purse.

"Well, if ain't the shark lady herself."

I turned to watch him attempt, and fail at, tossing his wadded paper towel into the waste can.

"Hi Bob," was as much effort as I was willing to expend on this Neanderthal.

He leaned against the wall in what I assume was a stab at looking seductive. With his lopsided grin though, he looked more drunk than sexy.

"I got some time right now, if you do, for a little afternoon quickie."

I fought between getting angry and laughing. "You're joking, right?"

"Nope, Blowhole Bob never jokes about matters so important."

Before I could form an appropriately worded comeback he laughed at his own inside joke and said, "They have a great snack bar at the Dolphateria, you want to join me in something hot and delicious?"

"No thanks Bob, I've got plans, you go ahead and enjoy your quickie on your own, won't be the first time will it?"

"Ha, Blowhole Bob loves a great zinger, even when they are aimed at him."

"Again, probably not your first. I gotta' go Bob, see ya'"

Although the day had gotten warmer, the skies were still clear and the always present breeze from The Gulf made the ride up Highway 41 a reminder of all that I loved about South Florida.

Punta Gorda, my destination that afternoon, had gotten the full force of the damaging winds from Hurricane Charley in 2004. It was a strong category four hurricane that left fatalities and billions of dollars in damage. To see it now, though, you would never have guessed it. The city combined both restoring the old with beautiful new renovations including parks, a harbor walk, and pedestrian and bicycle paths.

I parked my scooter at the entrance to Fisherman's Village and walked along the marina side to the end of the pier where Harpoon Harry's restaurant jutted into the Peace River.

I asked the host for a table on the patio, and it wasn't long before I learned who my blog commenter was. She knew me from the photos on my website and introduced herself.

Pam's *Harpoon Harry's* staff T-shirt hung off of her narrow frame like it had once belonged to someone larger. The white light from the midday sun shone golden off her chestnut hair and sun freckled face.

"Magpie I assume?" she said.

"Yes, but please call me Maggie."

"Ok Maggie, I'm Pam. I've got a big table," she nodded to a group of eight, a couple of tables over. "Their food is about ready to come out. I'll tell you what I know, but it's not much."

"I can't place your accent Pam, where are you from?"

"Oh, I am American, but I have lived in Egypt and Israel most of my life. My father is an archeologist and that is the, you must know, the mother-vessel for artifacts.

"And now you're a student here in Florida?"

"Yes, I am a student at The University of Miami but I'm here in Fort Myers with my father while I intern at the wetlands project here. I got this job last month to give myself funny money."

"I hope you mean fun money or..."

"Yes, fun money, thank you. Here, look at these, I'll be right back."

She pulled a stack of folded pages from her apron pocket and gave them to me. She walked away to wait on her customers, a group so browned and laid back I knew they must be residents and not tourists; the latter always more sunburned and exhausted.

The numbers that were scribbled on the pages meant nothing to me; they were random in the extreme. Some could have been longitude and latitude coordinates, and some were smaller numbers followed by the letters kHz. The drawings were even less helpful showing circles, some with the letters *a.s* .or *e.i.* in the center. Arrows pointed to what were either trees, stick people, or some random intersecting lines. Some of the arrows were longer, shorter, or diagonal, and all drawn to, and from, the predominant line drawing. To me they looked like the sketches of a six year old.

"Why did you save these in the first place?" I asked Pam when she returned.

"Curious, I heard them talking sometimes. They were kind of quiet but I picked up enough to know they were some kind of marine specialists."

"Do you know what any of these scribbles mean?"

"Maybe, I'm bringing them to a professor I know of. He's retired now and lives in Naples. He guest lectured for us once. He's very much awful, no one likes him, he's a recluse. Did I get that one right?"

"Recluse, yes, if you mean he doesn't get out much."

"Yes, he's a recluse. Easy for him, he has no family or friends, but maybe if I show him something interesting he will talk to me. I think he will find this interesting. He specializes in biological oceanography and if I'm right, he'd be the best one to give us an answer."

When I handed her back the papers she told me to keep them, they were copies of the originals she had at home.

"Do you know anything about them, do you think they are the same men you found in the net?" she asked.

"I have no idea, but I'll tell you what I did learn. Those men, the ones from the Gulf, all died of heart attacks. Heart attacks and then they drowned.

"That can't be right," she said. "That's...," she stared off as if she was trying to find the right word.

"I know, that's what I said too."

"How can they tell the men had heart attacks? From the autopsies I've assisted with in my marine biology clinics, I know that after some time in the water the tissues break down."

"They had holes in their hearts."

"Holy tuna!"

"Yes, holy tuna indeed."

I went home to blog without mentioning what Pam and I were looking at. If there was bad business afoot, I didn't want to tip my hand. I did write, however, that I had uncovered some things that could be a clue to what happened.

This blogger has been digging into, not only the identity of the men she found in the Gulf this past Sunday, but also into their cause of death. The information I have gained so far has me suspicious that this may not be a case of mere drowning. How they became tangled in the net, whether it was after they drowned or was the cause of their drowning is still not known. At least I have not found anyone to confirm or deny that entanglement in the net was the circumstance that lead to their drowning. I am still investigating and promise to keep on it until we're all clear.

Magpie.

When I went back to the blog after eating dinner, I had twelve comments. The first one asked if I knew what particular piece of music was played during a scene on *Hawaii Five O* and some conspiracy theories about aliens and killer dolphins. When I scrolled down to the last one though, my breath stopped, *Leave this alone or die.* Signed: *brassmonkey*

My fingers left the keyboard as if it were on fire, and I jumped back from my desk and stared at the computer screen. I moved two feet across the room, as though *brassmonkey* could reach through the monitor and grab me.

The anonymity of the internet leaves the door open to anyone with access to Wi-Fi, and I've had more than my share of people wishing all manner of bad stuff to happen to me. I learned right away not to take those personally. However, this was my first honest-to-God death threat. Because I had been covering, and was sometimes an unwilling participant in, the local crime scene since I'd moved here, I was like a combat soldier, hardened yet wary. I managed to talk myself down from scared to annoyed, with a lot of reassurance that there are people who do that kind of thing on any and all sites that allow comments.

My personal information was kept private; I'd hired a professional to do that for me when I first began the blog. I put *brassmonkey* out of mind, and when I noticed the time it was six o'clock, time for news.

I shut the computer down, fiddled with the antennae on my television, and sat down to watch one of the few channels for which I got reception. The two blonde anchor people got through the entire thirty minutes without ever mentioning the three dead men, but did show a commercial for *Dan's Dolphin Experience* that looked slick and expensive.

"Dolphin Dan, the money man," I said out loud to no one, "he blah blah blah's like no one can." I fell asleep trying to fill in the blah blahs.

SIX

Before leaving for work next morning I checked in on the blog. There were five comments telling *brassmonkey* he was a troll and to go away, and one telling me never mind about the *Hawaii Five O* song, they'd figured it out. That was it.

Pam called to tell me she was in touch with her professor.

"He's agreed to see me about the drawings. I'm going there tomorrow. Wish me good luck."

"Good luck, call as soon as you're done."

I did not know why Dan had me come to work before the park opened, but he was paying me well for doing very little which is my own version of heaven, that and pie. I helped stock souvenir salt and peppershakers, souvenir clocks, souvenir shot glasses, and, I was astonished to see, souvenir tampons. I busied myself with that as long as I could bear to, then took a stroll around the park. I counted that as legitimate work since I needed to familiarize myself with the place. I walked to the lagoon hoping to run into Big Kev, but saw no one there other than landscapers wrangling a rather large palm tree. When I watched it sway heavily to one side, my side, I beat a hasty retreat. I walked back toward the security shack and spotted Blowhole Bob leaving it. I tripped over my own feet to escape quickly. It was after one o'clock anyway and I was hungry.

Lunch at the *Dolphateria* consisted of menu selections that were mostly seafood, which seemed a little barbaric given the setting, so I got a salad and French fries. I found an empty table facing the window that overlooked a small playground. Sea-horse modeled swings hung from poles made to look like ships' masts, and the seats of the teeter-totters were in the shape of manatees. It was charming and I felt happy to be there.

I pulled up an audio book on my phone, stuck the headphones in my ears, and began tearing open salad dressing packages.

The tap on my shoulder was so startling I reflexively sent a crouton flying at the plate glass. "Holy shit, you scared the crap out of me," I said.

I turned to face a man the size of a Pontiac. He looked as though he were dressed for a prom in a powder blue pin striped suit, and he was wearing mirrored sunglasses.

"Excuse me," he said in a baritone so deep I felt my shoes vibrate, "but Mister Preston and his group will be sitting here, you'll have to move."

"Beat it Miami Vice," I said, "I'm not moving anywhere. Mister *whoever* can find another place to sit."

He used his elbow to turn back his suit jacket exposing his shoulder-holstered handgun.

I froze.

"Don't worry, I'm not trying to scare you, just letting you know who I am," said the man, grinning down at me from his neck-less head.

"Then who *are* you? And who the hell brings a gun into a park for God's sake?"

I surveyed the room. Teenagers staring into their phones and kitchen staff were all that I could see in the dining area, not a security guard in sight.

"I'm Mister Preston's safety agent and I'm asking you to move."

"What, like a body guard? Are you freaking kidding me? I'm calling the cops." I unlocked my phone, ready to dial.

"No need, the police chief is here as a guest of Mister Preston."

"Well, no surprise there," I said, picking up my tray. "This place needs a full time swat team."

My glass fell and water soaked my clothes; ice cubes littered the floor at my feet.

"Sugar shit and damnation! What next?" I yelled.

"Is there a problem here?"

The question came from a man walking toward us who was followed by an entourage of about a dozen. Everyone in the little gang, men and women alike, wore gray three-piece suits. Only their ties, or in the case of the women, scarves, varied in color. When the man in the lead had his back to them they edged and elbowed each other to secure a spot closer to the front. When he turned back to face them, they stopped and pretended to be using their phones or speaking to the person next to them. When his back turned again, they would resume their scramble. I had a feeling the head guy knew this and looked back from time to time just to screw with them.

"What's going on here, Esposito?" he asked the giant.

"Getting you a good table sir," said Esposito. His words, though accented, had no inflection.

Sir was attired more for a board meeting than a sea park. He was a man who had expensive taste in suits, and access to a gym and tanning bed. Wisps of gray at the temple off set the deep brown of his slightly thinning yet full head of dark brown hair. At over six feet, he was an impressive sight. He extended his hand to me while two of the gray-suited men cleaned the mess I had made.

"I am so sorry for this inexcusable intrusion. Please allow me to get you a new meal," he said.

He turned to another in the group and said, "Go and get our guest whatever she wants."

"Yes Mister Preston," said the gray suit with the yellow tie who then turned to leave.

"I don't want anything," I said. "I'll just be leaving. You can have the table."

I had barely turned my back when he said. "Please, don't go."

Then to Esposito he said, "Jorge, *you* go, you're fired."

I turned back to face him.

"What? No, please, don't fire anyone. It wasn't Espo–Jorge's fault, I'm clumsy, I spill stuff all the time. Seriously, it's no big..."

"I must be cruel to be kind," the man said.

I was mulling that last bit over when Dan came bounding toward us from where ever he had been.

"Mister Preston, sir, is everything alright?"

"Dan?" I asked. "I barely recognized you."

He was in a three-piece suit, his wild mane hidden under a Fedora. The hat would have been a good fit back when Dan had more hair and I'd imagined the last time he wore that suit he was dancing to the Bee Gees.

By now, the Dolphateria was cleared of everyone but the Mob, me, and dressed-up Dan.

"Mister Preston sir," Dan said, adjusting his hat and tie. "I'm really sorry, man." Then to me he said, "Maggie, what did you do?"

"I? What? I didn't..."

"I'm sorry, but, you're fired," he told me.

"Great, Esposito and I can go down to the unemployment office together," I said. "Want a ride big guy?"

"I'm not fired," Esposito said.

"But—just now—you..."

"He fires me three, four times a day," said the powder blue mountain. "Mister Preston is..."

"Great, thanks for havin' my back, Jorge."

"Don't interrupt, Maggie," Dan said, interrupting. "These people are..."

"Silence," said Preston.

Because his tone resembled the low rumble of storm clouds, the room became instantly quiet.

"I'm sure Dan didn't mean he was really firing you," he said. "That was simply a small joke, right Dan?" He glared at the terrified old hippie.

"Oh, yeah, of course, just kiddin' around Maggie," said Dan. "No way I'd..."

"See there? I knew it," said Mister Preston to his group." Then to me he said, "All right Maggie? May I call you Maggie?"

His smile was broad and crinkled his eyes into thin slits. They reminded me of cat's eye marbles in tones of deep blue and brown. He smelled good too, and I realized I was holding my breath; I also realized he was extending his hand.

As we shook I said, "Yes, Maggie is fine, it's my name, Maggie. Well, Margaret—Finn. But yes, Maggie is great, I mean, it's great that you can call me Maggie." I lowered my head. "I'll just be quiet now."

"Excellent Maggie, my name is Frank. And now that we're friends, won't you please join me for lunch?"

Mumbling broke out in the ranks, but no one addressed Frank directly.

"Thanks," I said, "but it looks like you've got lunch plans already." I looked over his shoulder at the entourage. Dan was shaking his head, the Fedora moving a half second behind. "Besides, my clothes are wet."

"Please accept my most sincere apology Miss Finn."

He snapped his fingers at a gray suit who pulled a card from inside his jacket and handed it to me.

"Please get in touch with my office about replacing your garments."

He looked at Dan. "From now on, her meals here are on me."

"Oh, you don't have to..." I said, but he extended his hand and cut me off.

"It was a pleasure to meet you."

I considered this an end to the conversation and walked out, disappointed at the abrupt dismissal. *The rich are different*, I thought. *I could never be involved with a rich guy anyway, no matter how much their eyes crinkled.*

ENTANGLED by Kathleen Cosgrove

SEVEN

I had only been home long enough for a visit to the bathroom when a knock on the door had me running to answer it, zipping my jeans, and cursing because I'd hit my toe on a chair leg. Thus was I, when I opened the door to find what at first appeared to be a ghost.

Standing before me was a woman who could find work as a corpse in Hollywood. Her skin was nearly transparent, she wore a black hat adorned with dusty, crushed, purple and blue flowers, and wore a black dress that hung on her like it was draped over a flagpole rather than a body.

"Misses Finn," she said in an accent that could have been from Transylvania.

"I am Sabina Fratada and this is my husband, Radu."

She extended a shoe-box-sized container that was gilded and covered in what I assumed were fake gems of red and purple. She pushed it toward me as if she wanted me to take it. I jumped back.

"Pardon me?"

"My husband, he is here," she extended the box toward me again. "Can we please go into your home? It is too bright here under the sun, the light, it hurts my eyes." She shielded her face with her free, withered hand.

"I'm sorry, please, won't you...?" I started.

For a ghost, she had extremely pointy elbows, and before I could fully open the door she apparated into my living room and was again offering me her dead husband. The box looked heavier than she, so I asked her to sit before she fell forward onto the linoleum.

"Would you like something to drink?" I asked, going to the kitchen for a cup of water.

"You have wine?"

"No, sorry, I have water and a bottle of lemon juice."

"You have whiskey?"

"Let me get you some water."

While throwing some ice in her glass I asked, "Maybe we could start by you telling me why you want me to take—I'm sorry, I've forgotten his name."

"Radu. Radu Fratada. He is dead three months."

"I'm so sorry, really," I said, returning to the sofa and handing her the water.

She took a sip and made a face. "You have no whiskey to put in?"

Once we established that there would be no alcohol this day, she at last proceeded to tell me why she had brought me the recently deceased Radu. She was not, in fact, from Transylvania, or even Romania, but from the neighboring country of Bulgaria. That is as North Carolina is to South Carolina, no one knows the difference with the exception of their inhabitants.

"How long have you lived in Florida?" I asked while watching the glass of water wobble its way to her lips. I wished I had put it in a plastic cup.

"Twenty years, twenty years we are here in this place while Radu puts the food in bags at the Publix store."

"Oh, that's nice, what did he do when you lived in Bulgaria?"

"He dig the graves, he dig graves since he come to me after the war. Before that, he dig the graves in Italia. He do that since he was boy of thirteen years."

"Oh really, I thought they used machines to do that." I said, half standing, ready to grab her water glass in case it didn't make it all the way to the coffee table.

"No, no machines in our village, just the shovel."

"I see, and what did you do, did you have children?"

"No, no children. I read the cards for the people in my village, to tell them what the future is to be. I talk to the dead for them. That is my gift, to see the things they could not."

"Oh, a fortune teller, of course, and your husband was a grave digger. And you came to Florida, why?"

"Oh, we come for the dolphin," she said finally making it all the way to the table with the water with only a minor amount of spillage.

"Doesn't everyone?" I agreed.

"Radu, he knows he does not want to go in ground when he die, he knows he cannot go to Blest Land that way. We come here where there are many dolphin to make the trip with him when he is dead."

It was on that part of the saga that she began dozing off. She startled herself awake when Radu nearly slipped from her lap, and then asked me if I had any wine. I told her I had not, in those few seconds, gotten any liquor deliveries and she went on.

"You will please bring my Radu and throw in to the dolphins so he can make the journey to the Blest Land. I have payment for you to do this. Me, I do not believe, but it was Radu's wish to do this so I make the promise that I will make this happen."

I stared at those black eyes that age had not dared to fade, at dried lips whose wrinkles held traces of red lipstick and spittle and I wasn't sure if I should fear or pity her.

"I'm sorry, I want to make sure I understand you. You want me to take the ashes of your dead—ex—of Radu, to the place where I work and feed them to..."

"No! Not to feed! Are you mad? No, you will make Radu for to swim with the dolphin. The dolphins they will know what to do. You give them the box, they will know."

"This is the custom of your people in Bulgaria? There are dolphins in the, what, the Black Sea?"

"Radu, he was from Italia. He come to my village, to Ritya, during the war, and I was pretty girl. He stay in Bulgaria but his heart always in Italia, in Roma."

"Oh, it's an Italian thing, I see. I never heard of that. I thought Italians were Catholic 'cause, you know, the Pope lives there and all."

"No, Radu not Catholic. Radu wishes to go to the Blest Land and needs dolphin to carry him there." Her voice had become sharp and emphatic. "He left money for this to happen. I pay you to bring Radu to dolphins, you can do this. You are smart lady who brings souls up from the sea."

As much as I wanted the cash, the last thing I needed was to bring a box of powdered Radu to work and ask if he could hitch a ride to the afterlife with one of the attractions.

"I don't think I'll be able to help you, I'm sorry. I'm only a guide shark there. They don't let us—well, I really don't think Dan—I'm sorry, I can't help you."

A crash of thunder hit the precise moment I uttered the final syllable and I literally jumped from my seat. The image of a threatening Radu demanding to be let loose from his glitzy box and set free to ride to heaven on the back of Flipper flashed before my eyes. Sabina sat as calmly as if a butterfly had flown by and was obviously not filled with terror as I was, of visions of ancient Roman gods daring to smite us with a lightning bolt. It was a bright, cloudless day and yet a bolt of lightning and boom of thunder had appeared out of nowhere.

"You know," I said. "Leave Radu here with me. I'll see what I can do."

I helped Sabina to her car since it was still a bit breezy and I imagined her whirling down the street, head over ankles, like brittle tumbleweed. Her sunglasses with the dark black lenses that reached eyebrow to eyebrow and ear to ear, made her look as though half her face had been redacted.

I leaned into the open window and caught a whiff of something that reminded me of some parties I used to go to when I was younger. I spotted the bag of twigs and leaves in a plastic freezer bag in the back seat.

"Sabina, is that pot in your car?"

"It was for Radu when he was sick, it is medicine."

"Well, I'd keep Radu's medicine at home if I were you, you don't want to get pulled over with that in your car."

"No one tells Sabina she can't have medicine, this is free country. Now, you be sure you tell you boyfriend not to disturb my

Radu," she said, placing gnarled fingers on the steering wheel of her massively large vehicle.

"Don't worry, I don't have a boyfriend, Radu is safe with me."

"You boyfriend *tell* me he is you boyfriend when he come out of the house."

"Wait, a man came out of my house? When, what did he look like?"

"A big man, and too young for you."

She pulled the gearshift into reverse and began backing out. I pulled my head out of the window, hitting it on the frame.

"You too old for a boyfriend anyway," she said and left the driveway without so much as a glance behind her.

Watching her drive off, a stick figure behind a jumbo-sized dashboard, I pulled my cell from my pocket and called in the cavalry.

"You didn't lock your door?" Rose asked while looking around my living room.

"I know," I said, overly dramatic.

"Remind me, aren't you the same woman half the state tried to kill a couple of years ago?" she asked, opening my bedroom door and peering in.

"Why are we searching for the guy now?" I asked. "The old gypsy said he left."

"Yeah, go back to that part," said Rose. "I thought maybe I didn't hear you right."

"No, you heard me ok. An old fortune teller from, I can't remember, Budapest or Bulgaria, one of those places, came here and said she saw someone leave my house before I got home. She must have tried finding me at home earlier."

"A fortune teller who makes house calls?"

"She wasn't here to read my fortune, she was here because, well, it doesn't matter. She said she saw a man leave my house, a big man. She was an oddball, but I don't think she was making it up."

While Rose searched the house, I looked under my bed. It was cliché, but I knew I was going to do it eventually and with Rose there, it seemed the best time.

"Who's mad at you now?" she asked, scanning the back yard from my patio doors.

"No one, well no one that stands out, except I've got a troll," I pointed her toward the computer. "He calls himself Brassmonkey."

"All blogs have got trolls. They're usually real ugly, sweaty guys with bad breath and no friends. They get off on causin' trouble, makin' threats," she said. "They almost never come out into the real world though, they're cowards."

"Except," I said, "he made a death threat."

"Just so happens I'm in cyber-crime class right now," she said, seating herself in front of my computer. "Hand me my bag, would ya?"

I did as she asked and watched her retrieve a pair of latex gloves from her satchel.

"Well, this beats anything I've seen and I've been on perv watch," she said, examining the computer monitor and pulling the gloves over her perfect manicure. Her nails were polished blue and had little gold stars at the tips.

As it happened, the screen was open to a page of old black and white photos. They were images of naval officers participating in an equator-crossing ceremony. One of the sailors was dressed as the bride of Neptune.

"When I looked up *brassmonkey*," I told her, "I discovered it was an old naval expression and then one thing led to another and before you know it, I wound up looking at men wearing mop wigs and coconut bras."

Rose shook her head in despair and continued in silence.

I was enthralled watching her type, never stopping, never correcting. She was like a machine on the computer, pausing occasionally to say, "Hmmm," or muttering a few words in Spanish.

"He's kind of quiet for a troll though," she said. "Most of them can't shut up. I bet he's trying to scare you; he must have seen it in a movie."

I stood behind her, looking over her shoulder, and that's when I noticed the copies of the napkins were missing.

"Well shit!" I said. "Shit, shit, shit. Someone really was in here. This proves it, look." I said, and pointed to the desk. "They took my freaking napkins."

"Took your what?"

"The dead guys, they used to eat at Harpoon Harry's all the time."

"Oh, I like that place," Rose said.

"Yeah, me too. Anyway, I met a server there who used to wait on them. They would leave behind papers and napkins they had scribbled on. She made me copies and I left them there." I pointed to the empty space near the computer.

"Is this like a quiz show? Do I have to guess at what's going on or are you going to explain?"

"Ok, well, I asked on my blog—look, scroll back up to read it," I said, pointing at the top of the computer screen. "Go to my blog folder."

She was already there.

"Now, go to my posting of the 16th, see, that's what I wrote."

Rose read it and I was quiet while she did.

"Now scroll way down and see where *biogradpam* writes that she may have seen them at Harpoon Harry's?"

"Yeah, this is brilliant," said Rose. "An entire investigation out there for every whacko and loony to see."

"Yeah, this system has its drawbacks, I'll grant you," I said, "but it's also pretty effective sometimes in getting good info."

"Ok, so maybe, and this is a gallon size maybe, maybe our perp wants to know what you know and breaks into your house. How does he know where you live? You used a pro to hide your personal information, didn't you?"

"Yes, of course."

"And that's all that's missing?" Rose asked. "No valuables?"

"If anyone wants my valuables they'll have to go to Junior's Pawn and Gun."

Rose walked through the living room again checking out the books on my shelves.

"Yeah," she said. "I've busted better decorated crack houses. I still think it was a simple B and E. The guy came in, didn't find anything worth stealing, and probably just came across the napkins and used 'em to wipe his prints."

She stood and grabbed her bag from the sofa. "I'll dust for prints anyway, probably a waste of time, but I like doin' it."

She took paper and pen from her bag, scribbled something on a note, and handed it to me. *Don't say anything, but there's a bug on your bookshelf.*

This is Florida, so it took me a second to realize she didn't mean a cockroach. She put a finger to her lips as we slowly walked to my bookshelf and she pointed to a small, black, button-sized object that was stuck near the bottom of my globe over New Zealand.

I gave her the wide eyed surprised look, then figured being silent was suspicious so I said, "So, does real dust make it harder to dust for fingerprints? You're really doing a good job dusting with that thing on my keyboard."

After I said it, I realized I not only sounded stupid, but also as though I were speaking to someone half a mile from me. Rose confirmed this by giving me a look that said, *shut up, are you that stupid,* and *I'm gonna have to kill you.* I know this expression well as she uses it a lot with me.

She dusted for prints on my keyboard next. "You know you got cookie crumbs between the keys and chocolate on the space bar?" she asked. Then she mumbled something like, "Can't stop eating long enough to..." and, "lookin' at men wearing coconuts on their manboobs."

EIGHT

Thursday at Dan's was like a dress rehearsal where friends and family of the employees could attend free of charge. The actual *swim with the dolphins* was limited to only a half dozen guests chosen randomly by their ticket number. Zig was there as a guest of the gift shop woman, so I invited Rose of course, and Pam who said she'd try to come by after doing something that had something to do with collecting seagull droppings. The fact that she was running up student loans to do so made me admire her even more.

The overcast sky kept the heat down to a reasonable temperature, and with the small fans inside the pockets of the shark suit I was fairly comfortable. I stepped out of the dressing room and into the park like an actress walking on stage.

Peacocks meandered lazily along a path that led to a shaded picnic bench where a mother was feeding an infant a bottle with one hand, and opening a box of raisins for her toddler with the other. Bird calls, laughter, and steel drum music filled the air, along with the smells of popcorn, cotton candy and hot pretzels from cart vendors. Children ran ahead of their parents eager to get to the small pools that held nurse sharks, rays and turtles. Lines began forming at the restroom entrances, and I remembered that some of the facilities were still under repair. Being this close to the beach always presents plumbing challenges.

I was taking all this in when a loud scream pierced the air like a smoke detector. A small child at my feet stared at me, eyes wide in horror, stiff as an ironing board and screaming, "A shark, a shark, it's going to eat me!"

Remembering I was not allowed to speak, I tried instead to make soothing noises. I realized too late that, through the latex mouth, the shushing sounded more like hissing. The poor child

ENTANGLED by Kathleen Cosgrove

screamed again and fell at my feet. When I didn't see a parent come it its rescue I tried, unsuccessfully, to pick him up. A crowd gathered and a young girl, brandishing a souvenir pirate sword, stabbed at me as I bent to try to help the fallen child. The sword found its way through the facemask and gouged my eye.

I inadvertently shouted an expletive. I was hoping the screams masked the curse, but the stabber's mother said, "Well, isn't that lovely, in front of children." She pulled the junior assassin away as more children began pointing at me and crying.

The father of the fallen toddler arrived and scooped the boy up muttering, "Who the (expletive), dresses like a shark in a place for kids?"

I wanted to apologize but was unable to do anything but shrug which probably only succeeded in making me look as though I was giving him the, 'up yours,' gesture. That's when I felt the pain of teeth on my ankle, the only part of my anatomy not covered in shark disguise. I instinctively pulled it away from the teeth of a small dog and in the process kicked a nun in the shin. She nearly fell, but two of her companions, another nun and a priest, caught her before she hit the ground.

"Oh, thank God," I said, forgetting the non-speaking rule.

"Indeed," said the elder of the three, and helped her limping companion to a bench.

"Who's in charge here?" yelled a large man holding a tray of cheese covered nachos in one hand and a Dolphin Dan's souvenir drink cup in the other. "These shark people can't just go around kicking nuns."

"Now there's a sentence you don't hear every day." said another man, this one carrying a lot of expensive camera gear. He moved quickly to my side and told the crowd there was an ice cream wagon just ahead giving away free cones. Within seconds camera-man and I were the only two there.

"You came just in the nick of time; they were becoming an angry mob." I said, readjusting my head.

He helped me situate it properly, then stepped back and asked, "You Ok?"

"I'm fine, though a kid with a sword knocked my contact out so you look both close up and far away."

He laughed, "That's not your missing contact, I really do look like that."

He was relatively young, I guessed early thirties, tall, and wearing the bright pink skin of a tourist. A brown mustache and beard covered the bottom half of his face and a large brimmed ball cap shadowed the upper half.

"I'm Howard, the park photographer." He extended his hand, realized shark fins replaced mine, and smiled.

"Your accent says *south,* your sunburn says *north,*" I said. "So, which is it?"

"Georgia born and raised, been living in what my daddy calls *Yankee Land* for five years," he said.

"How'd you end up here?"

"Like a lot of folks, came down for a vacation, decided it might not be a bad place to stay a while."

"Are you a nature photographer too?"

"Ahhh, yes, that's my main focus," he said and chuckled at his own, and I was certain well-rehearsed, joke. "Sorry, it's a horrible pun that I can't seem to stop myself from saying."

"But taking pictures of tourists pays better?"

"Well, it's steady anyway. I'm trying to get a local gallery to carry some of my stuff, but the competition here is pretty tough. I think this is where all nature and wildlife photographers come to retire."

"How'd you end up at Dan's?"

"Came here to see if I could get some shots of the dolphins, that lagoon is gorgeous. I suppose you've seen it?"

"Yes, and I agree, it's breathtaking."

"Dan said if I was interested, he happened to be looking for an official park photographer, just forgot to advertise for one. Hired me without even asking to see my work."

"I'm not surprised, that sounds about right for Dan."

A group of high-school aged kids approached us and he said, "Ok, Jaws, get ready, here we go."

The group of six teens, equal numbers of girls and boys, wanted photos with me, and all wanted those to be of them with their heads in my mouth. I obliged since they were having fun and not screaming or stabbing me. With that done, Howard left to photograph small children petting dolphins and I went inside to replace my contact.

With my vision restored, I searched for a first aid kit to try and get some peroxide and a band aid over my dog bite. The teeth didn't break the skin enough to bleed, but I was taking no chances. Florida is tropical and every manner of bug and germ thrive here, it's a bacteria Nirvana. The slightest thing can fester into something that would require a round of antibiotics and a living will. I wasn't able to discover where Frances kept the first aid kit, so I gave up my search and used soap, water, tissue, and tape. I stood in front of the air conditioning vent, luxuriating in one last blast of cold air before climbing into my costume. I made my way around the hedges that concealed the employee dressing room entrance and collided with someone who appeared out of thin air.

"Oh, sorry, I didn't see you." I said.

"No talking in costume."

The voice was unmistakable, echoing off vocal chords covered in decades of tobacco and gin. I hated that voice.

"Frances? What are you doing back here?"

"Not talking to you for starters and do I have to remind you again there's no talking in costume? And what are *you* doing here? Aren't you supposed to be out there doing what they pay you to do?"

I remained silent.

"Well?" she asked, raising the guttural level a few octaves.

The irony of her demanding an answer after telling me not to speak was lost on her, but I was enjoying it immensely.

She peered into the eyeholes of my costume for a moment and I saw a bit of raw anger in her stare. "I've got real work to do," she said at last, then turned and retreated in the direction of the Dolphateria.

I put Frances in her seventies, probably late seventies. She was about my height and build and her unnaturally colored red hair cropped short, framed sharp cheekbones over sagging jowls. An air of deep-fry grease and bitterness hung on her like a fog. As I watched her go, I'd hoped she wasn't anyone's grandmother.

My phone vibrated and I fumbled inside my pocket blindly to find the answer key and when I did, Rose's voice came through my earphone.

"Where are you?"

"Just go to the gift shop," I said into the hands-free mic, "I'll meet you there."

"Good, I like gift shops; I can look for shop-lifters."

"You're not on duty are you?"

"No, I'm not on duty, it's just a hobby."

"Oh wait," I said, "I can't talk anymore, people are coming."

A white haired couple dressed in his and hers yellow golf attire, stopped to ask for directions to the lagoon. I pointed with my fin while Rose continued speaking,

"This place is nice, I like it. It feels like bein' on a cruise ship but without the throwing up."

"You get sea sick?"

"No, but the cheap booze they serve you on those things along with the eight meals a day is…"

The phone went silent.

"What? Rose? Are you ok?"

"Hey, you'll never guess who's headed your way," she finally said. "It's old mister crinkly eyes himself, and it looks like he's coming straight for you."

She was right. I had the gift shop in sight and was nearly there when I spotted Frank heading toward me. His usual entourage including Dan, and now Howard the photographer followed close behind.

"Hello Miss Shark," Frank yelled and waved his hand. "Can we get a picture?"

There was no way out of it; I was going to have to interact with Frank Preston wearing an outfit that was even less sexy than a burka; one that forced me to walk like a drunken orangutan. Maybe, I thought, he won't know it's me in here. Maybe he's forgotten that this was my job. And even if he did, he couldn't know *for sure* it was me. After all, I'm not allowed to talk. I was home free. That is when I noticed Rose elbowing her way through the crowd. "Maggie, there you are," she said directly to me. "I've been waitin' on you for half an hour, I'm starving."

Rose and I opted for the Frozen-yogurt bar and took our cups to a nearly deserted area where we could talk openly. Rose filled me in on what she had learned about the bug she found in my home. We had agreed to leave it where it was so the department could try to trace the signal back to the listening end.

Rose was making her way through the avalanche of toppings covering her *Cookies and Cream* flavored yogurt when she said, "It's from a company that makes security devices for The British Secret Service, that's why it's taken so long to figure out where it came from. No one here uses their stuff, they're under contract with MI-6 not to sell to anyone else."

"That *can't* be right," I said, "MI-6? Why in God's name would anyone from M-I6 care anything about me? Whoever put it there must have bought it off the internet or something."

"No one thinks MI-6 is listening to you, but it's enough to get both the FBI and the Brits' attention. Not a full scale inquiry or anything, but they're curious to know how it ended up in your house."

"They're not the only ones. What about the break-in at my house?"

"The department can't just go start an investigation every time someone misplaces some napkins. Also, about your troll, Brassmonkey, his IP address goes through too many servers. I can't get help tracking from anyone because he's NST."

"NST?"

"Non-Specific Treat," she said, her shoulders moving in a sigh. "It's *so* hard to communicate with civilians."

"You say *civilians* like my granddaughter says *Muggles*."

"What in the hell is that?"

"You know, Muggles, non-magic folk. Didn't you ever read Harry Potter?"

"I am a half Mexican, half African-American woman making my way in a middle-aged white guy world, do you really thing I have time to read kid's books?"

"Well, he was *kind* of a detective; he had to track down Horcruxes."

"You know I'm not listening to you anymore, right?"

"I'm going to try to find Big Kev today," I told her, turning the yogurt bowl up to drink the part that had turned liquid. "I know you've already talked to him, but maybe he'll slip up and say something to me he didn't tell you because, well, I'm not a cop."

"That's not a bad idea, but try not to…"

"To what?"

"Forget it, the list's too long." she said, tossing her empty cup into the trash can free-throw style.

"Do you know anything else about what happened?" I asked.

A demonic voice came from somewhere behind us, "Maybe she knows how to get you back to doing what you're paid to do."

"You need to put a bell on that woman," Rose whispered.

"I'm not late," I shouted, looking at my watch, then at Frances. "Well, ok, ten minutes, but…" I tried to come up with an excuse then said, "Oh hell, never mind," I turned back to Rose, "You go enjoy the sights, I'll call you when I'm off work."

I was in the dressing room getting out of costume when I received a text from Rose telling me there was something I needed to see and it was urgent I meet her ASAP near the lagoon.

The path there was oddly vacant and the usual steel drum music from the hidden speakers was gone, allowing me to hear the chorus of birdcalls that I hoped were authentic and not merely a soundtrack.

I imagined the only thing that could make Rose hang around a lagoon filled with tourists would be a dead body.

My fertile imagination had no problem conjuring images of floating corpses, or hostage stand-offs, but it was no match for the reality of what I saw when I rounded the last Crepe Myrtle of the path.

A crowd of no less than a hundred sunburned backs lined the edge of the lagoon and beyond them, just a few yards from shore, was a stage. I heard a woman's voice singing Disney's "Let It Go," but it was not until I had elbowed my way to the front did I discover why there were a disproportionate number of men in the front row. I'm sure my mouth was as slack jawed as the ones surrounding me.

I got another text from Rose. *Are you seeing this?*

A woman of indeterminate age, a crown of flowers atop her bright auburn hair, was performing on the floating stage. With her head bent, her hair fell in soft curls to her shoulders partially obscuring her face. She wore a grass skirt revealing long, chorus-line legs, and a palm frond bikini-top over Vegas inspired breasts of tanned silicone. She sat on a rattan throne, drumming on a set of bongos between her knees, and belting out, *"Can't hold it back anymooorrre."*

Bare chested men in loincloths, their necks ringed with flower leis, flanked her on either side. They moved in 70's dance style, pivoting right and then left, arms bent at elbows moving up and down to the beat of the bongos. Lighted, inflatable palm trees waved in the breeze behind them.

Rose edged next to me displacing the sweaty man on my left telling him, "Move along, don't you have a wife and some kids back there or something?"

She nudged my shoulder with hers and said, "Now there's something you don't see every day, a bongo playin' hula-girl singin' Disney songs in the middle of a lake."

She lifted her cell phone over the baldhead in front of us. "I've got to video this 'cause there ain't enough words for what we're seein'."

When the park closed for the day, Dan assembled everyone for a staff meeting to discuss how the dress rehearsal went. He stood on a makeshift podium in front of the dancing-fountain play area. It was complete with a PA system, awning, and motorized fans. Joining him onstage was Frank Preston and three other men wearing Dolphin Dan monogrammed polo shirts tucked into slacks so expertly pressed you could have cut yourself on the crease.

Dan was wrapping up a standard pep talk of, *thanks and good job everyone*, when one of the polo shirts took over. He looked to be in his 40's with the standard issue blonde, tycoon haircut, clean-shaven face, and average body type.

"We, my associates and I," he nodded to the others, "are thrilled to be part of this magnificent new park. Far more than a place for families to come and enjoy themselves, Dolphin Dan's is dedicated to the kind of research that will help preserve our oceans and the precious life that call them home. Each of you play equally important roles in helping us achieve our stated goal; no matter how minor you feel your part to be. To us," he gestured with a broad sweep to the rest of his group, "you are all stars in this production. And speaking of stars, allow me to thank one of our great performers today." He looked right at me.

"Won't you please join us on stage?" he said, extending a hand in my direction.

Even more applause, along with whistles and shouts, followed that line and I noticed Frank Preston was one of the more enthusiastic of that group.

Me? I mouthed to the man speaking, and pointed to myself. He smiled and nodded.

I was feeling good about my job of *Guide Shark* but I hadn't thought anyone else noticed.

Frank was looking in my direction too, and I felt my heart flutter. I began making my way toward the stage when a strong nudge on my back nearly toppled me forward and a female voice said, "Oops, sorry honey."

I watched as the crowd parted to let the sashaying redhead through. Frank walked forward and offered her his hand as she took her place among the group of men.

"Ladies and gentleman, let's hear it for Miss GiGi and her Tropical Revue."

I looked around to see if anyone had noticed my blunder, but all eyes were fixed on Miss GiGi in her grass skirt.

With my shark head under my arm, I walked back to the dressing room certain that neither my absence, nor my tears would be noticed.

My cell vibrated while I was in the employee bathroom, finishing my little cry, and saw that the call was from my daughter, Megan.

I faked an upbeat voice, "Hello?"

"Happy Birthday Mom!"

NINE

One of my closest friends since arriving in Florida is my buddy Zig. He's a D.J at WWTF, a *music of your life* radio station in Fort Myers. He came here from Chicago where he was the morning-drive jock at a rock and roll station. Zig is my age, covered in tattoos, has longish hair, and drives an Indian motorcycle. Zig, his mother Dorothy, and Rose were at my house when I got there. Chinese take-out, cheesecake with candles, confetti printed paper plates, red Solo cups, and a punch bowl of rum cooler covered my kitchen table under a home-made banner that read, *60 IS THE NEW SEXY.*

I burst into tears.

I stopped crying, had a rum cooler, spoke to my two-year-old grandson on the phone, ate some cake, and had another rum cooler.

I sat with Zig's mother and told her what had happened earlier. Dorothy, who is in her mid-80's, is an ex vaudeville, and movie actress. She always appears as if she's having her portrait painted. She can dress down anyone, including a hired gun, and I've seen her do this, with such style and finesse that they thank her afterward.

When I finished telling her about my earlier embarrassing moment, she patted my hand, threw back her wine spritzer and said, "That reminds of the time I was at the Oscars. It was '51 or '52, I think, Zig was a toddler at the time. Anyway, seated next to me was a splendid actress, what the papers used to label, *Movie Star.*"

Dorothy raised her glass and flourished it above her head. "She had been absolutely sublime in the role for which she had been nominated. I thought she was a shoe-in for the statue as did everyone else, especially the actress herself. William Holden and Janet Leigh were on stage to present the award. I've always thought Bill Holden was overrated but that's a story for another time," she patted my knee. "So, Janet is grinning and ripping the envelope in the most inept way, and the actress beside me is squirming and alternating between holding her breath and sighing. The scent of gin overpowered her cologne and I worried she might not be able to walk onto the stage to accept the damn thing if she *did* win. Bill took the envelope from Janet, who was clearly too nervous to open the damn thing, and began to read the name. Because Bill had also had a few martinis for dinner, he slurred the name of the winner and the actress next to me thought it was her own; it was not. She had risen, the cameras on her of course, and realized too late her error. She nervously pretended to be adjusting her fur coat."

"Awww, the poor woman," I said, "how humiliating. Who was it?"

Dorothy's grin went ear to ear, "Why, it was Liz Taylor."

I didn't know if her story was true, but it made me feel better all the same. Either the likes of Elizabeth Taylor are not immune to my brand of humiliation, or Dorothy cared enough to throw the movie star under the bus for me. I thanked her and proceeded to the punch bowl for a refill.

Zig and Rose stood near the record player sorting through the albums that Zig had brought from his home. They were in the middle of a friendly argument over whose rendition of *Embraceable You* was the best. Rose went with Nat King Cole, Zig liked Ella Fitzgerald's. They asked my opinion and I told them I liked Michael Bubles'. They looked at me open mouthed, said nothing, and then returned to their debate. I returned to the rum and stared at the British spy- bug on my globe.

"You know what I hate?" I said, standing next to my bookshelf and speaking loudly in the direction of the listening device. "Tea, tea and crumpets. What the hell's a crumpet by the way, anyone know?"

My guests all turned to stare.

"I also hate rugby and...and fish and chips. They're not even chips are they, they're French fries."

More stares, I may have been slurring my words a bit.

"And the men are all sissies, have you noticed that?" I bent to insure I was speaking directly into the bug. "With their pasty white skin and fancy accents."

I finished the rest of the rum in my cup with one gulp.

"I'm going to go crush ice," I told them, carrying the globe to the kitchen with me. I sang The Star Spangled Banner and pointed the southern hemisphere toward the loud whir of the blender.

"Who wants coffee?" Zig asked. "I know I could go for a cup."

I dreamt that I was lying on the beach; Miss GiGi was pouring sand in my mouth from her bongo drums and singing Bibbity Bobbity Boo, while her back-up dancers kicked my head each time they side-stepped to the music. I took gentle steps to the kitchen and pushed the start button on the Mister Coffee.

I brought a mug-full back to bed and used it to swallow some aspirin. I didn't have to go into the park that day, thank God. It was closed to the public, repairing any glitches they found at dress rehearsal. I picked up my cell to call Zig. I knew he was on-air, so I left a message.

"Thank you so much for my birthday party. It was really sweet of you to put it together for me. Sorry I got drunk and stupid, but I really did have a great time. You want me to drop some cake by later? Call when you can and thanks again, you're the best."

Next, I called Pam and had to leave another voice message, "Hi Pam, just wondering if you heard back from your professor. I'm working from home today so please call as soon as you get a minute."

The last call was to Rose and she answered with. "How's your head?"

"About like you'd expect. Hey, I'm not sure if I told you, but Big Kev never showed up for work yesterday, which is why I couldn't find him to talk to him. Dan said Kev called in sick, migraine or something."

"I can't check on him on account of he's in the clear no matter what my..."

"I know, you weren't allowed to spit on him. Hey, I'm not supposed to be there today, but I may go in anyway as a favor to a...well, to a widow. I'll check if he's there and try to talk to him if he is."

"Don't tell me what you're doing. We got a Detective McKenzie on loan from New York helping out with the three floaters you snagged. I want in on it, and when that happens I won't be able to talk to you anymore."

"Shit, really? You won't be able to tell me anything?" I asked tucking my phone under my chin and pouring another cup of coffee.

"Nope, gotta go."

"Bye," I said to no one; she'd already hung up.

Friday, June 21st

There was an accidental drowning at the new Dolphin Dan's last Sunday, the same day yours truly had her own close encounter with drowning victims. In this case, it was a marine- life veterinarian. A witness stated the man appeared to have had a seizure while in the water. Information on the netted dead divers has been hard to get, but an un-named source tells this blogger the men may have died from heart attacks. Any divers out there want to address that? Though most of you still believe their deaths are related to the fact that they were entangled in an illegally sized drift net, police are still not calling this a crime. The deceased appear to have no ties to the fishing industry, although I am waiting to receive official confirmation of this. The local press is no longer covering this, but we'll stay on it here until we get some answers 'cause...We're all here to be clear

Magpie

I had some website-editing freelance work to do for a publishing house that specialized in Amish romance novels. I made what I thought were helpful suggestions, like having a shirtless muscular man on the front instead of always the same young women in bonnets. They felt that crossed a line so I suggested perhaps the men could just show their forearm, maybe roll their sleeves up a little to tackle that barn raising. I assured them a little man muscle would go a long way with the ladies who needed some excitement between churning and quilting things. The back and forth took up most of the day so it was pretty late when I stopped by Zig's to drop off the left-over General Tso chicken and birthday cake I had promised.

"You wanna stay and share this?" he asked when I walked it into his kitchen.

Zig lived in a neighborhood of small yet perfectly manicured pre-fab houses where his was the only one with a large motorcycle in the drive. The home had belonged to his mother, Dorothy, and when she moved into a large and swanky retirement community, he took over her old place. The house was a mixture of her antiques and his electronics, like The Jetsons meet Downtown Abbey.

His cat, Sheba, circled my legs, as she always did, and I wagered her affections were aimed more toward the poultry in my hands than to me. It was either that, or she wanted to kill me in a freak fall. I dropped her some General Tso to cover my bet.

"I would love to stay," I told him, "but I'm running by Dan's to...to kind of drop something off."

"Hang on, I'll go with you," he said, and grabbed his keys off a hook. "I've got to do a remote broadcast from there Monday for their grand opening. It will help if I can scope it out first. I'm guessing you came on your scooter and it looks like rain, we'll take my car."

He held the door open for me.

"O...K," I said, "but, well, the something that I need to drop off is kind of, uhm, sensitive."

"Sensitive? What's so sensitive, are you a drug mule now?"

"Very funny, L. O. L." I said, dropping into the seat of his sport's car that felt as though it were about an inch and a half off the ground. "No, I'm, well, I'm scattering someone's ashes if you must know."

"Whose?"

"A grave digger from Bulgaria."

"Yeah, that was going to be my first guess," Zig said, backing out of the drive. "Should I ask why?"

"His wife brought him to me because, I don't know, because I'm fated to always have these things happen to me I suppose."

I pulled the fancy box of ashes from my bag to show him.

"Yeah, it seems like that," said Zig, glancing at the package on my lap. "An Eastern European grave digger who wants his ashes scattered at a marine park in Florida. Yep, it doesn't get any more *you* than that."

While Zig checked out the bikini area of the gift shop, because, as he told me with a straight face, he thought the acoustics there would work best, Radu and I made our way to the lagoon. It was nearly five o'clock in the evening, but this close to summer the sky was only hinting at the reds, yellows, and oranges that would eventually fill the western horizon. I sat on the sand and watched slow moving dolphins rise to the surface sending up whooshes of moist air as dorsal fins made silent ripples in the surface. Sometimes two or three of them would rise and fall simultaneously, their movements coordinated in a type of slow dance. My eyes scanned the distance looking for the next appearance when I noticed a small boat coming from the eastern end of the lagoon behind the waterfall.

Because that area was in shade, I couldn't see who was in the boat and I scrambled to hide myself. I really didn't want to explain the box of deceased grave digger with me. The short palm bush I hid behind was wide enough to camouflage me as long as I didn't stand or move, and I had a clear view of the lagoon, though I had to hold open the palm fronds and peek though like a child playing hide and seek.

Dolphins circled the small dinghy as it made its way close to the mouth of the lagoon where it stopped. The person inside stood up, put his hand to his face like someone shouting, and began making large arm movements that soon became apparent were signals to the animals. In a few moments, a metal gate rose from beneath the water, cutting through the surface creating waves that sent the boat rocking in its wake. Dolphins jumped, dove, and circled. I didn't know if those were joyful or agitated behaviors. The gate made a slow descent and the figure on board appeared to be pulling things from the water onto the boat but he was too far away and backlit for me to see much else. The whole process took no more than ten minutes.

As he motored back to the waterfall, he made an abrupt stop. A cloud that had been obscuring the sun, had passed. It was now shining on the glass jewels on Radu's container that I had left on the sand. They shone like spot lights. Smaller clouds moved across the sky momentarily obscuring the sunlight then quickly moving away so that beams of light flashed on and off like a signal code. I closed the palm fronds to hide my face since I was almost certain I saw him holding binoculars. He stopped the boat, turned it in my direction, and stared at the shore.

I couldn't retrieve the box without coming out from behind the bush so instead I threw dirt onto it in an attempt to dull the surface. The sand was dry and slid off as quickly as I could throw it. The boat motored closer until it was only a few feet from shore directly in front of Radu.

I looked behind to see if I had an escape route, I did not. I willed myself to stay calm, telling myself I had only witnessed some kind of training exercise. The worst thing that could happen, I reasoned, was that I would be fired for trespassing or not asking permission to bury someone at sea.

"Deep breaths," I told myself. "Just breathe and stay calm."

The man, who I did not recognize, left the boat and tucked the binoculars into the waist band of his jeans, like police do with...*oh my God,* I thought, *is that a gun? No, of course not, but it looks like...no, stop being ridiculous...but still, it kind of looks like...*

He picked up the box of remains, opened it, dug around inside, and finding nothing to interest him, threw it back onto the beach, thankfully leaving most of the ashes inside.

He was so near that I didn't dare breathe until he was back on board, nor move until he disappeared behind the waterfall. I grabbed Radu, ran, and didn't stop until I reached the gift shop.

That is where I found Zig chatting with the shop's clerk.

"Hey," he said when I was nearly on top of him, "when did you get here? I thought I was going to have to send out a search party."

"Can we go now please?" I looked from him to the middle-aged blonde who was grinning impishly and holding a business card I assumed to be his, then back to Zig and begged, "Please?"

"See ya' Saturday," he called over his shoulder to the clerk as we made our way out of the shop. I was close to a run. Zig was sauntering which is how he always walks. I think if his house were on fire, he would saunter out of the door daring the flames to try and rush him. I stood by his car door and jiggled like a child who had waited too long to pee.

"I see you still got your friend," Zig said, nodding toward the box as we drove out of the lot.

"Yeah, it wasn't the right, I don't know, there wasn't a good time to do it. Can we go to your house?" I asked. "I might want a drink, do you have alcohol, or pie?"

"I have one of those things, I also have your scooter in my carport. Are you ok? What happened to you back there?"

"Oh, I just over-reacted to something I saw, I don't know why. Someone was working in the lagoon with the dolphins and I freaked out for some reason. It just looked, I don't know, not right. I dropped our friend Radu here and hid behind a tree like Wiley Coyote."

"It's understandable," Zig, said turning the windshield wipers on high after a sudden cloud burst. "You pulled a net of bloated corpses onto a boat less than a week ago, I think you're entitled to be a little jumpy."

The rubber blades were no match for the torrents of rain that were turning the glass opaque. I closed my eyes. The rhythmic movements of the wipers across the glass were relaxing and I zoned out for a minute before a bolt of lightning, literal and figurative, brought me back.

"A whistle, that guy was blowing into a whistle," I told Zig. "He wasn't shouting at them, he was whistling. Did I mention that one of the dead guys had a whistle?"

"I'm no expert, said Zig, leaning forward to wipe condensation from the glass, "but isn't that pretty standard animal training gear?"

"Yes."

"And don't divers carry them so they can call the person on the boat to, you know, come get them?"

"I don't know, probably," I said, moving slightly to break the suction of my legs from the leather seat. "Do divers carry guns?"

"If they're in a James Bond movie they do, why, did you see a gun?"

"It could have been a pair of binoculars."

"Bingo."

"You're right, I'm conclusion jumping again."

"Not necessarily, bodies are piling up here, it's suspicious. Stay on it, it's what you're good at."

"Then I'm gonna need some coffee, pull into that 7-11, there please," I pointed toward my left, "it's not raining on that side of the street."

ENTANGLED by Kathleen Cosgrove

TEN

They call him Flipper, Flipper, faster than lightening. No one you see is smarter than he. And we know Flipper, lives in a world full of wonder, lying there under, under the sea.

That was the theme song, albeit an awful one, to my favorite TV show when I was a kid. Flipper was much better than Lassie, in my opinion, because A), Sandy, the teen boy in the show, was cute and seldom wore a shirt, as opposed to Lassie's little Timmy who was merely adorable and clumsy. And B), Flipper lived underwater, which was alien and mysterious.

Standing near the dolphin exhibit, where photos from that TV show were part of the display, reminded me of those days when I wanted my own pet dolphin. Now, here I was, surrounded by those amazing animals, ready to ask Dan for a chance to work with the trainers.

I had spent the previous evening trying to learn all I could about dolphin coaching. Most of the Google hits were videos from various sea parks around the country that had their own *swim with the dolphins* experiences. I could find almost nothing to help me with deciphering the scene I had witnessed in the lagoon.

This was the last weekend before the grand opening and it was a media preview day. Everyone was busy fixing all the glitches in the system they had uncovered during the *family and friends* dress rehearsal. I arrived at dawn to look for Dan before things got too hectic.

The door to the shack was closed and no one answered when I knocked. I tried calling Dan's mobile but he didn't answer. I walked the park looking for Big Kev but had no luck. The Dolphateria was open so I headed there in search of Dan, Kevin and coffee, not necessarily in that order.

Since it was still an hour before the press would arrive, the room was nearly deserted except for a group of twelve or so. Three square tables had been pushed together to form a kind of long conference table where the group sat, oblivious to my entrance. The room smelled of coffee, bacon and cologne and my stomach made a rumble that I'd hoped was too far away to be heard. As my pupils slowly opened to the artificial room light, I was able to make out Frank Preston at the center of the table and the assorted gray suits filled the rest of the chairs.

The Dolphateria was arranged in a style reminiscent of a mall food court, but with a buffet type salad bar in the center. Three stations lined the back wall and offered either pizza, hot dogs and burgers, or sandwiches and chips. To the right of those was a fountain-drinks and coffee area, and on the wall to the left was the frozen yogurt bar.

Several dozen smaller tables-for-four were arranged to afford just enough space for maneuvering between them, and six high-top tables with two stools each were arranged in front of the desert area. One of the walls was made of floor to ceiling windows and afforded a view of the playground and picnic area. Frank's group sat in front of the windows and a man seated opposite him was tapping a stack of index cards nervously on the table. Frank reached his hand across to stop him.

"Go ahead," said Frank to the man. "If you honestly think these are better suited then I want to hear them."

The gray-suit held one of the cards and read, "Fluffy, Mittens, and Rover." He pulled another, seemingly at random and read, "Flip, Fin, Salty Beak," then another card, "Leftie, Mister Gray..."

"Stop right there," Frank said in his baritone. "We are going with Hamlet, Macbeth, Falstaff, Othello, Puck, and Lear."

Everyone was silent, glancing furtively at one another. The man with the index cards began to speak, but Frank gave him a look that advised him not to.

A woman at the opposite end of the table said, "But Mister Preston sir, you know, a couple of those dolphins are female."

"*Lady* Macbeth then, and we'll change Falstaff to Juliet."

The gray-suit with the purple tie wrote on a legal pad and said aloud, "Ok, so Juliet, *Lady* Macbeth, Hamlet, Lear, Othello and Puck."

"Then we're done," Frank put his hands flat on the table, scooted his chair back and began to rise when he turned and noticed me. "Maggie, what a pleasure to see you, won't you join us? We're naming the dolphins."

"Thanks," I said, "it sounds like you already have. Great choices by the way, only I'd have gone with Kate for one of the females. *The Taming of the Shrew* is a favorite of mine."

"Kate it is then," he said to the gray shirt with the legal pad.

I watched the man scribble out the name Juliet with a force that nearly tore a hole in the yellow paper.

"Sorry, I didn't mean to eavesdrop, I was looking for..."

"No, no, it's fine," he said and gestured for me to sit at their table. "Nothing hush-hush, no top-secret plans."

He pulled a chair out for me. I sat and glanced around the table smiling to the group. "I'm Maggie," I told them. "I'm the guide shark."

"Can I order you anything Maggie," Frank asked. "Coffee, tea, a sea lion?"

"Ha ha, I get it, and no, thank you, I'm fine," I said, "I'm sorry I interrupted."

I saw Frances scowling at me from behind the salad display.

"I'm not working yet this morning," I said loud enough for her to hear. "I'm just looking for Dan, anyone seen him?"

"He's sent a message he's a bit delayed." Frank said. "So tell me, what other of Shakespeare's plays are your favorites?"

I looked around the table at the clearly annoyed group, then back at Frank and said, "I understudied for Hermia in college. When *I* was in college," I felt the stupid need to clarify. "Not when Hermia was in college."

I made a small chuckle and Frank laughed in a way I took to mean that he was delighted. His cat's eyes crinkled and everything.

"Oh, *Dream* is *so* much fun isn't it?" he asked. "What was your Puck like? He's the one character I was never able..."

"Mister Preston, sir," interrupted the hound of hell, Frances. "I believe you asked to be notified when the lady arrived," and she motioned toward GiGi entering the room.

"Oh yes, thank you," Frank told her. "I'm sorry Maggie; I'm expected to consult on a performance."

"I understand, I never saw an investor take such an interest in the running of a place. That's—that's great."

"This isn't work at all Maggie, this is fun."

GiGi made her way toward us and half spoke, half purred, "Hello Frank, you're looking quite sexy today." She grabbed his hand and squeezed.

Now that she was only inches away, I was able to get a better look at her. I couldn't be sure, but I figured her for maybe early to late fifties. She'd had plenty of work done but the neck and hands were a dead give-away. Botox strained her smile and her eyes had a bit of a surprised look. I had to hand it to her though, she was gorgeous.

She turned to me and said, "Hello, I'm GiGi and you are Maggie, am I right, the park clown?"

"Guide," I said, "It's kind of a public relations position."

"And you wear a large rubber shark head to do that? Well, I can see you are perfect for the part."

"I saw your performance, by the way," I said. "It was, uhm, fascinating. I haven't heard bongo drums since Little Ricky played them on the *I Love Lucy* show."

We smiled at one another with teeth bared.

"Come Frank," she said, grabbing his hand. "You simply *must* tell me what you think of *myyyy* costume." She looked over her shoulder at me, then back to Frank.

There is no way he is falling for that bunch of baloney, I thought until I heard what came next.

"I need your opinion on whether or not it's too scandalous."

She put her arm through his and, walking away, moved her hips like she was using them to clear brush.

OK, I thought, *this is war.*

I bumped into Dan on my way out of The Dolphateria. The park had been open for only a few minutes and was already becoming crowded with landscapers, builders, and various staff. He didn't see me since he was looking over the heads of everyone toward the table where Frank and his group had been.

"Dan, just the one I wanted to see," I told him. "If you're looking for Frank, he's gone. The bongo player came and got him."

"Oh, Hi Maggie," he said, finally noticing me. "Do you know where they went?"

"I have no idea," I said. I had no intention of repeating the *scandalous outfit* line. "But Dan, before you go, I have to ask you something."

"I'm pretty busy right now, can it wait?" He pulled his cell from his pocket and dialed.

"I want to work with the dolphin trainers," I blurted quickly. "I'll do it on my own time. I won't be in the way or anything."

"Hang on dude," he said to the person on the phone, and then to me he said, "What?"

"I want to hang out with the dolphin trainers, only for a day or two, on my own time, just watching and not interfering or even talking."

"Yeah, I guess that would be cool. Go see Kev, tell him I said it's ok," he said and continued his call.

"Yes!" I did a double fist pump. "This is gonna be great."

I heard Dan say to the person on the phone, "Oh wow dude, I wasn't thinking, yeah, hang on."

He turned back to me and said, "Nah, that's a no-go Mags, sorry, I uhhh—changed my mind."

ELEVEN

"But Dan said I could," I lied to the guard at the security shack.

"Sorry ma'am, I have no way to confirm that. I am only permitted to contact Mister Dan in case of an emergency, or if anyone important needs to see him. Your situation does not meet those criteria."

I knew that; Dan was lunching with Frank Preston and people from the media and I figured it would be a great time to sneak in.

"You call him *Mister* Dan?" I asked, stalling until I could think of another lie. I tried to remember Dan's last name. Everyone just called him Dan, or Dolphin Dan, or variations of *nutcase*.

"Yeah, so?"

"Nothing, it just sounds a little like Forrest Gump saying *Lieutenant* Dan, that's all. Of course, not that you sound like Forrest Gump because you don't, not at all. That was a really good movie, don't you think," I glanced at his nametag, "Marty?"

"Yeah, whatever, now, if you'll excuse me, I got to walk the perimeter."

I wondered if that was a euphemism for taking a leak.

Marty was a short, thin, African-American man that I would place somewhere in his early thirties. I hadn't realized *how* short until he stood and walked from behind the desk of monitors. He wasn't a midget, or little person technically, but he was no more than, and probably a few inches shy of, five foot tall.

The room we were in was so small that, by comparison, he had appeared average sized before. Except for the desk where a television was tuned to Judge Judy, the bank of half a dozen monitors, and a couple of short stools, the room was empty. In addition to the elevator entrance, and a door leading outside, I spotted one clearly identifiable as a rest room so if he was going for a leak, there was no reason for him to leave.

"The perimeter of the building or the whole park?" I asked, thinking if he were going to walk the park on those legs I'd have the rest of the day and probably most of the night to get to the lab.

"Lady, I got shit to do, you go on now," he said, walking past me and sending out an odor of Axe cologne and nicotine.

So, I thought, obviously walking the perimeter meant smoke break.

I had an eye on the monitors behind him that surveyed the lab. The cameras were positioned too far from the tanks and at too awkward of angles for me to get a decent look at what the trainers were doing.

"Can I just sit with you and watch from here?" I asked, using my flirtiest persona.

"Do not make me have to call for back-up," he said, obviously not buying my act.

His key card was on the edge of the desk and looked exactly like mine. I made a spur of the moment decision and swapped the two when he turned his back to open the door to usher me out. With any luck, I thought, his would get me into places mine would not.

"Fine," I said, trying not to sound nervous, "Suit yourself, but I was going to get us ice cream and everything."

I had begun to suspect that Dan was treating the visiting members of the press to the type of beverages not normally available to regular guests of the park. I realized this when one of them asked why the costume I wore didn't include genitals. Like college kids on spring break, the tipsy journalists were one-upping each other in how ridiculous they wished to be photographed with the park's poor, hapless shark-mascot, me. Twenty dollars an hour suddenly didn't seem all that outrageous of a salary and in fact, I was tempted to ask for a raise.

The more inebriated the reporters became, the more loudly they laughed at each other's *we're gonna need a bigger boat* lines, or the more unrecognizable their imitation of the tuba in the Jaws theme song became.

Just about the time I was contemplating ways I could really bite one of them, Howard the photographer again came to my rescue.

"Hey folks, they've set up a tiki bar by the lagoon for the three o'clock stage show," he announced.

It was as though he blew the bugle at the Kentucky Derby. Within moments, the proud and drunken members of the fourth estate were off and running, leaving only Howard, me, and the post-adolescent photographer from the *Bonita Beach Banner*. The kid was trying to impress Howard with his photography techno-babble. I thought it only fair that I return Howard's earlier favor. I aimed the rubberized pointy teeth of my costume directly at the guy's head and rushed him doing my best tuba imitation "Dun duuuun dun duuuun dun duuuun."

"Hey," the kid yelled, "that's creepy, you wanna' back off?"

I did not, in fact, back off and he told Howard, "See ya' man, this shark is *definitely* not cool."

He zigzagged down the path like a metal ball in an arcade game.

"Should we tell him he's going in the wrong direction?" Howard asked.

I shrugged as much as an animated shark is capable.

"You're right," he said, "probably good for him to walk it off."

I nodded in the affirmative.

"Alright, I think you're safe now, they won't be back till the end of the Miss GiGi show; that's when the bar closes."

I raised my pectoral fin; he returned the high-five and said, "See ya' around Jaws."

Like taking off a bra the moment you enter the house, the first thing any mascot removes entering a dressing room is the head.

One can never fully appreciate the luxury of fresh air on your face until you've spent thirty minutes of a south Florida summer with your head in a latex box.

That rapturous moment of joy lasted less than a minute when the first person I encountered was Miss GiGi, in front of a mirror, adjusting her boobs. The floral print bikini top and matching floral skirt with slits from toe to hip barely concealed her toned and tanned figure. Her auburn hair was a near perfect match to the hibiscus lei and matching sandals. She was stunning.

"Hey ya," she said, still focused on her reflection. "I'm worried the pattern on this top makes the girls look lopsided, what do you think?"

I'd have rather stuck a fork in my eye than analyze that woman's breasts so I set the shark head in my locker and said, "You look lovely, I'm sure no one will notice."

"Notice?" she said in an alarmed tone, "*you* think they look lopsided too?"

"That's not what I'm saying at all, I'm just saying, no one would care," I told her, stepping out of my costume.

"Well, how would you know anyway?"

"I'm sorry, what?" I asked, pivoting so sharply I made a tread mark on the floor.

"Oh, I don't mean anything by that," she said, continuing to turn from side to side scrutinizing herself. "I just mean, no one is going to look at *your* figure, you're lucky like that."

I fingered the key-card in my pocket and wondered if it accessed a gunroom.

"Maybe it's not the top that's making them look lopsided," I added, standing behind her and using a concerned face. "Maybe one of them has sprung a slow leak."

She looked at my reflection behind hers and frowned, "Oh, these are not fake, they're real."

"Ok, why not," I said turning back to my locker. "That defies the laws of, well, biology and gravity, but ok, sure."

She stomped her foot, sending a flower petal across the floor and under the Coke machine. "Ugh! Why won't anyone *believe* me?"

I took the question to be rhetorical so I said nothing.

"Anyway," she said, rubbing lipstick off her teeth, "I have to be focused now; I'm going on-stage in a few minutes."

Then she turned to look at me baring her un-smudged canines and said, complete with dramatic pauses, "And—I have a date afterward—with *Frank*."

I was in the middle of putting deodorant on and froze, elbow at my ear, not breathing, afraid I'd give something away.

"That's nice," I told her, resuming my deodorizing. "I'll bet he won't mind the lopsided boob thing at all, don't you dare let it ruin your evening. Maybe you could wear a jacket."

She stomped again, this time propelling an entire flower across the floor. "Ugh—I—You—I have to go now."

"Bye," I answered brightly, "bitch," I added under my breath.

TWELVE

The thing about key-cards, I remembered too late, is that they are numbered. I realized, however, that it could take Marty a few hours to figure out he had the wrong one. That might give me time to get into the lab and swap them back if I could do it quickly, while he *walked the perimeter.*

I waited outside the shack for the nicotine urge to hit Marty. Five minutes after I'd begun surveillance, he walked out pulling sunglasses out of his shirt pocket with one hand, and a pack of smokes from his pants pocket with the other. He lit up, then pulled a cell phone from yet another pocket and started scanning the phone's screen while he puffed.

"Come on Marty, move away from the door Damnit," I whispered. "At least pretend you're checking the area."

Mosquitoes bit my legs, and although a bottle of repellent was only as far away as the bag on my arm, the smell from it would be too strong to take a chance. I was sure Marty would have noticed, even through the nicotine fog. I'd been squatting there no more than a couple of minutes, but my legs were cramping and my skin was drenched in sweat.

I'd have been better off in the shark costume, I thought, *at least it's bug proof and has fans.*

After another five minutes, Marty dug a small hole in the dirt with the toe of his boot and buried the butts, put his phone in his pocket and swiped his key-card. I held my breath; certain the door was not going to open for him. However, before he could try, a voice called out his name and Marty stopped, mid turn. It was Howard, making his way toward the shack, passing within inches of where I squatted, waving and calling Marty's name.

The expression on Howard's face was friendly, Marty's, not so much. They shook hands, the guard shrugged, and although I couldn't hear what they said, I got the distinct impression this was not the first time they'd met.

Howard held up something to show Marty, I imagined it to be a photo but there was no way for me to be certain. Marty followed Howard down the same path from where the latter had come. Torn between going into the shack and following the men; I chose the shack.

The door opened with the stolen key-card, as did the elevator access. Dolphins swam and circled frenetically outside the glass of the underwater tunnel, and I knew that meant there was a performance in the lagoon. I had a brief fantasy of one of them knocking Miss GiGi off the stage and smiled to myself.

After opening the final door, the one leading from the tunnel to the dolphin clinic, I stood at the entry and peered in from the side.

"She's coming around, she'll be able to swim on her own soon," a man's voice spoke from a corner of the room that was hidden from my view.

"I don't like it Harris," said Big Kev.

The entrance where I stood was raised allowing me to stand at eye level to the tank where Big Kev stood near a motionless dolphin. He looked to be holding it so its blowhole was above water.

"Her breathing's too shallow," he said.

I wondered who Harris was and wished he would move from where he stood so I could see him.

"It's the new anesthesia, she'll shake it off, you'll see," said Harris. "I'm a doctor damn it, just trust me."

As if on cue, the inert animal sent up a large plume of wet air from her blowhole.

"That's a girl Kate," said Big Kev to the dolphin, walking her slowly around the pool. "That's great, you're doing great." Then to Harris he said, "Yeah, but you're an MD, she needs a vet."

The animal made a few squeaks and thrashed her tail, sending water over the sides.

"Stop worrying, I know what I'm doing," said Harris.

"I still think we shoulda' waited for the new vet to get here," said Kevin, stroking the animal's sides.

"She's gonna be pretty spastic over the next day or two till she has time to adjust to the implant," said Harris who had moved toward the tank. "We'll keep her separated; don't want her freaking out the herd."

As Harris came into view, I recognized him as one of the partners.

"I'll hang with her tonight, you go home," he told Kevin.

"Maybe I'll stay tonight too," he said, "I'm worried about her. She's been pretty upset since Alden—you know, she misses him, loved him, I think."

My feelings about Big Kev made a complete one-eighty, he was a decent guy and I had totally misjudged him.

"What, you think I can't hold her freaking blow hole out of the water? Hell man, besides being a physician, I'm one of the investors of this circus and I've got a lot of money sunk into that pile of blubber. Don't worry, she's not gonna drown. Besides, maybe I'll invite Miss Hula down for her own private show."

Good Lord, I thought, *this guy is a real bottom feeder.*

"She's fine," Harris continued. "She's a freaking animal, you give her some food she'll love you too. Don't be getting all misty eyed over the damned thing."

He pulled his shirt off and made his way up the ladder to the tank. "Go on, beat it, I got this."

Big Kev said something I could not hear, and left down the same ladder. I exited the clinic the way I came in, pausing only a moment in the tunnel to watch the underwater show and to come up with a story to use on Marty in case he was there when I got back. I had decided to tell him that I had discovered the key-card mix up and was searching for him in the lab so that I could return his. I need not have bothered though, when I got off the elevator, the guard room was still deserted.

My phone showed three missed calls. One from Pam, one from Dave, my friend at the paper, and another from Rose. I called Rose first but it went to voicemail. Pam was next and hers did the same. With the call to Dave, I at last got through.

"Maggie, I thought you'd want to know, Stuart got a tip but it's still unconfirmed so don't blog it yet."

"Really? Thanks for calling me, what's the news?"

"You gotta promise first you won't write about it until we run it."

"Yeah, of course, I'd never screw you over, you know that."

'Ok, well, as long as you promise," he said and gulped before he continued. "Those guys you—ya' know, the ones you..."

"Yeah, I know the ones you mean, the dead guys in the net, go on."

"Ok, well, they flew to The Bahamas from San Diego three weeks before they— before you found—before you *caught* them. Anyway, they flew to Nassau on American Airlines, one-way tickets, and there's no record of them ever leaving. They didn't fly out, no boat charters, no missing person report. It's like they disappeared until, well until you found them."

"Hey Dave?"

"Yeah,"

"You are awesome!" I jumped up and down a little. "I am *so* getting you that gig at the Sun God. The phone chimed its *incoming call* tone and I said, "Thank you Dave, you're the best. Call if you get any more news."

The new incoming call was from Pam.

"How did it go with the professor?" I asked.

"He was interested, I could tell, even though he pretended not to be. Said he'd heard of this kind of thing but only as rumors."

"What kind of thing?" I asked, walking to a spot behind the shack for privacy.

"It relates to sonar, that much I'm sure of. It's why I brought them to him to start with. But what else it means, I don't have a cue."

"Clue, you don't have a clue."

"No, I don't, I need to see your copies, he took the originals."

"I don't have them anymore. You didn't make more copies?"

"No, I didn't have time. He's headed to Miami. He was getting his car serviced at the Jag dealer in Naples. That's where I brought them to him. He was running late and couldn't wait for me to stop and make duplicates."

"Well, whoever put a bug in my house took my copies."

"You have bugs in your house that, what, eat your papers?"

"Not that kind of bug," I said, cupping my hand near my mouth and whispering. "Someone planted a listening device in my house."

"Why would anyone do that?" her voice, also dropping to a whisper, asked.

"My friend Rose, the cop, is checking that out. A lot of stuff is going on right now and I may have gotten you involved too, I'm sorry."

"Do I need to be worried?" she asked.

"I don't know, I can't think of any reason you should, just keep your eyes and ears open. I guess we just sit tight until your professor comes back. When is that, by the way?"

"Tomorrow."

"By the way, what do you know about drift nets? You know that's what those guys I found were tangled up in. I've tried to research as much as I can online but there is almost nothing there. I even tried calling the Coast Guard and NOAA but they didn't seem to know anything about the laws regarding them either."

"You probably know then, that there are no regulations on the high seas, she said." Those things are sometimes eighty kilometers long, killing everything in their path."

"Yeah, I read that, it's pretty depressing. But is there some kind of organized crime associated with them? That's not exactly something that shows up in a Google search."

"I don't know, but it wouldn't be a big surprise to me. It is a billion dollar industry. So, do you think that's what all this is about, drift nets or fishing gangsters?"

"Honestly, I really don't know. Hell, the bug I told you about is from the British Secret Service."

I remembered to lower my voice but it wasn't necessary, the area where I was standing was still deserted.

"Well, that sounds pretty zany."

"Yeah, zany is not the word I'd choose but…"

I stopped listening to Pam because I heard squeaking and trilling sounds coming from the opposite side of the wall I was leaning against.

"Hey, let me know when you talk to the professor again," I said. "I've got to run."

The sounds I heard from behind the wall were unmistakably those of dolphins. The wall joined the shack on one side, and I followed it in the opposite direction toward what I thought was the lagoon. The closer to the water I got, the more trees and brush hid the wall from the rest of the park. I trudged between it, and the increasingly wild and difficult to navigate brush and weeds. Dead limbs and rocks made for an obstacle course, while branches scraped my arms and face and caught my hair. The thickness of the overgrowth blocked the sun and confused my sense of direction. My feet eventually became wet and muddy and I knew I had reached the edge of the lagoon. The sounds of rushing water told me I was behind the cave and waterfall.

Well, I thought, *this isn't on the guide map.*

THIRTEEN

I cut a path through the brush scraping legs, arms, and face. I wasn't bleeding but bug bites made me stop and scratch so much that by the time I stepped onto the beach of the lagoon my body was covered with the itching welts. I made straight for the water and waded in up to my knees, bending over to scoop water onto my arms, neck, and face.

"I'm going to have to talk to Dan about providing showers for the staff," said a male voice from behind me. It was Frank's; I froze mid-splash and contemplated jumping in and swimming to Mexico. Instead, I stood, turned to him, and said, "Sorry, that's probably not the view you came here to appreciate."

"An unexpected surprise," he said, a note of delight in his voice that made me forget the bites and scratches.

Frank was sitting only a few feet from shore, his jacket serving as a makeshift blanket, while his shoes and socks lay haphazardly on either side of him. He wiggled his toes and leaned back on his hands, all the while smiling that dazzling Frank Preston smile.

He nodded toward the bushes and said, "Should I ask?"

"Oh, I got lost."

"That's not good news coming from a park guide," he said, moving sideways like a crab and patting the jacket. "Would you like to sit a moment? Maybe get your bearings?"

"I probably should get back."

"Tell me, have you done much Shakespeare besides *Dream*?" he patted the jacket again.

I walked toward him brushing sand from my knees and pushing my hair behind my ears. I sat down on the jacket; my knees creaked.

"I was understudy in Lear, in college," I told him. "Even got to perform it twice before closing."

"Which sister, don't tell me you got to play Cordelia."

"I did, in fact. I think the director chose our Cordelias based on weight since our Lear was not exactly linebacker size. I was not a big girl, but in the scene where he had to carry me in, my feet dragged the floor and I had to move them a bit to keep us from falling."

"A dancing corpse," he laughed. "I would have loved to have seen that. What else?"

"I understudied in Twelfth Night, Viola," I said. "I never got to perform it except in two rehearsals. Always the understudy, never the star."

I regretted that last line, I didn't want to come off as pathetic.

"What about you?" I asked in my most non-pathetic tone.

"Oh, I've played a few good ones, Hamlet, Macbeth, Romeo," he sighed and smiled, appearing to be watching a young Frank Preston on stage. "Shylock, Prospero, and a lot of lesser characters." He looked at me, and seemed a little embarrassed. "It was a small town, small college, I had a deep voice."

We both sat silently, watching dorsal fins rise, fall, glide, and heard the occasional slap of water with tails. The sun grew larger and took on its late-day orange as it neared the horizon.

I would have traded an eternity in heaven for five minutes more of that moment.

A small electronic beep broke the serenity and it was coming from the region of my derriere.

I moved sideways from the jacket and allowed Frank to retrieve his cell.

He read it and his calm demeanor transformed instantly to a lined forehead and drooping mouth.

"I take it you're wanted elsewhere?" I asked.

"This C.E.O. business is not as glamorous as most people, including me, thought it would be."

"I've never known investors to be so—well, so hands on. But then, honestly, I've never worked in the corporate world before, unless you count newspapers as corporate."

"I have to tell you," Frank said, "I've fallen in love with this place. I've never been to Florida before, it never held any interest for me until I came here."

"That's funny, that's exactly how it happened for me. At first I loathed it, then it kind of grew on me, and now I can't imagine being anywhere else."

"There's something about being here, right here, this spot, watching those dolphins, that make me both grateful that I found it and sad knowing it can't last."

"Why can't it?" I asked. "Last, I mean." I turned to look at him directly, his cat's eyes had a melancholy, distant look.

"My life is pretty complicated, but..."

His phone vibrated and squawked; he glanced at it, then grabbed for his socks and shoes.

"I'm sorry to say I have to go, thank you for the company. It's not often I get to talk Shakespeare with anyone."

I stood up too, my knees telegraphing my age again, and said, "It was a nice chat, thank you for the beach blanket," with a nod to his damp jacket.

"Maybe some other time you can tell me more about playing Cordelia; Lear is one of my favorites."

He reached for his jacket and shook the sand from it.

"That would be nice. Have a good evening," I said to his back as he moved up the gravel path. My heart wasn't in that last line and I hoped it hadn't sounded as insincere as it felt.

Without the distraction of Frank, my body again sent urgent itching messages to my brain. I waded back into the lagoon, rinsed the sand from my legs, and relived those sublime ten minutes in a loop the entire way home.

Sunday, June 23rd 8pm

First thing, let me remind you of the grand opening of Dan's Dolphin Experience tomorrow. Gates open at 8am. The folks from WWTF will be there playing music and giving out prizes. Lots to see and do.

I'm still investigating the deaths of the three men found in the net Sunday. Some of the information I was able to obtain is as yet not available for me to share, but I will as soon as my sources release me to do so.

The drift net theory seems to be the most logical reasons behind what may have happened to them since they were, in fact, entangled in an illegally sized one. This blogger learned that deep-sea net-fishing is hard to regulate and fishermen will cut those nets free if they feel they may be boarded. Those nets will then float unmonitored and indefinitely, trapping and killing anything in their way as the currents carry them along the sea bottom. I've read estimates of millions of sea life lost in this way. Some of you think rival fishing gangs exist and I'm inclined to believe that now, although I'm still not sure if our dead trio are related to that in any way. Nets that are considered legal on Florida waters vary depending on the type of fishing being done. I don't know how that helps any of the creatures unfortunate enough to get tangled up in them though. When this is over, perhaps we should raise our collective voices to the Florida Fish and Wildlife agency and demand more be done. But for now, if anyone has any information that might help us solve this mystery, please leave a comment. Don't forget to shop with our sponsors.

We're all here to be clear
Magpie

I'm only going if they offer senior discounts. Signed ihatetheyankees137

Let me know when you pull up someone good, like Jimmy Hoffa or Amelia Earhart. Signed olddude42xl

The Japs and the Norways is the ones doing illegal stuff like whale harpooning and shit, I'll bet they got something to do with them nets too. Signed spankmegood

Talk to the folk in NOLA, they'll tell you about the escaped killer dolphins. Navy shot them, I heard, but some could have got away. Signed ufofreakandproud

Do you know if they serve Kosher at that Dan's place? Signed mahjongmimi

I hope this exposes all them net fishers, they're all pussies in my book. If you want fish, throw a hook in the water and wait like a real man. Signed buffetforprez123jb

Monday, June 24th Grand Opening

The route from my home to Dan's normally takes fifteen minutes, give or take a few. This morning's commute, however, was double that. The closer I got to Dan's, the slower the traffic became until a mile out it was at a dead stop. The money spent on the media blitz heralding the grand opening was, apparently, a wise investment. I'd have wagered a week's salary this was more visitors to Dan's than he'd had the entire time he'd been open.

There was no separate employee entrance so I sat in line with the tourists. The traffic began its slow crawl forward just as I had completed a deal with Gator's Choppers. They would fly me, at low altitude, over Dan's for ten minutes and I would give them ad-space on my blog for life, and perhaps longer. I really wanted to know about the dolphin sounds I'd heard behind that wall. Mostly because when Dan gave me the tour, he never mentioned a separate area for dolphins.

By the time I'd parked, angered a dozen or so guests by moving past them in line, and gotten into costume, it was 7:58; I was two whole minutes early.

The rain clouds passed leaving a refreshing breeze in their wake, the sky was a brilliant shade of blue, and there were new batteries for the fans in my pectoral fins. I was feeling good.

I made my way to the WWTF table, which was easy to spot with its ten foot banner reading *"Welcome to Dan's Dolphin Experience, The Biggest Little Aquarium in Florida,"* suspended above it. A dozen helium balloons were tied to the corners of the swag table where WWTF pens and post cards were being snatched up faster than the stations promo guy could set them out.

The sound of Nat King Cole singing *Those Lazy, Hazy, Crazy Days of Summer* filled the air, while Zig handed out drink cozies and Fort-Myers-Miracle baseball calendars. Enough of his fans wanted photos with me to keep me there through Mungo Jerry's *In the Summertime*, Jimmy Buffet's *Margaritaville* and half of The Beatles' *Yellow Submarine*.

The turtle-cove area was shaded so I walked there next, hoping that among the dozen or so children petting the reptiles, none would be fearful of my smiling, yet malevolent appearance. I was not to be that lucky. A baby strapped to its father in a backpack began to cry when it saw me. I moved to the opposite side of the cove but by then it was too late. The infant's cry became a scream of terror when the father told him, "It's ok little man, Daddy won't let that big ugly thing eat you."

Making a hasty get-away, I moved toward a sketch artist creating chalk portraits of the guests, illustrating them riding the backs of dolphins or soaring on the wings of pelicans. The ice cream vendor cleverly parked his cart near the line of those waiting to be drawn and was doing a brisk business. Many of the visitors wore Dolphin Dan's hats and t-shirts. They carried large souvenir plastic cups and cooled themselves with portable Dolphin Dan fans shaped like seagulls, the wings acting as propeller blades.

By eleven a.m., the late morning heat surpassed my costume's fans' ability to compensate, and I chose the sanctuary of the indoor aquarium. The low light apparently made my appearance less threatening because for the first time all day no one ran from me. The building was relatively small, and after ten minutes I had already reached the exit. I turned and repeated the tour patting the tops of small heads and getting leg-hugs in return.

After lunch at the Dolphateria, where I ate alone reading a National Geographic children's book about Dolphins I had picked up at the gift shop, I finished my last two hours of guide-shark duties for the day.

I spotted Zig on his way to the lagoon amongst the large crowd making its way there for Miss GiGi's two p.m. performance.

"Traitor," I said to him as he passed.

He stopped. "Aren't you off now? Go change and meet me there."

"Blowhole Bob relieves me at three," I whispered.

"Blow what?" he asked.

"You'll see him, he's the opening act. He's really—he's pretty unforgettable. Anyway, I have an appointment after work, gotta go, bye."

The dressing room was empty, but I could tell Frances had been there by the lingering scent of ashtray and Crisco. There was nothing to do about my matted hair or eyes reddened from dripping perspiration, so I donned a large hat, even larger sunglasses, and made my way to the security building. I wanted to try and get those key cards swapped back again before I was found out and fired.

The person answering the knock was not only *not* Marty, but was also Marty's complete opposite. I craned my neck so far back to see his colorless face that my hat fell off. I showed him my employee badge and reached back to retrieve my hat from the ground.

"Where's Marty?" I asked the freakishly tall, brilliantly white man.

"I don't know no Marty," he said with a voice that would sound angry just saying *hello*.

He had begun pulling the door shut, but I blocked it with my foot.

His grin was positively evil and he said, "That's gonna hurt."

"Wait!" I shouted. "Please, I work here."

"I know who you are and I got specific orders that you ain't' allowed in. Now move your foot if you want to keep it attached to that leg."

His smirk told me he would probably enjoy breaking my ankle. I pulled my foot away only a fraction of a second before the door slammed shut.

I contemplated that encounter on the way to the parking lot. Who, I wondered, would have given that giant orders to keep me away? Not Dan, he had no idea I'd been in there, no one did, as far as I knew. Moreover, what happened to Marty? I had assumed Howard took him away for some employee photo thing, but it appeared now that Marty had been replaced, been replaced by an evil albino giant. When you factored in the secret-service-bug in my house and the floating corpses, it had all the makings of a 60's James Bond movie. *And,* why did Howard come and get Marty, he's only a photographer? *And,* why didn't Dan tell me about the pool above the dolphin clinic? *And,* that thought reminded me, I had a date with a helicopter.

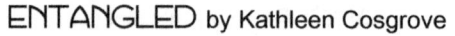

FOURTEEN

Gator's Choppers was one of only three private air services at the, '*so small you'll miss it if you blink airport,*' in Bonita Springs, its official name being *Sunset-Strip Airfield*.

Several small hangars dotted the perimeter of two runways. I spotted a large Army-green helicopter in front of one of the hangers. The alligator head painted on the nose was a pretty good clue that I had found Gator's Choppers.

A man, who I took to be Gator, sat at the hanger entrance. His seat appeared to have once belonged in the interior of a plane or helicopter, its seatbelts and straps dangled to the ground from torn fabric and exposed springs. If the seat looked old and rough, it was the perfect companion to the man.

Gator was most likely in his late sixties. He was bald everywhere but at the nape of his neck where sweat had plastered gray and white hairs to his skin. He wore a black t-shirt with the letters POW and MIA in white, over a silhouette of a man's face surrounded by barbed wire. Under the image were the words *Never Forget.*

"Gator?" I asked, looking down at the mirrored frames covering his eyes.

He tossed an empty can of Busch beer in the box beside him that held at least a half dozen more crushed cans.

"You that internet lady?" he asked, followed by a loud and onion-smelling belch.

I reached out my hand. "Yes, I'm Maggie Finn," I said, holding my breath.

I should introduce him to Frances, I thought, *what a pair they would make.*

"Come in, I got papers for you to sign," he said. He took one last pull from his cigarette before flicking it away from him. It landed near a small red can that I hoped did not hold gasoline. I sprinted away from it and into the hanger.

Gator's office consisted of a desk, whose size and shape were hidden under dozens, if not hundreds, of yellow legal pads, newspapers, manila file folders and at least three Rolodex's that I could count. A torn plastic office chair, a water cooler, and file cabinets of varying sizes filled the rest of the space.

Behind his desk, tacked to the wall with pushpins, was an American flag the size you normally see flying at used car lots. Framed photos of men in Army fatigues, holding rifles and posing in front of helicopters, or barracks, or tanks, covered the rest of the walls.

I signed the paperwork he wordlessly pushed in front of me, using a fountain pen I found in a stained mug filled with three more pens of the same type.

"Here's one more I just made up, it says you can't write about me, my business, my chopper, nothin' like that."

"But, don't you want to advertise on my blog? I mean, isn't that our deal?"

"The ads are gonna say what I want them to say." He emphasized the *I*.

"Ok, whatever you want."

I signed the handwritten document, ink staining my thumb and forefinger.

"You gonna want a camera?" he asked, lighting up another Marlboro.

"I have my phone."

He blew smoke, directing it out the side of his mouth.

"Like I said, you gonna want a camera? You can borrow mine for fifty bucks."

"Ok, sure," I said.

"Film's ten."

"A film-camera, ok, sixty then," I said.

He looked at me, not moving and I said, "Oh, of course, do you take Visa?" I pulled my wallet from my bag.

"You don't have cash?"

"No."

"Sixty five, the bank charges me for credit cards."

"OK, sixty-five," I said.

He put my Visa in an old fashioned credit card device, pushed it back and forth till it imprinted, handed me the receipt, and gave me the yellow copy after I'd signed.

He next handed me a 1970's era Nikon SLR with a zoom lens and a roll of Kodak film, and we left the office for the tarmac.

I climbed aboard the helicopter by pulling myself in with the aid of a leather strap hanging from the open entrance.

He patted the exterior. "Just like the one I flew in Nam, three tours, always a Huey."

Two seats, in the center of the chopper, sat side-by-side and were positioned inches from the open doorway. Gator assisted me with the harness and lap belt, handed me headphones, then went to the cockpit area while I loaded film in the camera and prayed. The scent of beer lingered even after he was gone.

He's been doing this for decades, I reasoned with myself. *If he could survive flying this in a war with people shooting at him, surely he could fly it with a snoot full of beer.*

He started the engine and as the blades moved faster, I tightened and retightened the harness, and pushed the headphones closer to my ears.

We left the tarmac, first vertically, then both vertically and horizontally and Gator's voice sounded through the headphones.

"We'll be at the park in about ten minutes, if you don't need anything I'm turning up the music."

Fear and exhilaration combined to make my heart race as we climbed over the hangars. The chopper banked to the side leaving me face down with the earth below. I put the camera between my knees and held onto the overhead strap with one hand, while I pulled my lap belt even tighter with the other. When he leveled the chopper, I took a breath and reminded myself this was his job, he was a professional pilot, I was not going to die, and people did this every day.

Golf courses, swimming pools, canals, lakes, and rooftops stretched to the horizon in the unbroken scene below me. I yelled into the microphone attached to the headset, attempting to be heard over The Rolling Stones' *Paint it Black*.

"How low can we fly over the park?"

"Five hundred feet," he yelled, temporarily muting Mick Jagger.

"We're just about there, gonna turn to give you a good look, hang on."

Again, the chopper leaned to the port side and I was looking straight down onto *Dan's Dolphin Experience*.

It took me about sixty seconds to orient myself to the layout but when I did, I pointed the camera at the pools, nearly hidden by trees behind the security shack, and shouted, "There."

Gator flew us directly over them, and hovered long enough for me to get a good view. Forgetting my fear, I let go of the strap and began snapping photos of them. I counted three pools. The zoom on the camera was long enough to allow me to see into the water where I could make out at least two dolphins in one of them.

"You got what you need?' Gator's muffled voice asked.

"Can you fly over the lagoon too?"

We did, but only long enough for me to get one photo before Gator said, "Ok, time's up, we're goin' in."

I had the zoom lens focused on what I thought was either my house or someone's detached garage, when I felt the vibrations of the phone in my back pocket. I answered and immediately my derriere left the seat as the helicopter dove rapidly down.

"Zig?" I said into the cell, "Oh God, we're going down."

"Maggie?"

"On the ground, five o'clock—fire," Gator yelled over the two-way.

"Zig, I think he's crashing us to the ground at five o'clock."

"Where are you?" Zig asked, speaking rapidly, which for him is a sign of panic.

"Gator!" I screamed. "What's happening?"

The drops and turns were so rapid I became dizzy and my stomach moved ahead of the rest of my body.

"I said fire Damnit!" he yelled, as we banked sharply to the port side, the side where I was seated. We were directly over a golf course.

"Are you in a fire-fight?" Zig yelled into my ear. "It sounds like you're in a helicopter."

"I am, I don't know what's going on," I yelled over the noise of the chopper.

The noise of the blades, a sound I had become accustomed to at the start of this ride, now thundered through my ears becoming more urgent as they whirred.

"Fire God damnit, what in the hell are you waiting for?" Gator ordered, his tone hostile, his face red, and eyes bulging.

He dove toward the greens again. Somewhere over his shouting and the loud whir of propellers, I could hear The Animals sing *We Gotta Get Out Of This Place*.

My view changed from sky, to grass, to water then sky again so quickly it was like cart-wheeling in space. When he held our position, at last, over the fairway, the players on the ground shouted, waved their clubs in the air, and pitched golf balls at us.

"Watch it, we got incoming," Gator yelled.

We swung and looped back, then ascended rapidly banking hard and barely clearing a water tower that read, *Welcome to Naples, Home of the Golden Eagles.*

"Zig, he's crazy. I think he thinks we're in Vietnam or something, he wants me to shoot golfers."

"I don't blame him," Zig said.

"Zig!"

"All right, sorry, you're not up with Gator by any chance, are you?"

By way of an answer, I screamed as Gator dove again and I lunged hard against my restraints. The call ended when the phone shot from hand out of the open doorway.

"You open fire now Private, or I'll toss your ass off this ship," Gator yelled to me over Credence Clearwater's *Run Through the Jungle.*

The helicopter banked hard in the opposite direction and Gator yelled, "They're on the run, get 'em before they reach cover."

"Yes sir," I screamed into my mic. "I'm gonna fire, I'm gonna fire a lot, see?"

I aimed the camera at the ground and made shooting noises, "Pow, Pow, Pow!" as men in pastel pants sprinted toward a stand of trees.

We climbed, circled, and then dove for the fairway again. This time the golfers hit the ground when our chopper dipped below the tree line, some dove into the lake.

He hovered, turned us nearly parallel to the ground and yelled, "Rice paddies, three o'clock."

Once again I aimed the camera like a weapon and made more gun sounds.

I looked at Gator who was shouting into his handheld while operating the lever next to his seat. "They're in the weeds, send the grunts in."

Gator moved us horizontally a few seconds, then forward at even faster speeds until I saw Interstate 75 below my feet.

"Supply convoy, nine o'clock, fire when we level," Gator ordered, then turned and dove at the highway.

My harness kept me in my seat, but my head jerked and bobbed like a dashboard Chihuahua.

I aimed my camera like a gun and strafed rush hour commuters to the sound of Steppenwolf's *Born to be Wild.* RVs, sports cars, and trucks pulling boats, passed beneath us, some pulling to the side of the highway, probably wondering if we were part of an air show.

"Go for the fuel trucks," shouted Gator, "blow their goddamn fuel!"

"Gator, I think we've been hit," I lied. "I see smoke coming from our tail—blade thingy."

We made an abrupt turn, climbed, sped up, and moved north.

"Tower, this is Golf Tango Romeo," Gator said into his handheld radio. "We're comin' in hot."

He silenced our 60's soundtrack and maneuvered us into a slower, steadier track as I watched the tiny airstrip came into view. Our Huey made several revolutions as it descended, then touched the pavement as gently as if we'd landed on cotton. I leaned back, closed my eyes and, aware I was still holding the camera like a gun, opened my mouth and laughed. I allowed myself a moment to note if I had peed in my pants, I had not.

A sudden return of panic hit as I spotted a woman running across the tarmac yelling and waving her arms, while a car came at

I guessed Terri to be somewhere in her late thirties and attractive in a tomboy kind of way. Loose strands of auburn hair fell from under a Miami Hurricane's ball cap, and she wore mechanics overalls with a grease-stained rag poking from a front pocket.

"What happened?" I asked. "I swear I didn't do anything to provoke..."

"No, no, 'a course not," she said in an accent straight out of a Tennessee Williams play. "No, daddy has a little PTSD, gets confused sometimes during a flight, he has flashbacks. He's harmless, never hurts anyone, just makes the locals nervous sometimes."

"Not just them," I said, putting my hand on the wall to steady myself.

"Usually all his customers are other vets who want a ride in the Huey, it's a nostalgia thing. Half of them's got the same hang-up, they understand. I'll take him back for some more out-patient at the VA."

"That's good, I guess." I said, not at all sure. I imagined it would be nearly impossible to completely wake from forty years of nightmares.

"I heard you over the radio by the way, you did a great job," she told me. "And I really appreciate what you did for Gator back there that was real nice."

"He served our country heroically, he deserves a break."

"We have a mutual friend, Zig. He's the one called and gave me the heads up. I'm surprised Daddy booked you, he usually only flies military," she said.

"He seemed to like the idea of advertising on my site."

"I'm gonna' go back inside now and make sure he's OK, you all set here?"

"I am, thanks, and tell Gator thanks for the ride, it was—thrilling."

"Will do," she said, smiled and winked.

We turned to go our separate ways when I remembered something.

"Oh wait," I said, "He never told me what he wanted for his ad."

"I can tell you what it is," she said. "It's what he always writes, *Jackie, come home, all is forgiven,* and sign it, *Gator.*"

"That's it? Who's Jackie?"

"My mom, she left twenty years ago."

Terri disappeared into the hanger and I drove away thinking about hope and love, forgiveness and understanding, and how much faith I had put into a crazy man and an old canvas seat belt.

FIFTEEN

Hands down, the best bridge I've ever driven over is the Skyway Bridge spanning Tampa Bay. It's the most exciting part of driving into, and out of, Saint Petersburg. At the topmost part of the bridge you're nearly two-hundred feet above the water. It spans a twelve hundred foot-wide shipping channel. Large vessels enter the bay right under you, and if you're lucky, you'll see dolphins leaping in the wake of those large ships. It's one of those times you can feel like a kid all full of wonder, and excitement, and the sheer joy of being part of such a spectacular world.

I made the decision to visit the Saint Pete Aquarium to learn how they operate, and how it may be different from what I'd seen so far at Dan's. I had the day off, a rental car I'd managed to swap ad time for, and clear blue skies.

I researched *The Saint Petersburg Marine Aquarium* online. It is a marine-mammal rescue, treat, and release facility. They bring in stranded dolphins, sea turtles, river otters and the like, treat them, and then send them back into their native habitats.

It was after-hours for the aquarium when I called the night before to see about making an appointment for a guided tour or something. I got a recorded message instructing me to call back in the morning, or if there were an emergency, a pager number I could use. I hadn't known pagers still existed and made a mental note to look into the cost effectiveness of having one. It might cut down on my cell phone minutes and had the added benefit of making me feel like a doctor in the 1980s.

I called in the morning and told them who I was and that I was interested in writing a piece about their facility. They invited me to come in ask for Charlie, he was the volunteer in charge of public relations that day.

Parking for the facility was a large gravel lot where a half dozen cars were crowded together in the only part of the area that had shade, said shade being afforded by an overgrown tree in the adjacent boat-repair yard. Since it was impossible then to find cover for my rental car, cracking the windows would have to do. I used one of the floor mats to cover the steering wheel, and another to cover the seatbelt buckles. The inside of a car in the middle of the day in Florida can get upwards of 140 to150 degrees. I also grabbed my water bottle, stuck it in my bag, and walked to what I hoped was the entrance. The building itself resembled a really large airplane hangar from the outside, with no signage of any kind that I could see. If they were keeping their place a secret, they were doing a good job of it. If they wanted to attract visitors, they were failing miserably.

The place was nothing like Dan's. It was clearly a marine animal hospital and not a tourist attraction. This was made obvious to me by the lack of a gift shop at the entrance. That, and because it was dark, drably painted, quiet, and no one was wearing costumes.

Charlie, my volunteer guide, was, as he explained, a marine biology major at New College of Florida in Sarasota. He showed me the various tanks with brief introductions to the different animals there, why they were there, and how they were being treated.

A sea turtle, a Kemp's Ridley, which had become tangled in discarded fishing line was being treated in shallow pool. Because poachers have nearly wiped out the species, the aquarium was very keen on making sure this one found its way back to where it belonged.

Another tank held a couple of river otters who had become ill after someone threw car batteries in the water near their habitat. Another small, shallow tank held a stingray with a ragged tear after it had a run in with a shark. Through an underwater view of a larger tank, I saw a manatee who had successfully been rehabbed after injuries from a boat motor, move lazily toward the surface.

"This is truly and incredible animal hospital, I wasn't aware places like you existed. You're not at all like the place I work."

"Yes," he said. "We don't train the animals to perform, that's not why they're here. It's a hospital where we treat them, hopefully they get better, and we send them home."

"You have dolphins here?"

"We do," he said, "follow me."

We walked up a few steps and were outside in a place that looked very much like the outdoor pool area at Dan's.

"This guy here," Charlie nodded to the dolphin in the tank directly in front of us, "was beached near Clearwater, and got a nasty sunburn, that's a healing ointment you see on his back. And that one there," he pointed to another dolphin swimming in an adjacent tank. "That one got caught in some fishing line. Coast guard spotted her. She actually swam to the boat, like she was asking for help. She got some pretty nasty cuts, but she's only days away from being able to be released back to the sea."

"This is so much more than what I expected. You must be very proud to be a part of this. You all are making a real difference, I love it. It makes me wish Dan's was more like this. I mean, they say they're dedicated to research, that's what the park is supposed to be all about but, I don't know, it seems a lot less altruistic I guess is the word I'm looking for."

"I've been reading about Dan's, been meaning to get down there in the next week or two."

"Tell me something, do you know where places like Dan's get the dolphins they use for the, you know, the shows?"

"Usually buy them from other parks. Used to be they'd be brought in from the wild but that's illegal now."

Interesting, I thought, because I was pretty sure Big Kev talked about getting the six at Dan's acclimated to captivity, like maybe they had been brought in from the wild.

"Do you think they like it, you know, being in captivity?"

"It's hard to tell. I mean, a lot of people will tell you that they're not capable of the same kind of feelings or emotions that we are, and probably just as many more will argue that they are. I've seen behaviors that mimic what I would call joy or sadness, but that may just be me, the way I'm looking at it, ya know?"

"I was reading online about some stuff, you know how crazy the internet can be and, well..."

Charlie eyed me suspiciously, "You're not going to ask about aggressive reproductive behaviors are you, 'cause I really didn't take you for...."

"Oh no, God no, no. No, but, I read—well someone keeps commenting on my blog about how the Navy trained some of them for combat."

I was speaking so fast now that I might have spit at him a little. "And that there were actually killer dolphins that escaped when Hurricane Katrina...."

"Oh, that, yeah," he said, visibly relieved. "Yeah, well that's kind of a half-truth. The Navy did use dolphins for their echolocation abilities to find stuff, mines mostly, but no, you can't really train a dolphin to kill. At least there's never been any legitimate reports of killer dolphins. They can be aggressive, it's how they hunt for food, but no, if they could be trained as killers, like in a war, you'd have heard about it from someplace other than random blog postings. The internet is the conspiracy theorists Nirvana."

"You're preaching to the choir here," I said. "My blog gets some of the craziest— well you know. Like I said, that's where I heard about the, you know, *killer* dolphins."

I chuckled over that last part in case he began thinking of me as a crazy conspiracy theorist too.

"But thanks for all the great info," I said, "and please, call me before you come down." I gave him my business card. "Let me have the chance to return the tour-guide favor."

I called Pam on my way home and left a brief message.

I tried Rose next, but that call went straight to voice mail too. I drove to the FMPD to see if I could catch her, or Miranda from forensics. Neither were in, but another cop I knew, Brian Hicks, saw me standing at the information window and buzzed me back.

"Hey, thanks Brian that was really nice of…"

"You want something to write about on your blog? You're gonna love this."

Brian walked me past the processing area where those who manage to get themselves arrested get fingerprinted and have their mug shots taken. Beyond that are the holding cells. In one of the cells sat an elderly woman wearing floral Capri pants and a Disneyworld t-shirt. Her few strands of hair were cropped short and colored a faded red with gray roots Her skin hung in loose folds, like someone had let the air out of her. Her cellmate was, I had no doubt, a hooker. The fifty something, extra plus-sized woman wore thigh high plastic boots. She had on short-shorts of a shiny gold material over which hung a fat roll large enough to have hidden a terrier in. Her breasts were tattooed and spilled over the tops and sides of her bathing suit top that, at quick glance, revealed a couple of long hairs in the cleavage. She wore a jet black wig made of an unnatural fiber and her eyebrows were penciled into the shape of pyramids.

"I brought them in an hour ago," said Brian.

"Together?" I asked. "You arrested them together? Don't tell me the little old lady was…"

"Hookin'? Nah, she hired Zelda there," he pointed to the younger, larger woman, "for her husband as a birthday gift. Turns out the old guy couldn't…"

"Stop, I get the picture."

"No, that's just the beginning. The wife tells the hooker she doesn't want to pay 'cause she says Zelda didn't do what she was hired to do. Zelda tells the wife that wasn't her fault. The wife says that her husband's, uhm, problem had to do with the fact that he didn't find Zelda attractive because of her weight."

"Zelda doesn't look like the type that takes criticism well," I said.

"No, and in fact, she found one of them pool noodle things by the back of the house and started swinging at the old lady who grabs another one and they have this weird noodle fight that turns into a full out wrestling match. The husband, who's watching the fight, finds his, uhm, manhood, calls back the last number on his wife's phone. He thinks he calling for a replacement hooker, but the number is actually the switchboard here. Turns out the wife was gonna turn Zelda in to get out of payin' her and ours was the last number on her phone. Get this, the old guy, it was his 85th birthday."

"Where is he now?"

"His brother, believe it or not I think it was an older brother, bailed him out. They're back at the house getting the wife's jar of bingo winnings and yard sale cash to bail her out."

"Thanks Brian, you want me to name you as the arresting officer or you wanna be anonymous on this?"

"Oh, no, use my name. If you don't get your name printed, you're not eligible for the uhhh…"

"It's cool, I know about the crazy civilian thing, I'll write it up tonight."

Brian walked me toward the back door which was past the men's detention area. I did a double take when I spotted Marty, the security guard from Dan's, sitting on one of the cells.

"Hey, Hicks, what's that guy doing in there, the pint sized one?"

"Oh, that guy? Not allowed to tell ya', it's Federal business. He's getting transferred out in the morning."

"He worked at Dan's as a security guard up until yesterday."

"Well, I'm not free to tell you anymore than I have."

"That's OK, thanks for the story."

As I walked to the parking lot he yelled, "Don't forget to mention my name in your story."

I raised my arm to acknowledge I'd heard him, got in the rental and drove home wondering how I was going to find out why Marty was wanted by the Feds.

After a shower and a dinner of bagel with cream cheese and applesauce in front of the news, I fired up the laptop and blogged a bit. I was too impressed with the Saint Pete aquarium not to write about it immediately. Since it was a crime scene blog though, and I didn't want my followers to think I'd gone too far off the rails, I led with the only other crime I had.

Tuesday, June 25th

On the lighter side of the police blotter, an elderly couple was arrested tonight in the North Fort Myers area on charges of solicitation and assault. The suspects are both octogenarians and the weapons used in the assault were alleged to be Styrofoam pool noodles. Officer Brian Hicks was called to the scene where he arrested the couple along with another suspect who is being charged with intent to commit prostitution. To get a more complete picture of the absurdity of the situation, I suggest you check out Darrell's mug shot website. www.ftmpmugshots.com

Log in tomorrow, he should have them by then.

Earlier today, this blogger visited the St. Pete Marine Aquarium to learn more about drift nets, fishing, and anything that might help with investigating the drowning case. I'm still piecing together what I learned there with what I know about how the bodies were found, and will get back with you when I have a better narrative. I will tell you this much though, there's a lot of crime going on in our waters that no one is being punished for except the marine life that call it home. Drift nets aren't the only thing killing off the life there. Fishing line, cages, plastic, and garbage become weapons that kill and maim the fish, birds, and marine mammals that come into contact with them. If you see anyone abusing our waters, please inform them that what they are doing is illegal and if need be, report it to the Florida Fish and Wildlife Department.

My phone rang before I could finish the post, I noticed Pam's number on the caller ID.

"Maggie?" she said in a quiet and muffled voice. "I got your message. My phone's been off, I'm in a hospital in Miami."

"What? Are you all right? I can come right over if..."

"No, I'm fine, it's Professor Ballanchi, he's been shot."

"What? Is he alive?"

"He is, but he's in intensive care. They had to induce a coma because he has swelling in his brain, or skull or..." Her voice trembled, then trailed off.

She was silent for a moment and I heard her inhale deeply.

"The police called me because mine was the last number dialed on his phone."

Her voice faltered again, she cleared her throat and said, "He was on Alligator Alley. He was talking to me about the drawings, wanted to know if I had more. Before I could answer him, he told me to hang on and he was quiet for a minute. I could hear the GPS voice in the background say something but I couldn't tell what. Then he said, 'I'll have to call you back, it's diverting me here because of an accident up ahead'."

Pam stopped speaking again and I was hesitant to interrupt, but after a particularly long silence I broke in.

"Pam, are you still there?"

"Yeah," she said, her voice just a whisper now. "He never called back. That road he took, led him into some remote part of the Everglades. According to the police, it's in an area known for drug ticketing."

"Trafficking."

"Yes."

"Damn," I said.

"Yeah, oh wait, hang on, his family is coming off the elevator, I'll call you back."

"OK, please call as soon as you can," I said and she was gone.

I dialed Rose and this time she answered, "Yeah, I know, I heard."

"About the professor?" I asked, stunned.

"I listen in on your phone sometimes, did I forget to tell you that?"

'Uhm, yes, you did. You can't do that, it's not legal."

"I'm trying to keep you safe, you're up to your eyeballs in trouble again, and don't go get a new phone. Since I can't talk to you now, this is the only way to make sure you don't end up in the Glades with a bullet in *your* neck."

I put my hand to my throat and shuddered. "He got shot in the neck?"

"If it's the same one I heard about at roll-call this morning, then yeah. Look, I gotta go, I'm not supposed to be talkin' to you anyway."

I heard the phone disconnect, my second in as many minutes.

A small amount of panic grew into full-throated fear the more I let my imagination run with each scenario it was capable of. The odds were not the kind I'd want to wager the rent money on.

The rest of the evening I spent checking comments on the blog, Twitter and Facebook posts. I researched dolphins, the rules for dolphins and other marine mammals in captivity, drift nets, and fishing laws as they pertain to the Gulf Coast of Florida. I wrote highlights of my findings in a spiral notebook that I could refer to later. Like books, I prefer to read paper and ink, even when they are my own notes.

I took the papers to bed with me, re-reading some and highlighting others.

Although my phone was in my pocket with the ringer on full volume, I still checked for any missed calls or texts from Pam. It was on my chest when the vibrations from it woke me. A glance at the clock told me it was two a.m., and from the way my eyes felt, I knew I'd dozed off with my contacts in. I poured solution into them that ran down my face and read the text from Pam. *Sorry I didn't call back. On my way home. Will call you in the morning.* I removed my contacts and went back to sleep.

It took a few moments of grabbing at both my phone and alarm clock before I realized the noise that woke me was a clap of thunder. Pulling the covers over my head was pointless, my brain was already calculating how much I had left of my budget for a cab ride in to work. This was an almost weekly discussion the two parts of my mind had with itself over the cost of taxicabs versus car payments. Realizing sleep was no longer on the morning's agenda, I gave up, shuffled to the kitchen, and pushed brew on the pot.

I fiddled with the television antennae and comforted myself with the knowledge that the lovely couple at the news desk had to get up even earlier than I. Moreover, if I put enough imagination to it, I realized we had similar occupations, that of being *entertainingly informative.* I mulled that over while I toasted a cherry Pop Tart.

After listening to the weather report three times, because I kept zoning out though them, I felt as though I had at last retained enough information to realize that it was going to rain all day. I don't know why I day dream through the weather forecast, but I always do, and end up only noticing the graphic that displays the temperature and size of the cloud covering the happy-face sunshine.

I eyed the cremation box on the bookshelf and said, "So, what do you think Radu? Think I should buy a car or just keep praying for dry weather? I know, I know, you like the scooter, so do I, but I'm sixty now, shouldn't that mean I'm getting too old for one?"

I threw back a gulp of coffee and said, "You know what, you're right, and once you're in a box you can stay safe and dry for eternity — well, in your case just until I get you to the lagoon, but I get your point. Live now, for tomorrow you could be someone's bookend."

When I was awake enough, I completed some work on a website I was editing. It was for a chain of dental offices. I had gently suggested their photos of diseased gums and abscessed molars may not be the best image for them, they disagreed, and so I edited the copy with one eye closed to keep from looking at their frightening graphics. They did, however, agree with me that the *dancing drill* may have been just a bit too unnerving for the audience they wished to reach.

Next, I checked the blog and found some good responses to my post about drift nets and illegal fishing. I copied the most helpful ones, pasted them into a document, and printed it to read on my lunch hour.

I opened my Twitter account and read a disquieting message, *you are being followed by Brass Monkey.* Though I knew being followed on Twitter meant only that someone was reading your tweets, the sentence *Brass Monkey is now following you*, gave me the creeps. I wanted to call Rose, I wanted to call Rose and have her tell me how stupid anyone was who would spend their time doing anything as ridiculous as tweeting. I smiled thinking of what she'd have said and even *that* made me feel better.

When Pam called I was already in a cab on the way to Dan's for my morning shift, which I anticipated would be quiet due to the weather.

"So, no pages of diagrams in the car then," I said after she related what the police had told her.

"No, the car was stripped clean, no briefcase, suitcase; they even took the radio and GPS," she said.

"Maybe they were in his pocket?" I asked, with a bit of hope.

"The family said the police were holding his personal effects. The hospital had to turn them over because it was a crime and his sister doesn't know what he had on him when he was taken into the E.R. I don't think she asked."

"No, of course not, I'm sure her only concern is his well-being."

"Well, about that," she said. "I don't think she and her kids like—well, I shouldn't say but, I don't think they are all that close."

"No?"

"I got the impression she was there because she was expected to be there. She has a couple of teenage sons and they were openly irritated about being at the hospital. You could tell she was too, but she was more, I guess, discreet about it."

"Well, you did say he was a bit of a, what did you call him, a shmendrik?"

"Yeah, I feel a bit bad about saying that now."

"Don't, bad things don't only happen to good people, you know what I mean? He wasn't married, no kids?"

"No, the sister said he was too consumed in his work to be bothered with a family. That was her word, bothered."

"Lovely."

"She's promised to call me when, or if he wakes up."

"Will you call me too?" I asked as my cab entered the parking lot at Dan's, the rain at its heaviest since I left the house.

"Of course, we'll stay in touch. I remember a little of what I saw and I bookmarked some relevant sites on my laptop. I wish..." her voiced trailed. "I wish I had just thought to take pictures of them with my phone. It never even dawned on me this would happen."

"I know," I said, "Listen, don't beat yourself up, just try to do the best you can with what you know and I'm sure it will be enough. And Pam..."

"Yes,"

"I don't mean to spook you, but, be careful."

"Spooks like ghosts?"

"No."

"I did not think so, but you think things are only going to get more complicated now, right?"

"I do," I said, paying the cabbie and opening an umbrella that immediately turned inside out. "Yes, I do."

Because it would be ridiculous for a shark to carry an umbrella, I did not. Instead, I stood under awnings and inside shops. I roamed the halls of the indoor aquarium, so much so in fact, that I was beginning to imagine some of the fish there began to recognize me, especially the sharks who swam closer and closer to the glass.

"Don't flirt with me guys," I mumbled to them as they passed, "you're not my type."

By 10:00 the rain had stopped, and by 10:30 the sun was up and the guests were arriving. I spotted Frances and turned to walk in the opposite direction, searching for something large enough to stand behind in case she had followed me. Why she wandered through the park like a rabid dog, and was not locked away in the kitchen where she had only the staff to frighten, was beyond me.

When I saw her walk toward Blowhole Bob to presumably harass him, I went to lunch.

I had just started on my slice of pizza, when the large albino entered the Dolphateria. I gulped two more bites before making a mad dash for the dressing room, got the key card from my bag, and sprinted to the guard shack.

I knocked, waited, knocked again, and waited a bit more. Then I swiped the card and entered. The room was empty, and after a trip down the elevator and into the dolphin lab, I realized the entire place was deserted, even the dolphins were gone. I used my phone to photograph everything, including documents and notes. I moved the cursors on the three computers until the screen savers disappeared, then took shots of whatever information was displayed on the monitors.

I found the doorway that I knew must have existed; the one that I was certain lead to the pools outside. It was at least twenty foot wide and equally as high. I saw, too, how they moved the dolphins. The ceiling was wired with tracks, pulleys, and wide hammocks that were used for lifting and moving the animals from the tanks. They were exactly like the ones I saw in St. Pete. The tracks disappeared beyond the doorway that opened onto a freight elevator.

The operation of the car was also controlled via key card. I entered and held my card to the security pad. The doors closed with an echoing thud, and above my head engines whirred as the car slowly ascended. It stopped with an abrupt jerk. When the door opened, the hooks, attached to more pulleys outside, moved forward and back with an *ack ack ack* sound.

I stood just inside the door and peered out onto a wooden deck, the kind you see around backyard pools. There were, in fact, the three pools I saw when I flew above the facility with Gator. They were separated from each other, but connected to the wooden deck along the length of the building.

I recognized the familiar squeaks and clicks of dolphins in the pool at the furthest end from where I was standing. I also heard the sounds of human voices came from that same pool. I leaned my head out as far as I dared and saw three people in wetsuits climb out of that pool and move in my direction. I swiped the key card and pushed the elevator button for the ground floor, hoping to descend more quietly than I had come up. Nothing happened. I swiped the card again, still nothing. I repeated this over and over as quickly as my hands would move but the doors would not close.

The divers sat on a bench, chatting, and laughing, removing pool shoes and face masks, and tossing them into a nearby plastic container.

"At least you get the playful one," one of the men said. "Mine is just plain stubborn,"

"I don't know," said a woman's voice, "Puck can be a handful too. He needs to be trained separately, he always instigates all the others into playing."

"You want to switch?" asked the man. "You take Hamlet, I take Puck. I'd rather a playful one than one who just head butts me all the time."

I looked around for any place to hide. Being found with a stolen key-card in a place I was told to stay away from would certainly get me fired and most likely arrested.

Between myself and the pool hung a large stretcher used for lifting dolphins. It was just low enough for me to climb into and that is what I did. As soon as the divers turned to get their towels and shoes, I sprinted to the hammock and climbed in. I lay there barely breathing.

The voices passed behind me and entered the elevator. I heard one of the men say, "Don't forget the gears jam, you have to engage the stretcher first or the door won't close."

Ahhhhh, I thought, *that's what happened*. Then the familiar *ack ack ack* sounded, as the stretcher I was in slowly moved in the direction of the pool, stopped, and then moved back toward the deck. With the trainers gone, I leaned to the side to roll myself out when I saw a pair of legs approach. Rather than give myself away, I rolled cautiously back into the hammock, froze, and held my breath. The legs moved closer. I saw the shoes just under my head. The figure walked back toward the elevator and I heard it close with a thud. The *ack ack* noise of the moving gears started. I tried to roll out but the ropes closed the canvas around me. I drew in a deep breath as the stretcher dropped into the pool.

In an instant I was cold, wet, and blinded. After a few seconds of raw fear and panic, I realized that the hammock was open at both ends with me inside of it like a big soggy burrito. I pushed with my hands at the sides and my feet on the bottom. My right foot, though, poked through an opening in the netting, trapping my ankle.

The more I pulled my leg, the more the rope compressed. Blood pounded against my eardrums. My lungs needed oxygen. I grasped the sides of the canvas again to pull myself upright, trying desperately to reach my foot and free it. I turned to my side, pulled, and twisted. A stabbing pain gripped my chest, the pressure suffocated me. I had become too weak to free myself. My movements were too slow, my muscles powerless. I grew dizzy as the water around me grew darker. Blackness and silence enveloped me. I was dying.

In the next second, the upper half of my body shot to the surface in one great movement. A force from below lifted my head just enough for me to gasp for air. I wheezed in a short breath. Then the pull of my leg on the rope dragged me back under. The dolphin who had lifted me, swam under me again, and then in a single rush, sent the stretcher, with me in it, rocketing to the surface of the pool in one mighty shot.

The dolphin supported me there, the hammock on its back. I choked and coughed as I inhaled air and water. I found my trapped ankle and freed it, then groped for the side of the pool and pulled myself up and over. In a blur of instinct and fear, I lay face down on the deck and, at last, breathed in great gulps of oxygen. Lying prone, my arms above my head and my face turned in the direction of the pool, I saw my savior and it had a blowhole.

Its head turned as it watched me for a moment, then moved and sent out a puff of air from the surface of its head and dove. I wanted to remember which one of the six it was so I raised my head enough to see the three notches on its dorsal fin.

It was then, I believe, I passed out, because at some point I felt myself awaken, the arm over my head numb and heavy. I moved to the side of the pool, dangled my legs in the water, and searched for my rescuer.

I watched and waited, then remembered that when I got off the elevator, I had not seen any dolphin in the pool I'd nearly drowned in. As much as I'd like to believe in miracles or angels in the form of cetaceans, I felt another answer had to be true. There had to be a way for the dolphins to enter and leave the pool.

I hated getting back in the water, but my desire to know the truth won out and I dove in. What I actually did, was to hold onto the side and slide in. I was a fair swimmer, but trauma is trauma and it was going to take a while to shake that off.

Still holding to the side, I moved around the pool with my face underwater until I found what I was looking for. A gate, about six or eight feet wide covered the side of the pool closest to the lagoon. Set off just beside it, was a metal plate about the size of a frying pan. It was exactly like one I had seen in the dolphin tank at the aquarium in Saint Pete. The dolphins, I deduced, would use that to open and close the gate that led them from the pool to lagoon and back. The dolphins would need only tap it with their nose to open the gate. It would then automatically close a few seconds later.

Once I'd gotten back out of the pool and grabbed a towel from the same cabinet I saw the trainers use, I heard the familiar *ack ack ack* of the pulleys. I turned and watched as the stretcher rose from the water.

A maintenance worker stepped off the elevator, and when he saw me said, "I'm here to fix this thing. You'll have to take the stairs till I'm done."

He nodded in the area of the far end of the building adjacent to the last pool.

"Thanks," I said, "no problem," happy he didn't know who I was and happier to know I had an escape route of my own.

Because I had not been tormented enough for one day, I ran into Bob, as in Blowhole Bob, entering the dressing room the same time as I.

"You taking this shark thing a bit too deep aren't ya?" he asked, laughing as though he had actually said something funny. Bob wore a pink golf shirt and plaid, knee length shorts, but my mind's eye added a large bow tie and squirting lapel flower.

"You get it? You're wet and I said deep?"

"I did," I replied. "That was a good pun."

"I'm good at that, that's why the folks love me. It's not just about dressing funny, you have to *think* funny, all the time. You know, you could use with a little lightening up, if you know what I mean."

I could only glare at him, unable and unwilling to search for a reply.

"Sorry to say it," he continued, "but you don't act like a real performer. I mean, did you even get a good shark name yet? 'Cause I'm tellin' ya, that's the most basic, first thing you gotta have right off the bat."

"So, first thing then, that's what you're saying? Because I'm not sure you were clear on that."

"Ahhh, I get it, sarcasm. That's OK, Blowhole Bob has known ridicule and understands that is the burden of a life in show biz."

"Bob, I'm sorry, but as you've already pointed out, I'm wet, dripping wet, and I'd like to just go inside and change."

"Hey, who's keepin' ya'? Not me, you go right ahead Miss Sharkey."

"Thanks," I said, squeezing by him, because he hadn't moved to let me pass.

"Hey, you're getting the threads all wet," he said, brushing at his shirt and pants.

"Sorry," I said, feeling icky about my breasts rubbing against his chest.

"That's OK, a little sea water on the pants was worth the price of a little man-eater action, ya' know what I mean?" He moved his eyebrows up and down Groucho Marx style. "Yep, Blowhole Bob is set for the day."

ENTANGLED by Kathleen Cosgrove

SIXTEEN

My phone was now nothing more than a watery paperweight, so I borrowed one from the cashier in the gift shop, called for a cab, and went to the entrance to wait.

Someone called my name, and I turned to see Gator walking toward me. Gone was the black POW t-shirt, and the ponytail. Instead, he sported a pale blue, button down, short sleeved, dress shirt and a military style buzzed haircut.

"Miss Margaret?" he called, raising his hand in greeting.

"Gator, what are *you* doing here?" I shielded my eyes from the direct late-afternoon sun.

"Comin' to see you," he smiled as he answered. It was the first time I'd seen that expression on his face.

"I want to say I'm real sorry about the other day."

"It's fine," I told him, "it all turned out OK. I got those pictures developed, thanks for the loan of the camera."

He shrugged his shoulders and his face took on an expression of sheepishness.

"What?" I asked.

"I feel kind of bad about that too, I shouldn't have charged you so much, well, I'm sorry."

"It's seriously fine. You look handsome in your new duds, by the way."

"Just came from the VA. I'm goin' three times a week now. I can't fly, well, not for a while, and, well, I want to do some— shrink says it would be good for me if I did somethin'."

"What do you *want* to do?" I asked, keeping an eye out for the cab, which I was told to expect in either five minutes or two hours.

"I'd like to—can I do anything for you? Terri said you helped..."

"Oh no, you don't have to do anything, it was no big deal."

He looked at the ground and pushed some gravel around with his boot. "I understand, you probably think..."

"Oh no, no, not at all, I just—hey, uhmm, if you've got your car here, I could use a ride home."

His face brightened. "Oh yeah, I'm parked just over there," he pointed to an end of the parking lot that was nearly deserted.

We chatted about the weather as we walked, then fell into an awkward silence.

"Here we are," he said, brightening when we reached his car, "Lucille." He gently slapped the rear end of the vehicle. "Ain't no one never drove her but me."

"It's beautiful," I told him, and it was. The Ford Mustang's black exterior had a better reflection than my bathroom mirror. The back third of the roof, the pinstripes along the sides, and the hubcaps were all a matching caramel color as was the upholstery, which was also impeccable.

"Thanks for trusting me to take you anywhere," he said. "You are all right, you know that?"

"Hey, I can't tell you how excited I am to even sit inside this, it's amazing."

He couldn't have looked more proud if he'd have given birth to it. "Come on," he said, "this ain't nothin', wait till you see her move. It's got four on the floor, of course, and can haul ass."

I prepared for a speed of light ride but, in fact, Gator was far more cautious with his car than his helicopter. We were overtaken by a school bus, a jalopy full of watermelons, and an old man riding a three-wheel bike. Still, I was dry, comfy, and listening to The Drifters on the car stereo.

"What do you think," he asked me, without turning his eyes from the road.

"It's the smoothest ride I've had in a car, like floating on air," I told him, and that wasn't a lie.

"Bought it in '69, right directly off the showroom floor. Took the money I'd put away in Nam and paid cash for her."

I sensed from his expression that he remembered every detail of that day.

"It's forty-five years old?" I asked, stunned.

"Yeah, and still got less than a hundred thou on the engine, which is original by the way. Know where I went when I left the car dealer?"

This time his face became a portrait of joy.

"Went straight to Jackie's house and proposed."

"No wonder she said yes," I told him. "Who wouldn't when you've got this to sweeten the deal?"

"Oh, she said no. She married Donny Gower six months later. That lasted longer than I figured, ten years, but I waited. There wasn't another woman in the world for me so's it was no trouble biding my time."

"You waited ten years for her? Gator, that's the most romantic thing I've ever heard of, you know, in real life."

"Nah, not romantic. I just knew what I wanted and I wasn't going to settle for less. She was as fine as wine, still is. I was kind of a bad ass. Ten years older than her, and folks didn't like me. Everyone thought we was all baby killers, you remember."

"Yeah, I do. That was a bad time for you guys, I hate that."

We were quiet for a long time and my mind began to wander.

Gator had a little bit of middle age spread under his belt, and in order to accommodate that, the steering wheel of the Mustang was angled to a near horizontal level giving both him, and it, the appearance of a man driving a bus. I thought of Ralph Cramden from the old TV series *The Honeymooners* and smiled to myself.

I suppose it was the trauma of the day finally hitting me, but the smile turned to a chuckle and from there I began laughing, and at times, I think crying, convulsively.

Gator looked from me to the road in such fast, short, jerking movements that he resembled a lawn sprinkler, which did nothing to help my cause. "I'm sorry," I said, when I could catch a breath. "It's just, I remembered a joke someone told me."

We had stopped at a traffic light in front of a supermarket when I had at last calmed myself from the fits of laughter.

"I'm really sorry," I said. "I don't know what came over me."

"I know PTSD when I see it," he said. "If you need to talk, well..."

I interrupted, "Oh, I don't...."

"It's OK," he said. "You don't have to tell me."

"Thanks," I told him. "I think what I really need now is pie, can we run into the store?"

The joy of sitting in that car with pie on my lap turned to angst when I spotted Sabina's car in my driveway as soon as we had rounded the corner to my street.

"That's my house there," I told Gator. "The one with the tank in the driveway."

"Whoa, that's a Pontiac Catalina I think, maybe '51, '52. That is out of sight!"

"Yes," I agreed, "and I wish it was."

After Gator admired Sabina's car he left and Sabina elbowed her way back into my living room.

"You sure got a lot of boyfriends for an old woman."

"He's not a boyfriend," I said, looking at my reflection in the mirror behind her. *Good God,* I thought, *I really do look like an old hag.*

"I come to see why Radu is not yet in The Blest Land. He tell me so in a dream that he is waiting. You please to take him soon."

"I will, I swear, it just hasn't been the right..."

She lifted the pie from the kitchen counter and said, "I hold on to this while we wait for you to do the thing. Then I bring it back, OK?" She grinned revealing every inch of her loose fitting dentures.

I looked at the still warm cherry pie in her hands and wondered how hard it would be to snatch it back.

What if she fell and broke a hip, I thought, *and I had to explain to the police and EMTs how she became injured. "Yes officer, I was wrestling this old woman for a cherry cobbler when she fell and..."*

Sabina left, pie in hand, and I looked at Radu and said, "So, I'm beginning to see why you want to spend your afterlife in some remote place, you're hiding from her, aren't you?"

Secure in the knowledge that nothing else bad could possibly happen to me that day, I prepared a bowl of Rice Krispies, opened my laptop, and pulled up the blog. There it was, third comment from the top, *Enjoy your swim?* It was signed, *Brassmonkey.*

ENTANGLED by Kathleen Cosgrove

SEVENTEEN

Rose called next morning with news that Detective Fergus McKenzie, on loan from the Brooklyn P.D., wanted to speak to me.

"Fergus McKenzie?" I asked, "Does he wear a kilt, 'cause wouldn't that would be awesome?"

"Not a kilt but—well—just come on in," she answered. "And try not to..."

"To what?"

"Never mind, the list is too long. Be here at eleven, then we can go get lunch after. I've been wantin' to go to Harpoon Harry's ever since you brought it up."

"I thought you weren't allowed to talk to me while..."

"Well, now I can. See you at eleven."

Wednesday, June 26th
While I cannot point to anything in particular that indicates foul play in the deaths of our three netted Navy men, I'm not yet convinced there isn't something, either.

This is still an ongoing police investigation, in that they have not officially closed the case, but the deaths have been classified as drowning. This blogger is not going to stop investigating, though, no matter how many threats she receives from anonymous, cowardly commenters on this blog. I still appreciate anything you all can give me. Some of the stuff I've gotten so far has been pretty useful, so please, keep it coming.

COMMENTS:

Dear Magpie someone told me you write about crime. My neighbor is watering her lawn on even number days but she lives in an odd number house. The police won't do anything. I think she is paying them off. Please investigate this. SIGNED mrspwhite1298799

I'd look at the place they bought their gear, all three tanks faulting at the same time sounds like bad tanks. SIGNED floridanative61

There are alien life forms from outside our planet. They are living on the bottom of our oceans, they have been there for thousands of years. The evidence is there but you all are afraid of the truth. www.enemybelow99.com. SIGNED wearenotalone6666

My neighbor waters whenever the hell he wants to also, why make laws if you're not going to enforce them? SIGNED sandinmyshoes

The government has been training dolphins for decades to murder, that's what did it. That's because the Russians are training Killer Whales to deliver nukes. World War Three is gonna happen under water, you watch and see. Go educate yourself. SIGNED aqualung74

And so it went for about fifty more comments. The whales with nukes thing made me giggle, but I thought the air tank idea was a good one. Most assuredly, though, the police have already checked that out. But, no death threats so I considered the post a win.

In the FMPD, I sat in an aluminum chair that I guessed was probably upholstered in the sixties, outside the office of acting detective Fergus McKenzie. The glass doors were not soundproof.

During the twenty-minute wait, I heard him bellow, in a heavy Scottish brogue, things like, "Ya bastards couldn't spot a bogus bill if it had Justin feckin' Beiber's picture in the center." And, "I think I'll go and get some wee ones from the nursery and send 'em out to do your job, 'cause I'm sure they'll know their balls from their ma's knittin'" He emphasized this last one by what sounded like a fist to the desk.

When the two uniformed officers, the subjects of his tirade, passed me on their way out, I would have sworn it looked as if one of them had peed a bit in his trousers. When it was at last my turn to enter the detective's office, I could almost understand why.

Fergus McKenzie had to be six foot six if he was an inch. I guessed his weight about two-fifty or more. Sections of his rust-brown hair clung to his face and neck, plastered there by the racehorse amounts of perspiration dripping from his pores. Rivulets of sweat cascaded from his brow, moustache, and full beard, giving the bottom half of his face the appearance of a compost pile after a good rain. The parts of the hair on his head that weren't wet, resembled a wig gone sideways. He wore a pale blue dress shirt opened at the collar, with sleeves rolled to his elbow on one arm, and falling back to his wrist on the other. Nearly all of the fabric was damp or dripping wet, and he smelled of Old Spice and mildew.

Before he closed the door behind me, he yelled to whoever was in earshot, "Can someone please, for the love of God and all his saints, turn the feckin' a.c. on? It's hotter than Satan's farts in here."

"Mrs. Finn," he said, looking at me. "I'm so sorry, the heat makes me fierce."

He lowered himself onto the torn leather office chair. "Please sit," he said, gesturing to the seat across from his desk, a twin to the one I had just left in the hall.

His sausage-like fingers rummaged through the dozen or so files on his desk while I sat quietly and looked around the office, which was obviously in a state of transition. In corners were boxes marked, *FM files* and *FM office supplies.* The tri-fold photo frame on his desk, where one would normally expect to see photos of a wife and children, held pictures of three different cats. At first, I assumed they were ones that came with the frame until I began to notice boxes labeled *FM cat toys* and *FM cat bedding*.

"Ah, here we are then," he said, apparently finding whatever it was he had been looking for. When he stood, his enormous frame blocked the light from the small window behind him.

"I've not introduced myself, I'm Detective McKenzie, on loan from Brooklyn's 83rd while the department here waits for its permanent replacement for—uhhh—that would be...," he fumbled through some more papers.

"Detective Nathan Gonzales," I said.

"Yes, yes, Gonzales," he said. "I met him once, consulted on a case involving—well, it doesn't matter. I'm returning the favor, and thought you might be able to help me tidy the place up a bit."

I glanced around the room at the boxes.

"I mean with a couple of cases I'm tryin' to close," he said with a small chuckle.

"Oh, that's good," I said, looking back at the man who's face instantly turned to iron. My throat constricted and my armpits begin to tingle.

"Do you have pets Mrs. Finn?" he asked in a way that sounded more like an interrogation than a conversation. I wondered if there could be a wrong answer so I stalled for time.

"I notice *you* do," I said, pointing to the photos on his desk.

"Ahh," he said, and grabbed the frame with his large hand and glanced at it. "That one there," he pointed to an enormous black and white cat, "is Willie. And that's Nessie in the middle, and the wee orange one is, coincidentally, named Margaret." He placed the photos back on his desk and asked, "*Do* you have pets?"

"Uhm, no, no I don't."

"That's a shame, I don't trust people without pets. You should get a wee bonnie kitten."

"Oh, well, I would of course," I said, my mind going through a form of gymnastics. It fumbled a bit on the high bar before it landed on, "But I have a fish, and you know that would never do."

"I thought you said you dinna have any pets?"

"Oh well, I consider—umm—Captain Hornblower one of the family. I forget he's a pet sometimes."

He raised a bushy eyebrow and squinted simultaneously, taking the *skeptical look* to a level I'd not seen since the time I told my father that my first child, who weighed in at close to nine pounds at birth, was four months premature.

"When I found my Margaret," he pointed to the photo of the orange kitten, "she was sparring with a dog three times her size over a bit of dead somethin', hissin' and scratchin'. Ran the mongrel off she did. It's why I named her after the saint. You know the one I mean?"

I knew the story of the saint, it was one my father told me often.

Sometime in the first century A.D., Saint Margaret, after refusing to renounce her faith, was sacrificed to a dragon that swallowed her whole. She escaped by killing the thing from the inside out using only her little cross as a sword. Being a child I had no trouble imagining the dragon, as hollow as a chocolate Easter bunny, able to pop little Catholic girls down like dinner mints.

"Oh, yes, I've always liked that story," I said, and wondered what he was getting at.

He put his hands on the desk and leaned in so close I could count the reddened veins in his bloodshot eyes. "Are you inside a dragon Margaret?"

"What? No, no, I mean..."

"Look, you're a journalist, I can't tell you what to do as long as you stay within the law, but I will tell you this." He straightened and moved in the direction of the door, "That dragon you're poking is meaner and uglier than you can imagine."

"You know," I told Rose when she joined me at Harpoon Harry's, "you could have warned me that he was a ginormous, sweaty, Scot with a bad temper and a thing for cats."

"I know, but it wouldn't have been nearly as funny," she said, grabbing a wet-wipe from her purse and cleaning the silverware with it. "Here, give me yours."

'No, I don't want my food to taste like toilet bowl cleaner."

"Alright then, don't ask me to visit you in the hospital when you're eaten up with Ebola or something."

"OK, OK, here," I said, pushing my utensils at her.

"Where's our buddy Pam?" she asked, scrutinizing each of the servers as they passed by us.

"I just talked to her yesterday. I think she's taking a couple of days off."

"Did you tell her to watch her back?"

"I did, she knows," I said, watching the diners coming and going.

Harpoon Harry's was a waterfront restaurant in Fisherman's Village in Punta Gorda. Since it can also be accessed by water, some of the fun is watching the different boats moving in and out of the marina. I watched two thirty-something couples come ashore from a yacht twice the size of my home and played the game I always do when I see the super-rich; I try to guess how they made their money. Sometimes the boat's name is a giveaway though, like this one, *The Class Action*.

"That reminds me," I told Rose. "When we leave here, I have to go buy a fish so I'm not guilty of perjury or something. Oh, and if McKenzie asks you, tell him I've always had the fish and his name is Captain Hornblower."

"Do you even hear the stuff that comes out of your mouth? No normal person says shit like that, you know that, right?"

I let that slide, and asked, "He seems to think I'm putting myself in danger, what did you tell him?"

"What do you think? I told him everything. He wasn't asking how often you dye your hair or how many men you've slept with, which in your case I'm guessing is a pathetically small number anyway."

"Ha, ha," I said, sipping the water our server had set in front of me.

"This is serious shit, and you really should be careful," Rose said.

"What do you know that I don't?" I asked.

"Mac thinks we can work out a little deal where you tell me everything you know, and I'll give you whatever little bits of info that won't harm the case."

"Well, that's a fairly crappy deal for me, and I wouldn't do it for anyone else but you, but, all right, we'll see if we each have enough pieces to put this puzzle together. So, what do you know that has your detective telling me dragon stories?"

Rose glanced at our server with what I knew to be her fake smile, and waited for her to walk away before she said, "How much do you know about Frank Preston?"

"Not much, he's difficult to Google. Everything is so generic, it's hard to figure out if it's actually *this* Frank Preston. I can't even find a picture that matches the one we know."

"He's good at hiding everything about himself, and that's because he started out in the security business. Even his client list is hidden. He sold the company for millions about ten years ago, but here's the part that has Mac a little interested. A subsidiary of an offshoot of the original company manufactured surveillance equipment, and one of their clients was, you're gonna love this, Scotland Yard."

I was at first taken aback, Rose made him sound like a super villain, but the more I let it roll around in my head, the less villainy he sounded.

"Let me see if I've got this right," I said. "You're telling me, a company he *used* to own a long time ago branched out into lots of other companies, and one of them *used* to make stuff for the police in the UK, am I missing something relevant?"

"Did you forget the little black dot over Australia?"

"New Zealand, and that's the kind of leap I would expect from a conspiracy theory nut, not a big shot New York detective. I mean, talk about a far stretch. He's got to have more than that, what are you not telling me?"

"That's pretty much all I can say for now except—well—I'm going to tell you something, and if you even talk in your sleep about it, I'll kill you. I mean it, I'll hurt you, and then I'll kill you."

"Maybe you shouldn't tell me then, I don't want to be responsible for you getting in trouble or fired or an international..."

"I like Mac," she said, then stared at me, waiting for a response.

"What? I don't think I heard..."

"Yes you did," she said, then leaned forward and whispered. "I like him, and, oh shit, this is stupid."

She turned and stared off in the direction of the bay.

"Wow," I said, more under my breath than aloud.

Rose looked awkward, maybe even a bit frightened and it was the first time I'd seen her so.

"I know what you're thinking," she said, still not looking at me. "You're thinking it's crazy."

"Well, yeah, 'cause, well..."

"I know, I know, he's way out of my league."

"What? Wait, no, I mean, *no*."

"I don't know what I'm thinking, he's a top cop in one of the most respected departments in the world and I'm just a..."

"Rose, stop it, you're killing me here. You are—I mean, geeze, look at yourself."

"I don't want to talk about it no more, don't bring it up again, I mean it."

"I won't, but Rose?"

"Yeah, what?"

"I think you're spectacular."

"I'm hungry," she said, "where's that girl with our food?"

After we had eaten nearly half our meals in silence, I asked, "I'm going to tell you something bad that I did—well, it's not illegal, well, it could be illegal, but I think it was just—I think I just exercised poor judgment, not in real life, but at work. I mean, I guess that's still real life, but..."

Rose waved a fork, skewered with a ketchup-laden French fry at me, and said, "This is the you that makes me wonder about your journalism creds. You have a way of puttin' words together that make my head hurt."

Then she popped the fry in her mouth and said, "Tell me what you did, I ain't gonna arrest you."

"I stole a key card from the security guard and went someplace I wasn't supposed to be."

"See how easy it is when all your subjects and verbs agree?"

"That's all you have to say?"

"I don't run Dan's, if I did I'd fire you, but I don't so..."

"Well, I think what I did was illegal."

"Are you disappointed you didn't get caught? Some perps are like that, but I don't take you for one of them."

"No, of course not, I just thought, well, never mind, I ended up getting caught in a hammock under water."

Rose stirred the lemon around in her water and didn't look up.

"Aren't you going to say anything?" I asked.

She looked at me, then back at her straw. "Where's the part of this story that's gonna surprise me?"

"I just thought that since I nearly drowned—whatever, never mind. Anyway, no one saw me except a maintenance guy, but he doesn't work at Dan's so he didn't know I wasn't supposed to be there, didn't even know who I was, am, even."

"And?"

"And so I get a message from Brassmonkey asking me if I enjoyed my swim."

She looked at me and grinned, "Now I'm interested."

ENTANGLED by Kathleen Cosgrove

EIGHTEEN

Rose was busying herself with calls to computer geeks when my own cell phone rang with a call from Pam.

"I got a call from the professor's sister," she said. "He woke up and wants to speak to me, said it was important."

"Are you going to talk to him on the phone?"

"No, he wants me to come there and I told her I would. Anyway, I thought you'd want to know."

"More than that," I told her, "I want to come with you, is that OK?"

"I was hoping you'd say that."

We arranged to meet in an hour at my house. Rose said she was re-opening the Brassmonkey threats, but only as an off duty thing unless she could convince Mac it rose to a legitimate threat. She wasn't confident that was going to happen though, but promised not to give up.

Pam and I made the drive across Alligator Alley and into downtown Miami in a little under three hours. We missed rush hour and Pam used a heavy foot in her Honda.

Entering Miami General Hospital was like stepping backward in time. I honestly felt Deja-vu every few minutes. The black and white tiles on the floor were most likely laid by men who were long since dead and gone. The walls were layered with so many coats of paint, that I was certain the hallways were several inches narrower than when they were constructed seventy some-odd years before. The staff was a mixture of old and young, with many of the nurses so aged that I guessed they didn't only wear their orthopedic shoes at work.

The elderly Pink-Lady volunteering at the reception desk insisted on telling us how to find the elevators. And although they were directly behind the desk she occupied, it still took her several minutes to relay that information.

A nurse, or someone in operating room garb, entered the elevator as we exited, and the overwhelming scent of old tobacco smoke that surrounded her, lingered in my nostrils and made me cough. I was reminded of Frances which gave me the creeps.

"Good God," I told Pam. "If I had to ride the elevator with that, I'd need my own respirator by the time we reached the first floor. What kind of hospital is this? I picture the doctors lighting up cigars at the patient's bedside, and nurses carrying flasks of whiskey in their garter belts."

"It's an old teaching hospital," Pam said, as we made our way toward the ICU. "It's the one the ambulances bring the Joe Blows to. They didn't know his identity right off so they brought him here."

"*John Does,* Pam, and in this city, I'll bet they get a lot of gunshot vic..."

Our conversation ended abruptly when an announcement overhead called for a Code Blue in ICU.

We watched as doctors, nurses and emergency staff made their way to one of the patient's beds.

"Unless they've moved him," Pam said, "that's Professor Ballanchi they're working on."

We stood in the hall, just outside the ICU, and watched the events unfold as if it were a play. At first, people moved in and out quickly, some rushing past us from elevators and others hanging bags to IV poles. Two nurses pulled things from a red cart in the room and the familiar, "clear," was spoken several times from the doctor in charge. After a few moments of this, the pace came to a near halt and everyone walked away except one, the one who pulled the sheet over the patients face.

The nurse at the desk confirmed for us that the newly dear-departed was indeed the professor. She was having the hospital chaplain contact the family so there was nothing left for Pam and me to do. We stood there, immobilized by our own thoughts, until I finally broke the silence.

"I thought he was out of danger, you know, up and wanting to talk."

"That was the impression I got too, that he was out of the forest."

"Woods. Do you think his sister will talk to you?"

"I don't see why not."

"I know I sound like a horrible person," I said, "but I feel less sad about the man's passing than I do about the information he's taking to the grave with him."

Pam let out a sigh and said, "Oh thank God, I thought it was just me. I was feeling guilty about feeling the same way."

"Nah, I think we're fine," I said. "We're trying to solve a possible murder, maybe prevent more deaths. No, it's all right."

"Still, I feel bad about the unkind things I said about him."

"I don't think dying changes who you were when you were alive," I said.

Pam was silent and I added. "I guess it would be bad to question his sister when she gets here though, that probably *would* be crossing the mark."

"Line. Yeah," I told her, "We'll wait a few days, or maybe just two, and give her a call."

"Or maybe tomorrow," Pam said.

I smiled and said, "I think I'm becoming a bad influence on you."

After a day's work at Dan's that consisted of one of my costume's fans falling into my underwear, seeing Frank and Miss GiGi having lunch together, and slipping into a regurgitated pile of something odious and yellow, I began mentally composing my letter of resignation.

I was thus distracted, browsing the gift shop, choosing the pet fish that would prevent me from knowingly committing perjury, albeit in the past tense.

"I'll need a male one," I told the clerk, who I was fairly certain knew as much about fish husbandry as she did about the plastic mermaid she was stocking on the shelf behind her.

"I don't know how to tell," she confirmed. "Dan just told me the pretty ones with the swishy tails have to be in tanks by themselves."

"I'll take that blue one on the right," I said, pointing to the one I thought looked most like an 18th century British Naval officer.

I was contemplating how to carry Captain Hornblower on my scooter when I spotted Gator in the parking lot.

"Gator?" I asked, when I saw him leaning against his Mustang he had parked next to my scooter.

"Maggie, Hi. I thought maybe you'd need a ride again, looks like rain," he said, and then looked up at the cloudless sky. "Well, maybe, you never know, these blue skies can fool ya."

"Are you auditioning to be my chauffeur Gator?"

He looked down, kicked some gravel around with the toe of his boot and mumbled something I couldn't make out.

"Gator?"

"Well, I heard from someone, someone who told me not tell."

He raised his head, looked at me, and continued, almost apologetically.

"Someone told me you might need someone, me, to look after you."

"There's a lot of someones in that sentence, you want to add a name to that list?"

"See, that's the deal, I'm not supposed to say. I'm just supposed to offer you rides. I figured, though, that you might think that's kind of creepy, me just showing up all the time."

"Because it *is* creepy, and so is someone being all secretive, going behind my back."

"I don't think it's creepy, I think it's nice. How come you don't think it's nice, someone looking after you?"

"You're right, it is nice," I said, getting into the Mustang. "I'm an ungrateful, horrible person. Umm, Gator?"

"Yeah?"

"You know you could be putting yourself in danger, right?"

He looked at me, his grin stretching sideburn to sideburn, "I know."

I put the bag containing my fish between my knees and buckled myself in.

"So, who's that for?" Gator nodded toward the bag.

"Me," I answered. "It's mine. I'm a pet owner now. I wonder," I said, examining the fish closely for the first time, "can you call a fish a pet even though you can't pet them? Now that I think of it, he might be more a decoration that I have to feed."

"No, if you name it, it's a pet."

I picked up the bag and asked, "It was Zig, right?"

"Zig, the fish?" Gator asked, confused.

"No, I mean, he's the one who hired you, right?"

"No, I mean, no I can't say, not no it isn't him, but it isn't." He hit the steering wheel with the palm of his hand, "Shit."

"Come on, you can tell me."

"Nope, I promised. Hell, I don't give up secrets, not even the time when that Gook tortured me in Nam."

"Gator?" I asked, raising an eyebrow. "You were for real tortured in Viet Nam?"

"OK, it wasn't Nam, it was Fort Gordon."

"They had North Vietnamese in Georgia?"

"My drill sergeant. But he was half Jap."

"Gator!"

"Sorry, he was Asian American," he said in what I perceived to be a condescending tone.

"And he tortured you for information?"

"Yep, and that's no BS. The guy put jazz on the HiFi and played it day and night, all the fu...damn time."

"Jazz? I gotta admit, that is torture. Was it the kind where they all play different stuff at the same time?"

"Yeah, saxophone solos that went on for like, hours and hours."

"Geeze, that would have made me give up my own mother." I said.

"Glad I found someone who understands, that shit can make a person crazy, do things, you know?"

"Did you? Do something I mean?" I asked.

Gator looked in his rear view mirror and said, "Remind me to tell you sometime, but for now, I think someone's following us."

I turned and looked behind us, trying to find a vehicle I recognized and wondering if we were going to have another PTSD stoked wild ride.

"Which one?"

He didn't answer but turned quickly off the main road down a residential street, making frequent glances into the rear-view mirror. After about a quarter mile, and three stop-signs he said, "Yep, here she comes."

I turned again and saw an unremarkable white car, the kind every third person here drives, about two blocks behind us.

"She?" I asked. "The driver is a woman?"

"Can't tell, I call all cars *she.*"

"What are you going to do?" I asked, "'cause I want to know who it is, don't you?"

"That's a fact Jack, watch this."

He pulled into the driveway of a home with a *For Sale* sign posted in the front yard and stopped. When the car in question passed us, Gator left the driveway and began following it.

"You're kind of close, they're gonna know we're following them."

"That's the point, and there she goes," he said quickly accelerating. The car was now trying to get away from us.

"I can't make out who it is, can you?" I asked.

"Nope, that is some high-end tinted glass though. I was gonna get that too, to protect the upholstery but—hang on, dude is stopping at the stop-sign."

Gator got out and took a couple steps toward the white car, that I could now make out was a Ford Taurus, when it took off quickly, cutting off a school bus coming from the cross street.

"He could have hit them kids," said Gator, getting back behind the wheel. "That is not cool."

"Maybe we shouldn't really chase him, we don't want to cause a wreck or anything."

"I'm not going to chase," he said, hunching over the wheel and loosening his neck like a boxer limbering up before a bout. "I'm just going to follow closely and meaningfully."

By the time we approached the next intersection, the school bus returned, this time breaking in the middle of the road, the STOP arm extended and red lights flashing. The bus driver yelled something to the driver of the Taurus who then took off, going around the front of the bus.

The children hung out of the windows, shouting and shaking their fists at the Taurus as their driver began pursuit with Gator following closely behind.

Our little convoy picked up a couple more vehicles of mothers who were waiting on corners to retrieve their children from the bus.

"There's a van and an SUV," I told Gator, leaning my head out of the window and looking behind us. "And a, wait, is that an El Camino? I haven't seen one of those in decades."

"Really?" Gator said, putting his head out and looking behind as well.

"Gator!" I yelled as the school bus stopped abruptly in front of a railroad track.

Gator swerved to keep from hitting the bus and accelerated at the same time, to avoid being hit in the rear. That maneuver put us in front of the bus and behind the Taurus again.

We left the residential area and followed the car past boat yards and campgrounds, leaving the rest of the convoy behind. We had gained speed to keep up, so when we made a sharp turn to follow it into an alley, we were going so fast that two of the wheels left the ground. We landed hard, and when we did, my seat fell back into a reclined position leaving me flat on my back and struggling against the force of our forward movement to right myself.

"Gator, where's the handle to make it go back up?" I asked, groping at the side of the seat for a lever.

"It's there, just feel around for it."

"This road is not helping," I yelled, as the Mustang bounced over the gravel surface with my hand *and* head, bouncing along with it.

"We're gonna be on it for a while, gravel's all there is out here, just hang on."

"My theet belt is on my face, I'm going to take it off tho be careful, don't crath into anything."

"What's the matter with you?"

"I bit my tongue, juth be careful, all right?" I said and found the clasp for the harness. As soon as it loosened, I fell between the bucket seats, hit the gearshift, bounced, and then hit it again.

The transmission made a grinding sound, Gator yelled a few expletives, and I crawled into the back seat.

"Stay there, he's going toward the bridge," Gator said, then downshifted and accelerated.

"Thouldn't we call thomeone?"

"Go ahead."

"My phone ith broken."

"Well, I ain't got one, don't like 'em. Just as well anyway. Remember, we're the one's following them, pretty sure that means we'd be the ones gettin' busted."

"Yeah, you're probably right," I said, sliding from one end of the back seat to the other each time he rounded a corner.

"I can't find the theatbelts back here."

Gator hit the brake hard when the Taurus made a sudden sharp turn to the right. The door to the glove compartment flew open and a flashlight fell from it and onto Captain Hornblower, tearing the bag and propelling my fish onto the passenger seat. In the next instant, the Mustang hit a large rut sending all three of us bouncing off our seats with The Captain going airborne and landing on my lap.

Fortunately, the bump also sent a bottle of water rolling toward my feet. I looked from it, to my fish, back to it, and realized there was no way I was getting him through the small opening. Instead, I poured the water into the Mustang's cup holder and threw The Captain into it. It made a surprisingly clean and waterproof fish bowl.

"Here we go," said Gator, "here's the bridge up ahead."

I glanced out the window just as we began our ascent up the drawbridge and saw a sailboat with what looked to be a thirty-foot mast.

"Gator, a thail—a thip—Gator, a tall boat ith coming, they're going to open the bridge!"

Gator turned hard into the next lane, throwing me across the seat behind him where I had no view but his bald spot. Water sloshed from Captain Hornblower's temporary home, and he circled the bottom like a fish gone mad.

"Well, he's gotta stop too," said Gator. "We can wait."

"What if he jumpths it?"

"This isn't no movie, people don't really do that. Anyway, this ain't like a real high speed car chase. It's like I said, we're just following, clo—what in the Sam hill?"

"What? What?" I asked, moving back to the spot behind the passenger seat.

"He's turning around, goin' back down."

Gator moved into the now deserted, oncoming lane of traffic, put Lucille in reverse, and began driving backwards down the bridge.

My heart felt as though I'd swallowed it.

"I'm really OK with not knowing, let's just go home" I said, turning to look behind us. At that moment Lucille gained speed.

"Gator, thtop, really, I'm getting thcared." I said, surrounding the cup holder with my hands to keep even more water from spilling out.

"I can't, the brakes are locked, hang on."

My body felt as out of control as the car. I dug my feet under the seat in front of me in order to keep from sliding on the leather upholstery.

"I'm gonna fall out of the back window, I juth know it!"

Gator ground the gear shift down and swung us around sharply as we leveled off onto the straightaway throwing me forward, where I climbed back into the front seat which, at that moment, righted itself.

The Taurus was gone and Gator pulled Lucille onto the shoulder where we sat, catching our breath. Miraculously, Captain Hornblower continued swimming in the two inches of water that was left in the cup holder.

From the corner of my eye I saw a large shadow moving toward us, then heard the sound of wings flapping.

"Gator?"

"Yeah?"

"A pelican landed on the hood."

"Yep."

"It's looking right at me."

"Yep."

After another moment I saw blue lights flash behind us. One of Fort Myers' finest walked to the car, leaned his head through the window and surveyed the scene.

Gator seemed unable to speak so I did.

"Ith there a problem offither?"

NINETEEN

Gator ran me by Wet Pets on the way home, funny, where I got a one gallon glass bowl, and a tin of food for the fish that I was not sure would survive the night. I placed the bowl on a shelf next to Radu in a kind of cosmic joke that I'm sure only I found and showered the days insults from myself.

I called Zig, thanked him for worrying about me, and told him I thought having Gator for a bodyguard/chauffeur was probably a good idea right now since apparently someone was following me. I got a reprieve from explaining the specifics by a knock on my door.

Rose came in talking.

"Mac says it's gonna take those Brits a few weeks to track that device, it's old so they consider it a low priority."

"Hi Rose, come on in. You want anything?"

"I could use a—hey, you got a fish," she said, walking toward the bookshelf. "He's kind of pretty. What crazy ass name did you give him again?"

"Captain Hornblower. It's the first thing that came to mind when I was talking to Mac, so now I'm kind of stuck with it."

"You should get one of them little boats they put in fish tanks," she said, dropping some flakes in the bowl.

"If he lives through the night I'll get him a purple heart, or whatever the British Navy equivalent is. He ended up dry docked on the seat of a Ford Mustang, then went air-borne before being thrown into the cup holder of a car speeding out of control backward down a bridge, all within ten minutes of leaving the gift shop."

"I heard something on the scanner, heard your name, figured I'd ask before Mac did. You look all right though," she said, walking back to where I was sitting on a bar stool in the kitchen. She pulled out the stool next to mine.

"So," she began. Your buddy got a ticket for improper lane usage, but you got fined for endangering wildlife? Can't be that one," she said, nodding toward the Captain.

"No, it was a pelican, on the car. I tried to make it go away and I may have accidentally hit it. It was a misunderstanding. I think it was all the pelican's fault personally. I think he was after my fish. But the cop was in no mood for excuses so, yeah, I gotta scrape up two hundred bucks for the fine."

I grabbed a handful of pretzels from the bag in front of me.

"He was nice about running the plate on the Taurus though, but only after I told him I knew you and Mac."

"That tag number doesn't match anything in the data base," Rose said. "As a matter of fact, it's not a real plate. Whoever it was took a big chance riding around with a fake plate on his car. It's probably your troll and the dude's doing a good job at hiding. You add that to the fact that he saw you at Dan's and it makes me worry. I've been reading your blog, trying to figure out what it is you're writing that makes him see you as a threat."

"Nothing I've written about is anything more than what the police know, so why am I threat, and why is he following me?"

"Let's think about what's happened since your last threat and today," Rose said, pulling a notebook and pen from her shoulder bag.

"I went to work today but nothing weird happened, well except, you know, the car chase after."

"What about yesterday?"

"I went to Miami with Pam, her professor died. Ohhhhh, her professor died."

"Hmm, and he told Pam he had information for her?" Rose asked.

"Yes, but what could he know about anything? I never talked to him, Pam barely did. She only showed him some sketches, the ones that may have been drawn by the dead divers."

"Maybe there really was something to them. But how would your troll know? Who did you tell about them?"

"I can't remember, but I don't think anyone, just Pam, her professor, and you of course. Did you tell anyone?"

"Of course, I told Mac."

"Rose, what if this is way bigger than we think? What if, I mean, it's kind of weird that Mac came to town just when..."

"Don't even think it," said Rose, waving her notebook at me. "Mac is a serious cop, he's practically a legend, and there is no damn way..."

"OK, OK, sorry, I suppose I've seen too many TV shows. But then that leaves that theory to die on the vine. I mean, no one knew about the sketches but us so that can't be relevant. What else?"

"What about Pam?" Rose asked, "I mean, how well do you know her?"

"If she's up to no good, why go through all the trouble of bringing the sketches to me and her professor? I'm no Sherlock Holmes, but I'd be willing to bet anything she's innocent. No one is that good at acting."

"I'm taking another look at Frank Preston," said Rose. "He's too smooth to suit me and I don't like it that I can't find out more about him. I put a call in to one of my friends at the bureau who's really good at getting info on people."

"I really don't want him to be a bad guy," I said. "But yeah, it does look a little shady."

"What else we got, what have you heard from Brassmonkey?"

"Nothing for a while."

"Then he'll probably be back, and he's bound to mess up soon, they always do. It's just..."

"What?"

"I don't like it's so hard to trace him either, and that bug. It's too high-tech for a troll. Mac is right, you're in way over your head."

"OK, so what do I do?"

"It's what you don't do. Don't blog no more, at least not about this. Leave it alone. Blog about—I don't know, what do regular people blog about?"

"Make-up, celebrities, health food, stuff I know nothing about. Besides, I'm pretty sure we need to know what this guy is up to and my blog may be the best way to find out. I'm no hero, and I fully expect you to look after me, but I'm going to keep going with this."

"We've had four drownings, and you almost made it five. Watch your back and call me if you see anything you don't like. I mean it Maggie, call me first, don't just go off being, you know, you."

"Spoken with love I'm sure."

The next morning I got up early and spent an hour writing website copy for a store that sells clothing for plus size women. The models they used did not appear plus-size to me. I thought they looked average size, like the people in textbooks. I suppose the fact that they didn't look like an image of an x-ray, made them heavy by comparison. All the talk about sexy curves and bold shapes made me remember how much I wanted pie. It was on my to-do list for the day, including looking for Big Kev at Dan's, going to find Miranda at the police station and beg for a forensics report, going with Pam to Englewood to see the dead professor's sister, and pawning my old wedding band, for the eighth time, to pay my fine for accidentally punching a pelican. I was not going to be able to get through the day without some kind of high fat and calorie filling on a Graham cracker crust.

I was going solo today since Gator was at the V.A. for his twice weekly group therapy session. The day was warm, but the breeze from the Gulf made being at Dan's and not in costume feel like a real treat. I knew the lagoon was closed to visitors from 8am to 10am while the trainers worked with the dolphins. As a park employee though, I was allowed to be there. That is where I was headed when I caught a glimpse of what appeared to be someone wearing my costume walking up the path that led to the guard shack.

My own costume was with Francis getting cleaned, and as far as I knew I was the only guide shark at the park, so I made a detour and headed up that same path to check it out.

I was too late to see much but the tail end of the costume cross over the threshold, and the albino giant's arm pull the door closed.

"Boo!"

After simultaneously screaming, jumping, dropping my purse and hitting myself in the nose with my right fist, I turned to see Howard behind me, grinning like a ten year old.

"Good grief Howard, you scared the bejeezus out of me."

"He started laughing, stopped, attempted a serious face and said, "Sorry," before resuming his laugh.

"No you're not."

"Yeah, you're right, that was pretty funny. What are you doing here, you working today?"

"No, I came to find Big Kev, you know where he is?"

"Yeah, I just saw him on the way to the lagoon, he's working with all six this morning."

"Thanks."

"No problem."

As I walked away, I stopped and asked, "Howard, have you seen anyone else wearing my shark costume?"

"That's a tough one to answer, I mean, how would I know if it's you or someone else in there?"

"That's true, but, I haven't been in it today, have you seen anyone in it?"

"No, but I just got here myself."

"If you do, would you mind asking who it is if you do?"

"No problem. Say hi to Kevin for me, tell him I'll be down there in about an hour for his shoot."

Shadows of fleeting clouds moved along the surface of the turquoise water of the lagoon. An intermittent breeze blew palm fronds together in a soft percussion while the soft whoosh of moist air from the half dozen gracefully swimming dolphins provided the melody.

Big Kev was working the dolphins from his position at the shore of the lagoon, while three other trainers were stationed on one of the raised platforms in the center. Kevin raised his arm, and one of the dolphin dove, then surfaced with a yellow rope, the end of it a ring that was around its snout. It was attached to a small yellow buoy, and the dolphin pulled it toward the shore. Kevin blew a whistle and rewarded the excited and squeaking animal with food.

As I watched, each of the other trainers, one by one, repeated the exercise with three different dolphins. Each dolphin dove, swam to, and slipped their snouts through the ring, then pulled the attached buoy to the one giving the command. It was impressive indeed.

While my eyes were fixed on two of the dolphins working in tandem, I was startled by a loud smack, followed by a spray of water that drenched my head and hair. A dolphin, not more than three or four feet from shore, was poking its head up looking at me.

"No, no, not me, I'm not the one with the food, go on," I said to it, and pointed toward Kevin. "Go to him, he's got your treats."

Instead of swimming away, it used its nose to splash more water in my direction, then turned on its side and swam in circles in front of me.

"I'm sorry, I don't understand," I said to it. "I don't know what you want me to do."

"She wants you to get in the water with her," said a voice directly behind me.

"Kevin, Hi, I didn't see you. Sorry I distracted one of your dolphins while you..."

"Kate is not part of today's exercises, she's off duty for a week or two. What are you doing out here today, enjoying the show?"

"I am, yes, it's really lovely to watch them, and you. It's amazing the way you communicate with them."

"Thank you," he said. "But Alden was the one who should get the credit, he was brilliant with them. I've never known dolphins to adjust to a captive environment as quickly as these six, and it was all Alden's work. He was so patient, only let them bring in one dolphin at a time. Spent nearly the whole two years on just getting the six acclimated to the place. They trusted him, especially Kate there," he nodded to the dolphin in front of us. "She had a special bond with him, she was the first one. I, well, no one else has been able to get her to respond like he could. That's why I'm giving her this time."

I thought his voice broke a bit, like it did when I heard him talking to that creepy Doctor Harris in the lab the week before.

That's when I remembered it was this dolphin, Kate that had been given anesthesia.

"I'm so sorry, by the way, about your friend Alden. He was a vet here, right?"

Kevin cleared his throat, and I thought for a big guy like him to get so sentimental was kind of sweet. I hated taking of advantage of it, but not enough to stop prying

"Yeah, he uh, he uh, I think he came here at first because he wanted to, I don't know...."

He stopped and wiped his eye.

"You think he was worried this place wasn't going to be on the up and up?" I asked. "That maybe the dolphins would be harmed?"

"Oh yeah, maybe, I'm not sure, he was always lookin', always askin' questions. Wanted to know what everyone was up to all the time. Not just with those guys," he nodded to the dolphins in the lagoon, "but all of 'em, the sharks, the...," he waved his arms up over his head. "I don't know, everything, the, the damned flamingos."

"Do you think he was spying?"

"Maybe, I saw him wearing a *Water Warriors* hat once, I asked him about it. He said he got it for donating money one time, but maybe he was into them more than...," he shrugged. "I don't know, listen to me goin' on."

"Do you guys ever, I mean, have you ever seen anyone be, well, not, like you would want them to act?"

"Huh? He asked, his brow furrowed.

"I guess, if you were worried that maybe anyone here was not being as good to the animals as you think Alden would have wanted, that maybe you could tell me. I wouldn't say where I heard it or anything. But, I'm friends with Dan and I could...."

"What? No!"

He looked angry and I was afraid I'd screwed up.

"It's OK," I said, trying to quickly regain his trust. "I mean, I know you would never let anyone ever, I just thought, if you had any kind of complaints at all. Anything. Maybe more hours to train, that kind of thing. Maybe I could put in a good word, that's all."

"No, it's all fine, thanks. Listen, I gotta go, but you, you can stay here if you want, she seems to like you." He nodded to the still splashing dolphin in front of us.

"Kevin, hey, thanks for saying hi, and it was really nice to meet you."

"Yeah, ok, see ya."

I watched him walk toward the pier where the other trainers were gathered. His shoulders slumped and he stopped for a moment, looked at me, then turned away and left.

"Well Kate, that was pretty interesting, huh?" I said to my perpetually grinning buddy.

She made a clicking sound. I figured that was her way of agreeing with me.

"By the way, I know it was you, the one who saved me that day in the pool. Don't deny it, I remember those three notches on your—your back fin thing there. Anyway, thank you."

She made some more clicking sounds and used her tail to send up another dousing of lagoon water at me.

"Thanks," I said, "good talk."

I knew my visit to the Fort Myers P.D. would not be nearly as magical or beautiful as my visit to the lagoon, so I treated myself by stopping in at DeeDee's Delights bakery on the way there. I purchased a strawberry pie and put it in the ice chest I always carry with me to keep my water bottles chilled.

The pretense I concocted for getting past the lobby was that I needed to speak with Mac about some information I had learned. My plan then would be to poke my head into Miranda's forensics lab to chat, and maybe get her to tell me any new information she had on the three dead divers. It was a long shot, but I was feeling lucky.

"I've got to buy myself a lottery ticket today," I said to myself, because as I pulled into the parking lot, I spotted Miranda on her way out. I drove up next to her and put my hand out to gesture her to stop.

When she put her window down I asked, "Where ya' going? I was just coming to see you."

"I'm getting something to eat, I've got like twenty minutes and then I gotta' be back. Bye."

"I've got a fresh baked pie I just picked up. We can eat it in your office if you want, save you a trip going out."

"What kind?"

"Strawberry, from DeeDee's."

"Can I have it without talking to you?"

"No."

She sighed, "All right, come on, follow me."

Walking to her lab we passed Mac who was too engaged in conversation on his phone to speak, but he did acknowledge my presence by way of a wave. He was in the middle of telling the poor sot on the other end of the line, "What do you mean you dinna have the report yet? Er ya' waitin' till the victim gives you a statement? 'Cause if you are, you might want to remember he's in the morgue and his health ain't up to chattin' right now."

Seated inside Miranda's office, I watched her take some paper plates and plastic forks from a drawer of her metal file cabinet while I untied the string on the bakery box.

"Oh my God Miranda, look at this, have you ever seen anything so beautiful?" I asked, as I pulled the top open.

Miranda cut herself a healthy slice and handed me the plastic knife.

"I was hoping you had something you could share with me now that the case on those dead divers is closed," I said.

"Who said it was closed?" she asked, feeding herself the first bite.

"Oh, I thought you ruled them all heart attacks, didn't you?"

"Not me, the M.E. did."

"But, that's kind of weird, huh, all of them having heart attacks at the same time?"

Miranda looked at me as though I was as stupid as my question made me sound.

"Yeah, I guess that's why the case is still open." I said, cutting my slice of pie to avoid seeing her roll her eyes.

"Were you able to find out if their diving gear was to blame?" I asked.

"Yes, and no it wasn't. All their gear was good. They got it at a dive shop in the Caribbean. If you feel like taking a trip I'll be happy to give you the address. Take your time, enjoy the sights."

"Yeah, but thanks, no, I'll take your word for it. What about that whistle I saw one of them wearing, do you know if that was part of the gear they got in, where, The Bahamas?"

"I didn't say it was The Bahamas and no, the whistle wasn't from there."

I had the first fork-full of pie half way to my lips when Detective McKenzie poked his head in.

"Come on Chase, that meetin's about to start. Oi, is that pie? Bring it with ya', and the plates."

The helping on its way to my mouth fell, instead, to my lap, as Miranda scrambled to grab the pie and plates. That left me with nothing but some whipped cream on my pants and when everyone was gone, I scooped it up with my thumb and tasted it. Even with the lint, I could tell it was an amazing pie.

I ran by Junior's Pawn and Gun before meeting Pam. The transaction was brief and Junior joked about putting in a drive-thru window just for me. The day's earlier tragedy of once again being denied all but just the sight and smell of pie, had made me peevish and I took it out on Junior by not smiling at his lame joke. I put the two hundred in my purse and walked out into a sudden downpour.

"Nope," I said to myself in the rear view mirror as I moved my damp hair around, "no need to buy that lottery ticket today."

Today's rental car was more a loan from Zig. He was out of town for a long weekend with someone who I'm sure looked much like the person he spent the last long weekend with. All his lady friends are tall, what I like to call *fancy looking*, and they drive pricey convertibles. That last part works out well for me because I get to use his little sports car, which is not much larger than my scooter, but does include doors and a roof.

The professor's sister lived in Englewood, a town about an hour's drive north of Fort Myers. I was scheduled to meet both her and Pam, at a little waterside pub called The White Elephant.

Englewood has a large retiree population, who are not quite as well-heeled as some others on the southwest coast, namely those in Venice and Sarasota to the north, and Naples to the south. Still, the town is a lovely little spot, with all the charm of small-town Florida.

The White Elephant nestles on a patch of Englewood beach, a part of Manasota Key, and lies a mile or so west from the center of town. The pub looks out onto a small inlet where boats are moored. It is just a narrow, two-lane-road span from it, to the beach, so a lot of pub guests are attired in beachwear, and smell of salt water and sunscreen.

I was early, so I crossed the street to the beach, to enjoy a view of the Gulf. No homes or businesses blocked the view of white sand, blue water, and primary colored umbrellas dotting the horizon between them. People waded far from shore in waist-high water to the sand bar. Others walked the shoreline, stopping from time to time to gather up shells that are carried there with each wave, leaving a carpet of softly colored gems under their feet. Englewood Beach is noted for the unbelievably large number of shells and sharks teeth that line the shore.

Twenty or so seagulls formed a perfectly lined regimen staring off into the sea, until a rushing toddler sent them flying up and out, squawking loudly in protest. Other than that, it was peaceful, quiet, beautiful. It looked like the kind of beach they use to film vacation get-a-way ads. I deemed it my new favorite beach and planned to come back with a blanket and umbrella.

The breeze blew at my back as I made my way toward the Jimmy Buffet music coming from the rooftop speakers of The White Elephant. As I passed through the front of the restaurant, I paused to allow my pupils to adjust to the shaded interior. A few steps more found me on the patio that lined the bay. Wooden tables topped with blue umbrellas painted a portrait of the quintessential tropical tiki bar.

A menu of some truly mouthwatering and exotic drinks made me wish I had a designated driver, but I opted for a ginger ale with a pineapple garnish while I waited for Pam.

I glanced around for any likely candidates to be the professor's sister, but the only ladies there, were accompanied by men in golf shirts and ball caps, so I sipped my drink and waited. Boats bobbed gently up and down on the inlet as small waves rippled the water between the pub, and the tree lined shore several yards away. My mind was a million miles away when I heard my name called.

Pam only half-sat on the stool next to mine.

"Kathy," she said, "that's the sister's name by the way, called me on my cell not more than five minutes ago to say she wouldn't be meeting with us. Not couldn't, but wouldn't."

"Why?"

"She didn't say except that she didn't want any trouble and to please just leave her alone."

"How did she sound?"

"Tense, she sounded tense, like, you know like Barney?"

"I'm sorry, like who?"

"You know, Barney, Barney the knife."

"Barney the knife, Barney the knife. Oh, Barney Fife. I'm confused."

"The skinny one from black and white television."

"I know who Barney Fife is. I mean, I'm confused as to why all of a sudden she won't talk to us and sounds scared. Obviously someone has gotten to her, but who and why?"

"I'm sorry we came out here for nothing," said Pam, tapping her sandals on the foot rest and chewing her bottom lip.

"Hang on, sit tight, order something. I have an idea."

I pulled the cell from my purse and dialed. Rose answered on the first ring. She had just come out of the meeting that Miranda and Mac absconded to with my pie.

"Hey, can you get an address for me?" I asked.

"If it's not a public place then you know I can't."

"But what if I suspect the person is in some kind of danger?"

"Then we'll send a squad car over, what's the name?"

"No, don't do that."

"What are you up to?"

"It's the professor's sister. You know the guy that was shot off of Alligator Alley?"

"Why do you want to be bothering his sister?"

"The napkins, you know, the ones someone took from my house. He had them and now we want to get them back, but she changed her mind at the last minute about meeting us."

"That doesn't sound like she's in danger, sounds like she's met you."

"Ha, ha. But really, Pam did say she sounded nervous on the phone, like Barney the—I mean Barney Fife."

"I can't send a squad car to someone's house because they talk in a whiny, high pitched voice. We'd have squad cars at every other house in Naples."

"I know, that's why we want to go there ourselves. Oh wait, never mind, I have an idea," I said. "Bye."

I was fortunate to be in a town so small that there were only two florists. This made narrowing down the one that sent flowers to Kathy Ballanchi this week, pretty simple. I figured that surely, no matter how awful her brother was, someone would have been decent enough to send flowers to his sister, and I was right. *Audrey's Flower Garden* had sent an arrangement to Kathy Ballanchi only yesterday. They told me this when I said I wished to order something for her and didn't want to send a duplicate. I gave Audrey part of my pelican-punching fine-money for a cheap bouquet, then waited outside the shop for her van to make the delivery.

Ms. Ballanchi's home was on Manasota Key, the same stretch of land that is home to Englewood Beach. We followed the van back over the bridge on Beach Rd, circled the roundabout, passed The White Elephant, and entered a neighborhood of small, pastel homes built in a time before siding and Cuban tile roofs made every house identical to its neighbor.

We stayed several houses behind the van, and parked in the driveway of a home that appeared vacant. We watched. Kathy Ballanchi answered the door for the florist, and then retreat back inside. Pam assured me that even though I, with my nearsightedness, couldn't make out whether it was the woman we were looking for or a Yeti, she was able to see well enough to be certain who it was.

After the delivery van left, Pam knocked at the front door. When Kathy Ballanchi opened the door her eyes widened and she gasped.

"What are you—how did you…?"

"I'm so sorry Kathy," Pam said, "but we were worried about you, you sounded so…"

I was afraid for a moment she would say Barneyish.

"…you sounded so nervous."

"Because I *am* nervous. My brother was shot and killed. Strangers show up, call. I don't want any part of whatever he was involved in, now go away."

"I understand," I told her. "But if you could just tell us if you saw some drawings in with his belongings…"

"His belongings were stolen by the thugs that shot him, now please, just go away. I'm serious, I don't want anything to do with anything…"

"Of course," I said, "but if you find any kind of papers, drawings, before you throw them away or anything, if you could call me."

I handed her my card and Pam and I walked away, then turned back before she closed the door and asked, "When you say people calling and coming by, did you mean people besides Pam and me?"

She gave me a pleading look and closed the door.

"Someone else is talking to her," I told Pam, "and she's scared."

TWENTY

"**Gator,**" **I asked, when he** picked me up from work the following day. "Do you, by any chance have a boat?"

"Yep, a small one, almost never take it out though. Why, you want to go fishing or something?"

"Maybe, in a way. It's just—well—one day I saw someone at Dan's letting some dolphins into the lagoon. He opened a gate that led out to the Gulf. I'm kind of curious, ya' know?"

"You are a nosy one, Miss Margaret, no wonder you need a body guard."

"Are you my body guard, Gator?"

"Ha, I always thought that would be a good job for me, my Army combat training and all."

Gator kept an eye on his rear view mirror, and I suspect he was hoping to spot the white Ford Taurus, but the rest of the ride home was uneventful.

"But you flew helicopters, not much hand to hand, or even pistol to pistol, combat there."

"No ma'am, but the Army did teach us some effective ways to stay alive, if you know what I mean."

"You mean, they taught you how to kill or be killed?"

"Well, I suppose if you want to be blunt about it, yeah."

"Do you remember any of that?"

"Sure I do, just, you know, not a lot of chances to use it here, stateside."

"No, I guess not."

"Haven't had Foxy Lady in the water much lately, not sure she's sea worthy. I'll take her to a guy I know tomorrow."

"Thanks, and you're gonna pick me up tomorrow morning?"

"You got it."

I put the key in my front door and remembered something vital to tell Gator. I ran back to the street and waved my arms at Lucille's tail lights, but he turned the corner without seeing me.

"I can't believe I forgot," I mumbled to myself, sulking into my home. "I can't believe I forgot to tell him I needed to make a pie stop."

I was in the middle of reading blog comments and conspiracy theories that ranged from, weaponized animals, murderous fishermen, and the price-gouging of erectile dysfunction meds, when my phone rang.

"Just giving you a heads up that Mac is calling in your buddy Pam to question her about the men she got those napkins from," Rose said without so much as a *howdee do*.

"When? I want to be there with her when she sees him. Do you think he'd be OK with that?"

"Yeah, he wants to see you too, that was gonna be my next thing."

"You know, that could have come first but, whatever. Anyway, what time? You know I'm off tomorrow?"

"First thing in the morning."

"What do you consider first thing, 'cause on my day off I consider ten to be pretty early."

"Ten's the middle of the day, be here by six."

"If you meant the middle of the night, you should have said so. OK, see you at six."

The thud of the newspaper hitting my front door woke me from a really great dream I was having about Miss GiGi and Frances serving little cocktail wienies to the guests at my wedding to Frank Preston. Once I was fully awake, I realized, not only was I not getting married, I also do not get newspaper delivery.

After checking the peephole in the front door and leaving the chain-lock in place, I looked down at the front stoop and saw, what in the dim light of early morning, appeared to be someone's slipper. After closer examination, I realized it was a two foot long, bug eyed, gray and smelly dead fish.

I closed the door quickly, turned the dead bolt and called Rose while I hit brew on the coffee pot.

"I think Brassmonkey has watched The Godfather one too many times," I told her. "He left a dead fish at my front door and didn't even have class enough to wrap it in newspaper."

"Leave everything like it is, I'll be there in twenty or thirty."

"Could you bring us some doughnuts?"

"You're kidding, this is police business not, oh never mind, chocolate or jelly?"

"I'm gonna go talk to your neighbors, see if anyone saw who did this," Rose said, licking raspberry filling from the palm of her hand.

"It's five in the morning."

"I've seen your neighbors, they're in their 80s. They got up and had their bran flakes an hour ago, I guarantee it."

"They're gonna be pissed, I hope you have your gun."

I fed Captain Hornblower and promised him a nice little ship for his fish tank since he had proven himself as brave and hearty as his namesake. By the time I had packed paper and pens, and filled two to-go mugs with coffee, Rose was back with some helpful news. My neighbor across the street remembered seeing a white car slow down in front of my house, then speed away. She saw this, apparently, while outside watering her lawn.

"She was watering her lawn at five in the morning?"

"Nope, four in the morning. She's in an odd number house, today is the 16th. I saw the water pooling in her grass, had to promise not to turn her in to the water company."

"I've got to find Sabina, show her some pictures of white Ford Taurus' and ask her if it looks like the car the man was driving the day those copies went missing from my house."

"Who?"

"Oh, an old gypsy I know. I'm scattering her husband, the grave digger's, ashes at Dan's."

"I get it, if you don't want to tell me just say so, you don't have to be sarcastic. Unless—hold on, is that...?"

"Yep, true story."

"I'm gonna win the *Crazy Civilian* pot this week for sure," she said, slamming the palm of her fist on the steering wheel.

"The what?"

"Yeah, don't tell anyone I mentioned that."

"How often does my name come up?"

"Since I met you, I've made enough money to take one of them murder mystery cruises. I always wanted to go on one of them."

"Glad I could help. By the way, what did you do with the fish? It smells like you put it in your pocket."

"It was slimy, it slipped out of my hands and onto my shirt when I was putting it in an evidence bag. You can really smell it?"

"Do you want to go home and change before we go to the station?"

"No time, we're already runnin' late and I don't have a change of clothes on me either. What have you got?"

"I've got strawberry scented hand sanitizer."

"Good, give it here."

I handed it to her, and at the next red light she rubbed it into her shirt, then onto her neck and wrists like she was applying perfume.

"It'll have to do," she said, handing me the now nearly empty bottle. "Is that better?"

"Yes, sure," I lied, rolling down the window, "all better."

Sitting in the police station lobby next to a woman for whom a bottle of strawberry scented hand sanitizer would have been useful, I waited for Rose to do all her necessary checking in. I leafed through a copy of last Christmas' edition of Guns and Ammo and watched the clock. It was 7:30 before Rose came and rescued me from the lobby that had since become filled to capacity, and included two crying babies and one crying drunk.

She led me to a room that was painted a pale blue and where the walls were hung with paintings of orange and pink sunrises. I guessed this was probably because someone, somewhere, wrote a psychology paper on the Feng Shui of police stations.

"Big room," I said, "are we expecting company?"

"I chose this one. I need some airing out space," she said, pulling at her shirt in a futile attempt to rid it of fish odor.

"Good call. What else did you put on, it smells a little, uhmm, something familiar. Oh, I know, my granddaughter's hamster cage."

"Damn, I knew it," she said, blowing on her shirt now. "I remembered this stuff in our evidence locker. We picked up a guy selling exotic animals from his house. I thought that if the stuff they put at the bottom of those cages was good at masking ferret urine or mouse shit or something, that, oh hell, now instead of just dead fish, I smell like a dead fish in a petting zoo."

"Well, I can smell the strawberry a little, that helps, kind of. Just stand close to the open door."

"Good idea."

Detective McKenzie walked in quickly yet purposefully, surveying his surroundings, like a bear approaching a bee hive.

"Where's the other one?" he asked, setting his coffee mug on the 60's era conference table.

"Just spoke with her," answered Rose. "She's in the parking lot. Wes is gonna show her back."

He looked at me, narrowing his eyebrows like he had to squint to get a good look.

"You," he said, and pointed at me with an unlit cigarette. "You're still poking sticks at that dragon."

"Yep, I guess I am," I said, and watched him put the cigarette behind his ear.

"I hear you got a message today."

"I did, not a very original one, but yes."

"Shelton," he said to Rose, who was standing in the doorway. "Come over here, I want you to go over this with me, tell me what I'm lookin' at."

I expected to see her hesitate because of the fish smell, or shoot me a panicked look or something, but she didn't. She threw her shoulders back and walked to the side of the table where the big man sat, as though not a thing in the world was on her mind but work.

I watched them put their heads together, discussing something I could not make out since my hearing was just a few decibels shy of needing one of those old timey ear trumpets. Instead, I studied Rose for any telltale signs that she was nervous, excited, shy, infatuated, or acting in any way different around the big Scot. I studied him too, trying to see what traits she found attractive that I might have missed. The most I could come up with was that he combined confidence and an iron will, with an odd kind of charm and wit. Although not my type, I was beginning to understand a little of what Rose might see in him.

At the moment I became aware of the fact that I was staring, Pam and another woman, whom I did not recognize, entered the room. The other woman looked like a circus performer or a heroin shop proprietor. Her head was shaved on one side, and lavender colored strands of uneven hair hung from the other. The tattoos that covered her arms like sleeves, were so numerous that they ran together into a seemingly endless mural of comics, M.C Escher drawings, and crop circles. Her t-shirt sported the letters, STFU, and it took me a moment to realize those weren't the initials of a university somewhere in Florida. The overwhelming smell of tobacco permeated, not only the air around her, but probably penetrated several layers of our planet's atmosphere. I assumed the officer showing her into the room was mistaken, and had meant to bring her to an interrogation room, or prison cell, or the bus terminal.

"Ah, you must be our sketch artist, Brittney," said McKenzie, pushing his chair back and extending a hand to the woman who was about the size and weight of the detective's forearm.

"Brit," she said, without shaking his hand. She made an effort to throw herself into a chair, but was so tiny she merely floated onto it.

"And you must be...," said the detective.

Pam walked forward and shook his hand, "Pamela Sutton, so thankful to meet you."

McKenzie shot Rose a sideways look.

"Pleased, she's *pleased* to meet you," I added. "Pam grew up outside the U.S."

"Ah, and myself, American English is a real bastard to get the hang of," said McKenzie.

After we were seated, and coffee and water offered by the same person who lead Pam and Brit into the room, Rose spoke.

"Detective McKenzie would like you two," she pointed to Pam and me, "to recreate the drawings you say those men left at Harpoon Harry's. Also, Pam, please describe as best you can remember, what those men looked like. Brit here, is going to sketch them for us."

Rose gave Pam and I each a sketch pad and pencils.

"Maggie, you start on those drawings while Pam gives her descriptions to Brit."

"I'm gonna need a smoke break first," said Brit, in a flat, even tone, not bothering to look up.

"You just had one," said Rose. "Here chew some gum."

Rose pulled a pack of Juicy Fruit from her pocket and slid it across the table to the artist who sighed and rolled her eyes but said nothing. As she picked up the pack, pulled out a stick, and began chewing and popping her gum, she opened her own large sketch pad, glared at Pam for a moment and said, "So, you gonna start or what?"

"Oh, yes, sorry," said Pam, straightening in her chair and leaning forward toward Brit.   "OK, well, I'll start with the crab-cake and Corona guy first. Is that all right?"

"Sure, whatever, look through these."

Brit slid a page of facial shapes across the table.

"Which one most likely matches the head shape of your crab-cake man."

"Oh, well, this is interesting," I said, looking at them over Pam's shoulder. "They look like those faces you move hair onto with little magnets don't they?"

While Pam chose eyebrow and mouth shapes from the pages in front of her, I began my own sketches, wishing I had both better memory, and drawing skills.

When I was a kid in school, the art teacher spoke to me as though maybe I was blind and couldn't see what it was I supposed to draw.

"See, the banana is curved and yellow with a brown marking on the side," she would say. "Your picture looks more like, well, I don't really think it looks like anything. Have you had your eyes examined dear?"

Of course I could see the banana, I knew what one looked like from memory, but I just couldn't make my fingers recreate it. The only thing I could draw was a kind of stick house with stick chimney and door. That did not take me very far either in school, or today in the police conference room. I did the best I could, and counted on Pam to do a better job.

By the time Pam had finished with her first sketch, it was time for Brit to take a smoke break, and the rest of us to stretch our legs.

"What's this about?" I asked Rose when we were alone in the ladies room.

"I can't tell you much, Mac will have to do that, but I'll give you this. If the guys from Harpoon Harry's are the same as the ones you fished out of the Gulf, it will be the best tip on where they were and what they were doing the days right up to their death that we've had. That means we know that all three of them were doctors too."

"No kidding? That's awesome, I'm so glad someone's finally putting that together. What took so long?"

"A lot of background stuff I can't..."

We were cut off by the door opening and hitting Rose in the back. She had stood there just for that purpose, to keep our conversation private, but she got a whack on the back of her head for her trouble.

"Oh sorry," said Pam. "Did I hurt you? I didn't know..."

"No, I'm fine, it's OK," said Rose. "I was in the way. I want to tell you, you're doing a great job in there."

"Oh, thank you. I hope the artist can work with my poor describing skills."

"She can, she's real good."

"She doesn't look that much like a police officer to me."

"Brit? A cop? That's hilarious. No, she's not. She's working off some trouble she got herself into. She's good, probably a great artist. Got her masters in Fine Art, and working on her PhD at some college up north. Came here to vacation with her boyfriend, got stopped with weed and a small dusting of coke. She claims it was her boyfriend's. Mac saw some of the drawings she made when she was in holding. He made her this deal. She comes in here, helps us out till it's time to go back to school, he expunges her record. Judge Bethune loves him, will do pretty much whatever he asks. So, we got a legit artist to work with for about another three weeks. I'm glad we've got her for this."

Back in the conference room, Pam and I each showed the detective our sketches of what we remembered from the ones the men had left at Harpoon Harry's.

Miranda was called into the room to check Pam's composite drawings against the photos she had of the dead divers. After the M.E. had obtained the dental records, it was pretty easy to find both California Driver's License photos, and U.S. Navy ID photos, to compare them to.

You'd have thought from the sketches Brit had made, that the men sat for them. They were eerily close to being perfect matches.

"Good, now we have a trail we can follow backward from Harpoon Harry's," said McKenzie. "Great work everyone."

"I drove Miss Finn here sir," said Rose. "You want me to bring her back, or get someone in traffic to do it?"

"No, you do it, and see if you can track down anything on that car."

"Yes sir."

"Shelton, just another wee minute please."

"Yes sir," she said, and waited as the rest of us left the room.

I stood outside the door for her and she passed by me a moment later like she was shot from a rocket. I sprinted down the hall to catch up to her.

"What's the matter? What did he say?" I asked.

"Come on, my car's out here," she said, and opened a door at the end of the intake hall.

Rose didn't say anything until we had driven a couple of miles down Tamiami Trail.

"I know you want to ask me but I don't want to talk about it."

"OK," I said, "I won't ask. Just tell me this, was it bad?"

"He said..."

I waited for to go on.

"He said he don't normally approve of cops wearing perfume but..."

"Oh, that," I said. "I'm sorry."

"You don't get it, he liked it. He said I reminded him of home."

"Brooklyn?"

"No, Scotland."

"You think people really smell like strawberry scented dead fish from a hamster cage in Scotland?"

"I am never going to go there and find out."

"Ditto that buddy."

TWENTY ONE

Rose looked at security camera footage at all the gas stations within a square mile of my house, and had another couple of cops check some even further out. When I remembered there weren't all that many near me that were open that early, the task didn't seem as daunting as I'd initially imagined.

While Rose busied herself with that, I revisited my notes from earlier in the week adding this newest bit of information to what I had.

The three men were ex-Navy, and from San Diego. I looked back at my notes and saw that Alden, the veterinarian who drowned at Dan's, was also from there. I wrote coincidence with a question mark next to that one.

After all, San Diego is a common place for both. I made a note to learn as much as I could about Alden and moved to the next set of facts.

I was receiving death threats on my blog from someone calling themselves Brassmonkey. That name being a Naval term, I drew arrows connecting the three Navy guys to Brassmonkey.

I had a dead fish thrown on my doorstep. Fish of course, are not part of the Navy but at least the territory of where the Navy operates. A few steps of separation, so I drew a dotted line from it to the others.

I was being followed by a white Ford Taurus which matched the description of the one that tossed the fish on my front stoop. I drew a solid line from it, to the fish, and Brassmonkey. I didn't know that he was the one in the Taurus, the one who saw me nearly drown at Dan's, but he was number one on my suspect list.

Next, the professor knew something about those drawings that was important enough to call Pam, both from the road and from the hospital. He's dead, and his sister is being intimidated by someone.

There was something Pam had said about him that sent up a red flag somewhere in my brain, like a connection to something else, but I just couldn't pull it out and take a good look at it. I made another note to learn some more about the professor.

By far, the weirdest piece of the puzzle was that damned, untraceable listening device that, whoever stole my notes, placed in my house. I drew a triangle with the word *sketches* at the top, *listening device from England* in one corner, and *professor* in another. I stared at it a while unable to come up with anything, drew a circle around it with a yellow highlighter as a reminder to come back to it, and started a new thread.

The last piece of the puzzle was the odd behavior surrounding a lot of what I saw at Dan's. The guy in the boat with the underwater gate, and the fact that I may have spotted a gun on him. The security guard, Marty, being hauled off to the Feds after being summoned, it seemed, by Howard of all people. Then there was Dan's more than strange, even for him, behavior. The conversation I heard between Harris and Big Kev. That was the hardest part to put together even on its own. Whether any of it might fit into the rest was a complete mystery to me. And, in the back of mind, was the small voice that nagged at me day and night asking, *what if Frank Preston is behind it all.*

I looked at the jeweled box on my bookshelf and said, "So Radu, what do you think? I could use some input here. Nothing? What about you Captain?" I asked my new pet. He swam behind the plastic plant. "Thanks guys, love the input. For right now, I'm going with the idea that Frank Preston is one of the good guys. And no, no matter what you think, it has nothing to do with his twinkly eyes. Well, OK, maybe a little."

Happy that I finally had roommates to bounce ideas off of, I decided my first step was to learn about Alden and what he did before Dan hired him as veterinarian. That meant trying to track down Dan at work the next day, and that would not be easy. He had become increasingly elusive, and I began to wonder if he had bitten off more than he could chew with this place. He was used to being a free spirit. Now he was answering to no less than a half dozen investors, and at least one of them, I had learned, was not a very nice person.

I went to bed thinking about all the calories I saved myself by not having pie, and said a prayer that Brassmonkey would not up his game and throw a tuna at my house next morning. But before I could get into a nice dreamy sleep, the phone rang and I answered it to a fairly distraught Pam.

"Are you OK?" I asked when her initial hello sounded a little panicky.

"Remember how you said someone put a fish at your house today?"

"Yes, though I think what I said was, that I was the victim of a drive-by fish hurling. Why do you ask?"

"Because when I got home tonight, I found a dead fish by the front door as well, this one had its eyes removed."

"Were you aware that the three dead men I pulled up from the Gulf also had missing eyes?"

"Yes, I'm aware, and I think the fish delivery man does too."

"You make him sound like the pizza guy, but yeah, I agree. I'll call Rose and let her know."

"Should I leave it where it is?"

"Probably won't have to, but wrap it up in plastic or something, maybe put it in your freezer for now. I'll ask Rose when I get her on the phone what to do next."

"Does your friend Rose think they'll be able to find out who this person is who has been, what did you say, pitching these fish at us?"

"I'm not sure. Do you have anyone you can stay with for now?"

"My father is due back in country tomorrow, he has a home in Sarasota. Do you think I should ask him to stay with me?"

"If you can't stay with him up there, then yes, that's a good idea."

I have work and study here, the commute wouldn't work. It will be easier for him to stay with me. I will ask him to bring his weapons."

"Weapons, you mean guns?"

"We've lived in war zones, of course he has guns, many guns."

"Wow, OK then, that's good. I'm glad you'll be looked after. If things get hairy I may come bunk with you guys."

"You don't really mean hairy when you say hairy, do you?"

"No, I really don't. Also, I didn't mean bunk beds when I say bunk if that's what you were thinking."

"That's good, call me when you hear from Rose."

"Good night Pam, lock your doors and call me if you get nervous, I'll come over."

I didn't hear from Rose until 5am.

"You know there's other cops you can call besides me? We're not all assigned our own individual citizens. You get that, right?"

"I hate calling the switchboard, they know my number. They're annoyed before I even say anything."

"So am I."

"I know, but you're annoyed in a good way, we're friends. They absolutely don't like me."

"They don't have to like you, they just have to patch you through to the duty officers."

"I know all that. Anyway, what do you want Pam to do with her dead fish?"

"She can cook it up for supper if she wants to, we don't need it. We're not gonna dust the thing for fingerprints. Just tell her to come in and give us a statement."

"OK, I'll call her. Hey, you know her and her father have lived in war zones? He's an archeologist, and they've lived most of their lives in the Middle East. He has a lot of guns apparently"

"Great, next time I have a case involving roving gangs of mummies with guns, I'll know who to call. I gotta go. Call the day officer's desk. Bye."

I called Pam, gave her the number for the Fort Myers PD, and got ready for work. Since I'm disguised as a grinning man-eater all day, my choice of wardrobe for work is casual in the extreme. Usually the fewer the garments the better, at least as few as an over fifty-year-old woman who is not Miss GiGi can get away with. I wear my hair half way to shoulder length so I can put it in hot rollers when I'm wearing real clothes, and a ponytail when I'm in costume. Of course, makeup would be useless, so I usually just smear on some moisturizer and call it a morning. All this means I can cut my getting ready for work time down from forty five minutes to about ninety seconds.

I called Gator and told him I was taking the scooter in to work, but to call when he could.

The parking lot at Dan's was filled with school buses. At the front gate a line of 3rd graders were waiting, poking, pushing and generally being 3rd graders. I braced myself for what I knew would not be a good day to be a land shark.

My morning went as expected with half the children, mostly the girls, posing politely to allow Howard to get their photos. The other half, mostly the boys, either bit me, kicked me, or in the case of one of the bigger ones, tried to wrestle me. Their teachers were nowhere in sight and I suspected they were off looking for the beer concession.

My lunch break was spent looking for Big Kev who was not in the Dolphateria, which was the first place I checked. When I tried the lagoon, I didn't find him there either. What I did spot was a small boat entering the lagoon from the mouth, where it led to the Gulf. I hid behind the same palm as before, for no apparent reason, since I was allowed to be there. I watched it slow down to its no-wake speed, approach the little cave, go behind the waterfall, and disappear.

I wanted to get back there too and knew that after hours would be the only time to do that. I was anxious to talk to Gator and ask him if *Foxy Lady* had running lights.

I did find Big Kev at last, in the staff locker room, having a loud discussion with Frances.

Kevin said, "But I promised his mother I'd send her anything he left here."

"You had no business speaking for Alden, he didn't work for you," said Frances.

"Yeah, well, he didn't work for you either. Besides, why do you care? You're the friggin' lunch lady. None of this is your business anyway."

"Watch your mouth you, I don't let anyone speak to me that way. And the reason I keep my eyes on the likes of you is because Dan expects me to."

"What, you're like the park snitch?"

"If you're not doing anything wrong, you don't have anything to worry about. Now, you leave Alden's locker alone. Dan can send his things to his mother. How do I know you weren't going to steal what was in there? Your kind can't be trusted, everyone knows that."

"My kind?" Big Kev's voice was strained with tension and anger. "Just what kind is my kind?"

"With that brown skin, you ain't exactly Irish."

"Why you little bi..."

"Hey guys, I didn't know anyone was in here," I interrupted, before Kevin ended up in jail for assault.

"Oh great, another useless one," said Frances. "Where did Dan find you all, at some school for the simple minded? I can see it now, the bunch of you, just wandering around bumping into each other, trying not to get run over by the parked cars."

"Frances," I said, "always good to see you. Shouldn't you be brewing toads and newt's eyes in a cauldron somewhere?"

"A great joke from our park clown," she said. "I'm sure you'll have them all in stitches down at the unemployment office. I'm leaving now. And you," she pointed her tobacco stained finger at Kevin, "you stay away from Alden's stuff, you hear? I have my own fingerprint kit."

"Bye," I said to her. "Try not to let a house fall on you."

When she left, I asked Kevin, "What was that about?"

"I don't know, she's crazy. I mean, seriously, just bat-shit crazy."

"I agree, scary crazy, because she's also mean. And why didn't she want you to get into Alden's locker?"

"Because she really is honestly crazy I guess. The thing is, what she didn't know was, I had already opened it. When she walked in, I was just locking it back up. You think she really has her own fingerprint kit?"

"I'd only be surprised if she didn't. What was in the locker anyway?"

"Nothing, which is weird, because he kept all his notes and log books in there. He was really conscientious about noting everything, every detail. He had volumes of notebooks in there. I knew his mother would want them, she's a biologist, they'd have meant the world to her."

"Any chance he emptied them out himself before he, before he died?"

"Sure, there's a chance I suppose," he said, sitting on the bench in front of me and pulling sneakers from his bag. "But why? As far as I know he wasn't planning on going anywhere."

"Where are you going?" I asked, watching him lace up.

"Down to the lagoon, you want to walk and talk?"

"Sure."

I felt as though Big Kev and I had bonded now in a kind of a, *the enemy of my enemy is my friend* way. It was us against Frances now, and we had become brothers in arms.

"How well did you know Alden?" I asked.

"Pretty well. We worked closely ever since I got here a year ago. I mean, we didn't hang out much socially or anything, just a couple of times for lunch or beers after work. Maybe a half dozen times is all. He practically lived here."

"That's a very loyal employee," I said

"That's a pretty a pretty cool design," I said, pointing to the tattoo on his forearm of two elaborately drawn dolphins with something I couldn't make out in the center.

"It's a tat of the submariner's badge."

"You were in the Navy, in submarines?"

"Yeah, despite what that hag says, I'm an American and a veteran. My mother is Iranian, my father is from Iowa. I was born in California, Sunnyvale."

"Sunnyvale, nice, I've been there, it's a gorgeous town."

"My dad worked for Google. He was a great designer, was there from the start almost."

"Was? Did he retire?"

"Passed away, colon cancer, seven years ago."

"I'm sorry," I said, and put a hand on his shoulder for a moment.

"That's when I quit school and joined the Navy. I guess I was in a weird place in my head. Don't get me wrong," he said, stopping for a moment to gaze out over the water. "I'm glad I joined, the Navy was a great experience, but I'm even gladder to be out."

"Alden was from San Diego, right? Was he ex-Navy too?"

"Nah, Alden was a boy genius, scholarships to all the best schools. He got his undergrad at The University of Miami as a matter of fact, then his PhD at U.C. Davis. I think it's ranked number one or two in veterinary sciences. He worked with some really great marine mammal guys in San Diego. Coming here to run his own program was a dream for him. He was thrilled to have this job, even though he didn't like what Dan or the rest of them were doing."

"How so?"

He glanced at his watch and said, "Hey look, it's late, I've got to go. We can have lunch tomorrow if you want. I can meet you at the Dolphateria at noon."

"That sounds great, thanks. I'm late getting back to work myself. See you tomorrow."

I walked back to the locker room thinking how odd it was, that even though knowing Big Kev was ex-Navy I felt certain he was not Brassmonkey. In my mind, Big Kev was definitely a standup guy, and the Navy thing was just a coincidence. On the other hand, the fact that Alden was *not* in the Navy didn't fully convince me that his fate was not somehow tied to the others. I needed to find out just who those great marine mammal guys he worked with in San Diego were, and if they could possibly have been Navy. Fortunately for me, I had a friend I could call with just such a question.

Shelby and I met when we worked for The Tennessean in Nashville. She married a Naval Officer she had met when she visited her sister in San Diego. It was a whirlwind romance that ended shortly thereafter in a hurricane-force-wind type divorce.

She got a good job working for the San Diego public television station producing nature documentaries, so she stayed. I had three different jobs in three different cities since then. When you work in the newspaper business, you never completely unpack.

I called her when my shift at Dan's was over.

"Shelby, how are things in sunny California?"

"Probably the same as where you are, but less humid and more earthquakey."

"Hey, I hate to bring up your ex but..."

"Then please, don't."

"Ok, but does *He Who Shall Not Be Named* have any friends you stay in contact with?"

"Yeah, some, why?"

"I want to know if there's a naval program there that works with dolphins."

"Oh God, you're not writing one of those killer dolphin articles are you? Please say no, even if you are, I hate to think of you in that way."

"No, and if I told you what my latest job is you'd think writing killer dolphin articles was a promotion."

"OK, tell me, you know you're going to eventually. Just go ahead and get it over with. I won't laugh."

"Of course you will, you always do, you can't help yourself."

"I know, it's what you love most about me. But seriously, first tell me what you're doing, then we'll get to whatever else is going on."

"I'm working as a mascot at a sea park. I dress up in a shark costume and have my picture taken with children and old men, both of whom bite."

There was silence at the other end so I asked, "Shelby, you still there?"

"Yes, I'm waiting for you say you're just kidding and tell me what you're really doing."

"Wait no more, that's the bare and inglorious truth."

"Now you'll have to excuse me while I laugh my ass off, hang on a sec."

I heard her tell someone in the background, "Hey, you think your job sucks, you remember me telling you about my friend Maggie in Florida? Her job makes yours look..."

"Shelby!" I yelled, "talk to me."

"Oh, yeah, sorry," she said, her laughter subduing. "I'm just picturing you in that. So, what do you need to know?"

"There was a guy here, a veterinarian who specialized in..."

"Hold on," she said, as she began another round of laughter. "Sorry, I thought I was done." She took a deep sigh, "OK, go ahead, I think I'm good now."

"Glad I could brighten your day. As I was saying, this veterinarian, who also happens to be *dead,* is from San Diego, at least that's where he was before coming here two years ago. He specialized in marine mammals, mostly dolphins I think."

"Give me his name, we've got a good database here for that."

"Alden Gower," I said, and spelled it out for her. "Thirty-two, graduated U.C. Davis, and before that U of Miami. I need to know if he was working with the Navy on anything."

"Got it," she said, now serious and business like. "How'd he die?"

"Heart attack in the water."

"Pretty young for that."

"No kidding. Here's where it gets even more weird. You know how I told you last week about those guys I pulled up in the net?"

"Yeah. I read about it on the A.P. too."

"I'll bet you didn't read how they died."

"Not drowning?"

"Heart attacks, all three, and all three of them doctors too."

"Whoa," she said and whistled. "What's the Navy connection? Oh wait, I remember you told me they were all Navy. But this guy Gower, he wasn't?"

"No, and that's why I'm curious to see if he worked for them as a civilian. Any chance you can find that out?"

"I can try, the ex has moved away with his demon offspring. There's no chance of running in to him, so I don't mind going there myself and seeing what I can find out."

"Thanks so much."

"No problem, it will be fun. I haven't done any investigative reporting since I took this job."

"So where'd Pete, sorry, I mean The Dark Lord, where'd he move to?"

"You're gonna love this, back to his home town in West Virginia."

"Perfect place for them. Didn't you say his daddy used to make moonshine and flavor it with, what was it, Jolly Ranchers?"

"Yep, not sure if he's going into the family business there, don't care either. I just know he's two thousand, three hundred and ninety seven miles from here."

"Yeah, but who's counting, right?"

"Not me. Anyway, I'll ask around tonight when I get out of here, but it may be tomorrow or the next day before I know anything. In any case, I'll call you as soon as I do."

"I owe you big time."

"Nah, the image of you in a shark costume is payment enough. Talk to ya' later."

TWENTY TWO

Gator was waiting for me in the parking lot when I clocked out for the day.

"Miss Margaret, hello," he said, and waved.

I walked to where he stood next to Lucille.

"Hey Gator, thanks for coming, but I have the scooter here, I'm going to drive it home."

"Yeah, I figured, but I had some news for ya' and I wanted you to know right away."

I was not aware that Gator's grin could be so large, the rest of his face nearly disappeared in it.

"That Taurus, I spotted it."

"Really, where?"

"I followed it to Donny's Salvage Yard over off of MLK."

"Are you sure it was the same one?"

"Sure I am, it had that same decal in the same spot, right rear window."

"What decal? I don't remember seeing one."

"Yeah, the submarine one, with the two dolphins."

"Gator, are you absolutely sure and positive that's what it was?"

"Miss Margaret, I have been in and out of the V.A. more times than the Pope. I've seen that decal hundreds of times."

"Gator, this information is huge, I mean, you have no idea how huge. Can we go to that salvage yard right now?"

"Sure, I figured you'd want to. Get in," he said, and opened the passenger side door for me.

As we headed up 41 toward Fort Myers, I asked, "Gator?"

"Yeah?"

"I don't think the Pope ever goes to the V.A."

"Yeah, it just came out, I wasn't thinking."

"No problem, it's kind of how I say stuff all the time. I'm going to call Rose and tell her to meet us there, she should be able to stop them from crushing it until she can get a warrant or something."

Highway 41 from Bonita Springs to Martin Luther King Blvd cuts right through the center of Fort Myers, with traffic lights every couple of miles. Shops, car dealerships, shopping malls, and fast food restaurants line the sides of the road. Depending on the time of year, it can take you either half an hour, or double that, to get where you're going. June is off season so we made it there in forty five minutes because Gator drives like an old woman. That gave me time to call Rose who agreed to meet us there.

The office of Donny's Salvage Yard was an old single wide mobile home. Beyond that was the typical graveyard of wrecked and rusted vehicles in various degrees of cannibalism. In Donny's case, that number was relatively small, in that there were less than fifty as far as I could tell at first glance. Beyond that, however, was a mass of metal so densely packed there could have been several hundred cars in the fifty square foot yard.

A large black dog, wolf, bear, type creature ran toward Lucille as we entered the lot and Gator's face took on a look of fear and panic as the beast galloped closer to the Mustang's pristine paint job. Coming within inches of the car, the animal stopped dead in its tracks and we could see it was attached to the fence with a chain. A man too well dressed to be an employee made his way slowly out of the office door.

"Can I help you?"

"We're looking for Donny," I said.

"You found him."

Donny was a young man, and in my book young man is anyone under forty. He was clean shaven, his build filled out his six foot and some frame nicely, his haircut looked expensive and as I stated earlier, his clothes were better suited to a job interview than a day's work at a junk yard.

"Someone hauled a Ford Taurus in here earlier," Gator told him. "We think it might have been stolen."

Donny's face remained expressionless when he asked, "You the police?"

"No," I answered quickly, "but they're on the way."

"Then they're wasting their time," he said. "I didn't take it in. No title, no sale."

"Yeah, but I coulda' sworn I saw you drive it into the back," said Gator.

Barely perceptively, Donny's jaw tightened and his eyes narrowed, but his voice remained calmly unchanged.

"Well, you are wrong. I did take in a white Honda earlier, but it's already gone. I have a friend who needed the engine and tranny. I'll leave you to explain your mistake to the police when they come, I have an appointment."

Donny drove off in what Gator informed me was a '09 Jeep Wrangler. We watched him turn left on MLK toward Interstate 75.

"What did you think of that?" I asked Gator.

"You mean about me never saying the Taurus was white?"

"Yep. Did you get the tag number of the Jeep?"

"Sure did. Now what?"

"Now we wait for Rose," I said.

"I think we should go out back to the yard and wait, let's see what we stumble on," said Gator walking in that direction.

"What about the extra-large dog monster thing?"

"He's on a chain."

"Uhhh, I don't know. It looks like a long chain. You test it out first, I couldn't outrun a rock."

"OK, wait here," said Gator, as he walked away.

"They can smell fear," I called to him. "Act confident, I'll try and distract him."

Gator walked into the office and entered the yard from that building's back door. I walked to the far end of the outside perimeter. The dog followed me on his side of the fence, barking. Hair stood up all along his neck and spine in a kind of dog Mohawk.

The salvage yard was covered in sand, gravel, and lug nuts. Cars on jacks with ragged tires, missing doors, and hanging mufflers, were parked helter-skelter, creating a jungle of rusted, twisted metal. Oil soaked blue rags lay on or near the vehicles, along with discarded cigarette butts and Coke cans. Gator moved slowly through the maze of junk, stepping quietly and deliberately.

I stood on the other side of the gate and said, "Hello nice dog," in the kind of friendly, upbeat tone you can use when you have a seven foot high chain-link fence protecting you. The dog looked at me with its head cocked to one side and appeared rather cute in a snarling, drooling way.

"That's right," I told it, "you just look at me and pay no attention to the big man trespassing on your property."

The dog had gone from barking to a low growl when I heard Gator yell, "Oh shit!"

Then the ear splitting screech of a cat who had just had its tail stepped on, sent Gator, the dog, and cat into a frenzy of running, yelling, barking chaos.

Gator was trying to run in a zigzag motion, something he probably learned in the Army, but at his present age and size came off looking more as though he were drunk and stumbling.

The cat was ahead of them both and leaped onto the rear end of a pickup truck giving Gator the, *I don't have to run faster than the dog, I just have to run faster than you,* look. It worked, the dog gave up on the cat and was gaining on Gator when I yelled to him.

"I think he might only have a couple more feet of chain. Get up on that car, quickly. Oh, and don't forget, don't let him smell fear."

Gator scrambled onto the hood of something that wasn't much more than a frame and some tires. The dog followed him, mouth open, snarling and yelping. Gator scrambled to the roof, slid back, got a foothold on the fender, and pushed himself up, but the fender gave way sending the man back to the ground. The now terrified Gator tried crawling under the car but it was not high enough off the ground to accommodate his girth. He lay prone, kicking and screaming, only his head under the hood. Fortunately, the chain had tangled around a couple of Coke cans that rattled just enough for the dog to become startled and confused, stopping him in his pursuit. This gave Gator time to jump into the bed of a pick-up.

By this time, I knew I'd have to try and rescue him. I ran through the office to enter the yard through the same door Gator had used. Slipping on an oily spot on the floor, I caught myself on a desk and inadvertently hit the start button on a CD player.

George Thorogood began singing *Bad to the Bone* through speakers on the back wall.

Baaad, bad to the bone.

Normally I can't throw further than I can spit, but hyped up on adrenaline as I was, I pulled off one of my shoes and managed to hit the dog, who had since resumed his pursuit, in its hind end.

It was not enough to stop him, but it distracted him enough for Gator to climb up and over the roof. I found the chain and pulled, sending the animal to the ground. As I pulled the dog toward me, its hind-end dragged through the dirt.

About the time I lost my grip on the chain, the angry, growling, dog-beast got up, turned and charged at me. I stood frozen, my legs unwilling to move.

Gator, feeling he was now a safe distance away, whistled and hollered but the dog didn't care. It wanted me, I reeked of the scent of fear.

Through the pounding of my ears I heard George singing *B-B-B-Bad*, Gator whistling, and the sound of the bear sized dog gnarling.

Gator was mid-leap, attempting to throw himself on the dog like a soldier on a grenade, when from somewhere behind me a voice yelled, "Opie, down!"

The dog was immediately silent and went into a sitting position. Gator fell onto a wrench, and I unfurled myself from the fetal position.

The rotund man in the ball cap behind me then said, "Opie, come," and the animal walked through the gate and stood statue-still next to his master's left leg.

"Who are you?" I asked.

"Donny, I own the place, who are you?"

We both turned with the sound of tires on gravel, and Opie growled while still sitting obediently.

Rose's car approached us just as Gator made his way through the front door of the office followed by the cat, who sat at his feet and began grooming itself.

Rose and a uniformed officer stepped out of the squad car, and I walked to meet them, followed by either the real Donny or an imposter. Gator moved toward them also, but at a much slower pace since he was limping and out of breath.

"You the one who called me about the wreck up on 75?" Donny asked the patrolman who stood next to Rose. His voice held a barely controlled rage and when he looked at Rose his lips curled into a sneer. He looked away and spit at the ground behind him, then took the lead off of Opie's collar. I could see this was not going to go well.

"No sir, I haven't heard of any vehicles in need of a tow on 75 in Lee County in the past hour," said Rose's partner, emphasizing the word sir in what was shaping up to be a real pissing match.

This version of Donny was built like Grover Cleveland and wore a similar mustache. He was in his fifties or early sixties and wore a tropical design shirt open just enough to reveal a zipper of stitches down his chest. He carried a package of Marlboros in his pocket, and a really bad attitude.

"That's because you a-holes sent me up to Hillsborough f'in County on some chicken shit, wild goose chase," he said, and spit again, this time I thought too close in the direction of Rose. "Now I come here and find these two trespassing on my property. What are you yahoos gonna do about?"

I was about to lose my temper and I think Rose sensed it. She moved a step closer to him, pulled a pad and pen from her pocket, and in doing so revealed her shoulder holstered Glock,

Donny's face flushed red and a vein on his forehead bulged, but he stepped back and, for the time being, kept his saliva in his mouth.

"Sir," Rose said, "I'm sorry about the confusion regarding the phone call you say you received from us. I can tell you it is not this department's policy to request local businesses render aid to other counties. I will follow up on this when I get back to my office, but I suspect you may have been sent there by someone misrepresenting themselves."

I was so proud of Rose I was probably beaming. She kept her cool and spoke so professionally and courteously to this nasty, ignorant bigot that I wanted to go give her a hug. I didn't though, because she would have punched me in the throat, but I wanted to.

"Just who in the hell would want to do something like that? Besides, don't you think I got caller I.D? It read Fort Myers Police Department right on my phone."

"You see?" said Rose, "that's interesting, because our calls don't identify that way on caller..."

"Rose," Gator interrupted, "I mean, sorry, I mean Officer Shelton. I really think you guys should come back here and see this. I think it might explain a lot."

He was limping badly and the bottom of his jeans were torn, showing a large scratch across his leg that appeared to have only just stopped bleeding.

"Gator, are you alright?" I asked.

"Yeah, sure, I'm OK—just—you gotta see this."

"Unless you Keystone Cops have got a warrant, no one is going back there," said Donny. "This here is private property."

"Of course, you're right," Rose told him. She turned to her partner and said, "Ray, go ask the Captain to call the judge about getting a warrant on suspicion of a stolen vehicle on this property. And while you've got his attention, tell him that Donny's Auto Salvage appears to be in violation of several OSHA laws and probably won't be able to take any of our business for the foreseeable future. Tell him I'm suggesting we go with Manuel's Salvage on Edison and eighth. Also, call the ASPCA, and have them pick up this dog, make sure he's up on his shots, looks like he might have bit our man Gator."

"Forget it," said Donny, simultaneously coughing and lighting up one of his Marlboros. "Go on ahead and look, I ain't got nothin' to hide. You people are all alike, ain't got no respect for nothin'. And before you get your panties in a wad, I don't mean anything against *you* when I say you people," he looked at Rose. "I mean all you government bastards, hassling honest businessmen. There's going to be an uprising, you'll see."

Opie chose this moment, the one of his owner's grandstanding, to squat and grunt, and leave an Opie size meadow-muffin on the gravel, effectively stealing Donny's thunder.

Donny walked over to the impressively large pile, kicked dirt over it and grumbled, "Damn it Opie, this ain't the place for you to take a..."

"Umm, buddy?" I said to him. "You may want to quit while you're ahead here. Step back and chill out, you're going to give yourself another heart attack."

Donny walked into his office but not before hacking out one last wad of spit while Opie lifted his leg on the front fender of Donny's pickup.

"Good boy Opie," I said under my breath, "good boy."

Gator, Rose and Donny were so far back in the salvage yard I was only able to spot them when I watched Opie lope in that direction. The three were near a white Ford Taurus that appeared to have had its driver's side door removed, front window smashed and, with the hood open, I could see the engine had been removed as well.

"Yep, said Donny, "anyplace you'd find the VIN is gone. Ain't you a real Sherlock Holmes?"

"But look here," Gator said, his chest puffed as he grinned. "Someone wrote the number on the inside of the owner's manual," he pointed it out to Rose. "See? It's kind of small but it's there on the bottom of the parts ordering page."

"I ain't got nothing to do with this," said Donny. "I didn't pull this car in, you can't..."

"Don't worry," said Rose. "We don't think you did either, we think whoever called you away brought it here."

"Hey guys," I said, walking to the back of the car and pointing the decal on the rear window. "Take a look at this. You know who has a tattoo that looks just like this? Big Kev, I mean Kevin Hale, the trainer at Dan's. Man, I trusted him, I really thought he was a good guy. When I see him I'm gonna ring his neck"

Rose was reading something on her tablet when she said, "Before you go get yourself arrested for manslaughter you should probably know that this car is not registered to Mister Hale."

"It's not?" Gator and I asked simultaneously.

"Then who's is it?" I asked.

"Joseph Douglas, M.D."

"Do we know who that is?" asked Gator, walking to her side and peering over her shoulder.

"Ask Maggie, she pulled him out of the Gulf of Mexico along with two of his buddies."

TWENTY THREE

Brit and I were seated at Rose's desk, and she was doing the best she could with the description I had given her of the man who had impersonated Donny. I assured her she would have a much easier time when she worked with Gator, who was currently giving his description of the getaway Jeep to a uniformed officer.

Rose was working with Detective McKenzie to solve the puzzle of the dead doctor, and his now infamous white Ford Taurus. I would have much rather been working with them than sitting here trying to remember what kind of shoes the Donny imposter wore. I couldn't be sure he was even wearing shoes, and told this to Brit. That statement was met with her predictable eye roll and an announcement that she needed a smoke break. I didn't blame her, my powers of observation are so abysmal I'm surprised she didn't say she was taking that smoke break at a bar.

Outside, I stretched my legs and took a respite from the arctic temperatures the acting detective demanded the precinct's thermostat be set to. I remembered a sweater I kept in the trunk of my car and was headed in that direction when Zig called my cell.

"Hey Mags, mom has a couple of tickets to see a play and asked me to go with her, but I remembered how much you liked the theatre and…"

"And you'd rather have your eyes gouged with a toothpick than go see the play," I said, my head in the trunk of my car, rummaging under beach towels and flip flops for the sweater.

"It's a musical for the love of God, a musical based on Macbeth. If I remember that play from high school, it's a three hour stab fest."

"It is pretty dark, I'll give you that. I wonder whose idea it was to turn it into a musical."

"You're in Florida Mags, it's *Florida*."

"Touché."

"Does this mean you'll go? Please say you'll go."

"I love your mom, I'd sit with her and watch paint dry, of course I'll go. Besides, who can't have a good time with your mom?" I said, shaking sand from the sweater I'd found. It was under a stack of the reusable grocery bags I always carried, but seldom remembered to use.

"Great, ok, it's this Saturday night. She'll probably hire a limo for the two of you, but if not I'll pay for a rental car for you. And she'll probably want to go to dinner first, that will be her treat, and then after..."

"After, she'll want to go have a drink somewhere."

"Yeah, probably that new piano bar by the mall."

"I'm looking forward to this, thanks."

"No, thank *you*."

When I returned to the back door of the building, I spotted Brit standing beside a small hill of cigarette butts.

"You know there's an ashtray right over there," I said and pointed to the one seated above a metal waste-can, not three feet from where she was standing.

She rolled her eyes again, which I was beginning to think was some kind of turrets manifestation, and said, "Duh."

"You know, with a little effort you could string those sounds together into an actual word. Then maybe later, when you're ready, an entire sentence."

"Ha, ha." she said.

"You do see the irony of that last one, right?" I asked.

"Look, I get it, you're hilarious. Now, if you see that old guy over there watching us," she pointed to the homeless man I'd seen on that particular corner every day that week. "He's gonna come over here when we're gone and get these. That's why I'm not smoking them all the way down, and why I'm *not* smashing them into that filthy ash tray."

"I had no idea you smoking band of brothers had such a lofty standard of hygiene. I have been put in my place for sure. You coming back in?"

"Be there in a minute," she said, and blew perfectly concentric smoke circles at a 90 degree angle.

"You'd be great at kid's parties with that."

After another couple hours at FMPD, being home and barefoot felt like a vacation.

The night's crime blog was about a woman who held up a convenience store using a red lace bra to partially cover her face. She neglected, however, to cover the name and number of her son's football jersey that she wore during the heist. Her son was also arrested at their home for allegedly robbing the Victoria's Secret store at the Bonita Springs Mall earlier that day. Her name was Bunny and his Clive, which made for the best headline I'd ever written.

I was asked by Detective McKenzie not to blog about any of the events surrounding either of the drownings until he had cleared me to do so. It was not an order, but a request. I honored that since I was hoping that Brassmonkey would become nervous at my silence, not knowing if I was on to him.

I called Pam to make sure she was OK and that her father had indeed gotten into town and was staying with her.

"Thanks for checking, yes he's here," she said. "He's resting now at home, it is thirteen hours of flight time from Cairo to Miami, not counting a five hour layover in Spain. Then, of course, the three hour drive here from the Miami airport, he was exhausted. He will unpack most of his things at his home in Sarasota, and then he will be here in the morning."

I sat in front of the television watching the news, and picked up my notebook from the coffee table and began going back over my notes. Something was nagging at the back of my head, and I was sure if I could just piece all the facts together in the right order it would come to me.

I re-wrote the facts on another sheet of paper, then cut those into individual strips, like papers in fortune cookies. And just like piecing together a jigsaw puzzle, I began arranging them in various orders. Once I had them arranged, I'd study them a bit, then rearrange them to find a pattern or clue.

When my back was sore from being bent over the table for so long, I got up and walked to the bookshelf where Captain Hornblower was swimming in to, out of, and around his little plastic sailing ship, like he was making a routine inspection.

I dropped a couple of flakes through the hole in the top and said, "You're absolutely right Captain. You leave no pebble unturned, no mast unexamined. I'll go back and work harder at seeing if Frank Preston is part of this hornet's nest, or simply a really handsome billionaire who likes to hang out all day in a sea park."

I looked at the box containing Radu and said, "Yeah, when I say it out loud it really does sound ludicrous. OK, back to the drawing board. Thanks guys, you're the best."

Before revisiting the puzzle, I went to the kitchen to put some kernels in my hot-air popcorn machine. I had just turned it on and was getting a bowl from under the cabinet when a Jaguar commercial came on the television.

Every vehicle is equipped with state of the art GPS systems that connect you to a live operator when the path ahead is not clear. You're never alone on the road when you drive the new Jaguar. See your local dealer for details.

I quickly went back to my puzzle, wrote Jaguar on one of the slips and placed it between *professor* and *diagrams.* Then I spotted the slip that read *British bug* and put them together. Jaguars are made in England and I added that on another slip. I stared at them for a moment and remembered something Rose had told me, Frank Preston had some kind of ties to a firm in England that made security devices. I wrote *Frank Preston, UK security business* on another slip, added it to the grouping, sat back and sighed.

"Rose," I said to her voicemail, "call me when you get a minute. I agree with you and Mac that Frank Preston nay have something to do with that bug in my house."

I found the broom and swept the popcorn from the floor since I had neglected to put the bowl under the popper when the Jag commercial came on. I was just attempting to the move the stove an inch or two to get some kernels that had fallen between the cracks, when my phone rang. I held it under my chin and continued pushing the stove.

"Hello?"

"Maggie, are you alright?" asked Pam. "You sound distressed."

"No, not distressed, just sweeping up popcorn. What's going on? It's kind of late, are *you* OK?"

"Yes, I'm fine. My father is not well though, he is in a great deal of pain in fact. I am driving to his home and taking him to the emergency room."

I stopped trying to move the stove and said, "Oh no, it's not his heart is it? Maybe he should call 911."

"No, it's not his heart, it's, well, it's lower than that."

"Maybe a kidney stone?"

"That was my first thought too. I just wanted to give you a face up because I know you were expecting me for lunch tomorrow. I didn't want you to worry that maybe that pesky fish-guy was causing trouble."

"Drive safely and call me as soon as you know anything."

I was sorry for Pam's father, but at the same time glad she was in a hospital in Sarasota and not here. I had no idea what to expect next. Things were getting intense now, and I didn't know from what direction the next hit would come. Better Pam be out of the line of fire until this was resolved.

My blog had some funny comments regarding Bunny and Clive, but most wanted to hear how the drownings investigation was going. Nothing from Brassmonkey, which was both a relief and a bit disturbing. If he wasn't commenting here, what was he up to? Maybe he was the Donny imposter, he was certainly at the top of my list.

I set my alarm for 5am so I would have time to go to the police department and learn what I could there, before going to work.

Then I sent a text to Gator telling him not to come and get me. I figured he needed to baby his leg after he'd scraped it on a rusty tailpipe at Donny's. I was glad when Rose insisted he get a tetanus shot, although for someone who had been through three tours of duty in Vietnam, he sure put up a fuss about going to get it.

TWENTY FOUR

I fell asleep trying to visualize Frank Preston in his billionaire's high rise kitchen, gouging eyes from fish and giving orders to have them chucked at my front door. As hard as I tried though, I could not see him doing that, nor to imagine him as some evil super villain. Yet all the signs seem to be pointing right at him. I tried envisioning him again, stroking a large white cat with one hand and speaking on a red phone with the other, and giving orders to blow something up. That seemed more plausible but yet, it still didn't fit with the man who laughed about my walking corpse episode in King Lear. Thus were the thoughts that kept me awake, tossing and turning, and staring at my alarm clock.

By five I was already leaning over the kitchen counter, waiting for the coffee to finish brewing and counting the popcorn kernels on the floor that I had missed the night before. Without caffeine, the thought of bending down to pick them up seemed insurmountable so I looked out the window instead. It was still dark, but the neighbor across the street was already watering her lawn. A large egret walked down the middle of the street like it was on parade, and mourning doves sang their soft melancholy ballads. I stared at the horizon and watched the first glimmers of dawn turn the landscape from black and white, to the soft pastels of early morning.

I finished the second cup of coffee while watching the news and pulling a t-shirt over my head. During the commercial break I put my contacts in and threw my glasses and phone in a purse. I sat on the sofa, emptying the last few drops of coffee from the cup, and tied my shoes.

It's going to be a pleasant morning with a temp of 79 by noon, reaching a high of 84 on the coast and 87 further inland by 3pm.

Expect scattered showers mostly to the east of I-75 in the late afternoon, when those clouds start rolling in from the west.

Up next, beach goers should be aware of rip tides causing dangerous and even life threatening conditions for swimmers up and down the coast from Clearwater south to Naples, especially in the late afternoon and early evening. Our own Kelly Spencer will give us tips on what to do and how to survive getting caught in one. But first, a look at today's fishing forecast brought to you by our friends at Dan's Dolphin Experience in Bonita Springs.

I turned the TV off with the remote, threw my bag over my shoulder, and by six was on my way to the downtown Fort Myers police department to meet with anyone there who would talk to me.

The first thing I heard upon entering the precinct was the voice of Detective Fergus McKenzie bellowing to one of the front office clerks, "…and don't use any other word but coffee when you order it either, I'll not be havin' one of them Nancy-boy drinks."

"The coffee maker is out," the clerk told me as she buzzed me in. "I volunteered to go to Starbucks for him because McKenzie without coffee is too frightening to imagine."

"He's that bad huh? When do you get your permanent detective?"

"Not soon enough. I mean, I like him ok, but he's an acquired taste to be sure. You gonna be here awhile? I can pick you up something too. I love an excuse to get out, and the more orders, the longer I'm gone."

"You could buy a new Mister Coffee with the money you're spending on this run."

"I know, but don't tell Mac that. So, you want something?"

"Thanks, I'd love to, but I have to be at work and in costume by nine. Bathroom breaks are challenging when you're wearing dorsal fins and a tail."

"Hahaha, gotcha'. Rose isn't here yet, she had to pick up a DUI on her way in, but Miranda is in if you want to talk to her."

"Great, thanks, enjoy the coffee run."

I found Miranda in her office doing battle with a mountain of paper, a look of surrender on her face.

"Hey Miranda, sorry to bother you, you look busy. I just had a quick question, but I can come back."

"No, it's alright," she said, dropping into her desk chair and motioning me toward the only other seat in the room. "I've got a minute, what's up?"

"Were you able to pick up any prints from that Taurus?"

"A few, most had too many layers to get anything useable. We got Gator's of course, and Doctor Douglas' off of the owner's manual, and that was pretty clean. One from the passenger side seat belt, and another on the cigarette lighter. They're being run through the national data base now, we didn't turn up any matches locally. Your buddy Rose could have something this afternoon."

"Was the doctor the original owner?"

"Yes, bought it new."

"I may be stepping out of line here, but I heard a rumor that all three doctors had holes in their hearts, what could do that?"

"You heard right. Massive heart attacks will do that. The bodies, I don't have to tell you, were not in the best of condition when the M.E. got them, but he feels pretty certain about that conclusion. The cause is one that has everyone baffled. The bodies were too decomposed to offer any real answers."

"But there weren't any gunshot wounds?"

"Guns? No, why do you ask?"

"Just curious if they could have been killed, and then dumped."

"If they were, it wasn't with a gun. All right, now I really do have to get back to this pile of horrors."

"Sure, of course, I appreciate your time. Just one more quick question please. Why is everyone being so nice to me?"

"Oh," she said and chuckled. "Sparring with you is fun so don't expect this to last, but Mac said you've been really helpful to him and we should be nice to you."

"No kidding?"

"No kidding, but I gotta tell ya', I don't think the pie hurt."

In the locker room, cooling off during my first morning break, I checked my phone for any texts or messages and realized it had gone dead. Though I was sure I had left it on the charger all night, I wasn't one hundred percent certain the charger was plugged all the way in. This was the new phone I had gotten after the last one drowned the same day I nearly had also. It came with one of those heavy ac adapters that drooped and tugged, and I made a mental note to replace it with a less Jurassic Park version.

Blowhole Bob came in just as I was about to put the phone in my locker.

"Checking your fan mail?"

"Exactly. What are you doing here? You're not supposed to relieve me till two."

Today Bob sported a t-shirt with a photo of Captain Kirk and Spock. They were *photo-shopped* to look like The Blues Brothers. Under this were knee length khaki shorts and a pair of leather sandals over black argyle socks.

"I'm looking for Dan," he said. "I haven't seen him for like, two days."

"Yeah, I wondered about that too. I guess he's out of town doing his big picture thing. If I see him I'll let him know you're looking for him."

"Thanks Sharkey, I'll go find Frances in the meantime. That broad is sharp, she could run this place better than him anyway."

"Sure she could, as long as you didn't want to have any guests or employees. I think even the animals would go on strike."

"Nah, she's alright. She comps me all my meals, and yesterday she gave me an entire key lime pie."

"You're joking, you're seriously joking, right?"

"Blowhole Bob never jokes about meringue. Unless, of course, it's on someone's face."

I put the shark head on to cover the shocked and stunned look that I was sure was my expression, and headed for the exit.

"Bye Bob, see ya at two," I said.

"Bye Sharkey, and have I told you how much I admire your tail end? Get it, *tail* end?"

"Bye Bob."

At lunch, I borrowed a phone charger from the guy working the ice cream cart and made some calls while eating my *non*-comp'd hamburger and fries in the Dolphateria.

I returned the call from Pam who said her dad did, in fact, have kidney stones and that they had used some kind of noninvasive procedure to break them up. He was waiting to be discharged within the hour and was feeling fine. So fine, in fact, that they were coming straight down here after leaving the hospital.

I called Zig's mother, Dorothy, to confirm our plans for dinner and the theater that evening. After that I left a message for Rose to call after two.

After Bob relieved me, I stopped by Dan's office before leaving for the day. His door was locked, but I noticed the key card entry panel to the right of the door and swiped it. The knob turned. I glanced over my shoulder to be sure no one saw me, and stepped inside.

The overwhelming scent of pot hit me before I had even crossed the threshold. On the corner of his desk sat an ashtray in the shape of an iguana. It held a marijuana roach that was attached to a small metal clasp. His laptop was closed and a half empty coffee cup sat on top of it along with a wadded up McDonalds wrapper. Framed blueprints of the park and lagoon hung on the wall behind his desk. Next to those, a photo of Dan on the set of the 1996 remake of Flipper standing next to the star, Paul Hogan.

My eyes were adjusting to the dim light of the office when I stepped and hit my foot on an old Army locker that was wedged between the desk and a file cabinet. It protruded enough for my big toe to find. Glancing over my shoulder again, in what was now just a reflex action brought on by guilt, I found a lock. It wasn't fastened. I thanked heaven for Dan's less than responsible nature, and opened the lid.

At least a dozen spiral notebooks, which I instantly knew would be Alden's, and as many composition books along with a half dozen sketch pads filled most of the space. I lifted the first couple of books and spotted three plastic bags, the freezer storage size, filled with what I was certain must be pot, lining the left side of the stack. An old cigar box was wedged sideways behind the books. I opened it and found a revolver inside. When I heard footsteps approach, I dropped the books back to the top of the pile and without thinking, picked up the gun and put it in my purse.

I held my breath as someone knocked, then jiggled the knob on the door. It must have automatically locked behind me because whoever it was gave up. I moved to the window and peering through a small slit in the blind, saw Bob's retreating form.

A loud gush of air involuntarily left my lungs, and I realized I had been holding my breath. I stuffed as many of the notebooks into my bag as I could without it looking like I had stuffed notebooks in my bag. I was grateful I had taken to bringing a large tote with me to work. I took another peek through the blinds, stood a moment in front of the door and looked around to see if I had left any clue that I had been there. When I was satisfied I hadn't, I slowly opened the door, stepped onto the pavement, turned to close it again quietly behind me and heard a familiar gravel voice say. "Well ain't this somethin' to see."

"Hello Frances," I said, relieved for once that it was only her and not the scary albino or even Bob. "I was knocking but Dan doesn't seem to be in."

"I thought I heard the door close," she said, with her narrow cobra-like eyes staring at my own.

"Nope, just knocking. If you see Dan, could you ask him to call?" I said, with a faked airiness.

"Do I look like his secretary to you?"

"Bye Frances, have a nice day."

I walked away as fast as I could without looking like I was fleeing the scene of a crime, put my things in the scooter's saddle bags and left in a cloud of dust. I needed to run by the store and buy pantyhose for the evening, but I wanted to read what was in those notebooks more, so the trip home was non-stop.

My hands fumbled with the door key, and I kicked my shoes off as I walked inside, anxiously grabbing the first notebook from the bag before I reached the sofa. I began reading as I sat and threw my bag on the coffee table. The loud thud reminded me that there was a pistol I'd forgotten was in there.

I debated on whether or not to tell Rose what I'd done, or just break into Dan's office again and put the gun back. Reading the notebook drew my attention away from gun matters and focused me on a new set of questions. Why was Dan hiding Alden's notebooks in an Army locker in his office along with some bags of pot and a gun? Alden's notes were tough to decipher since they were mostly scientific and medical, and I knew I'd need some time to go over them more carefully with Pam, but now was not that time. I had a date for dinner and the theater with Dorothy, and just barely enough time to get ready.

ENTANGLED by Kathleen Cosgrove

TWENTY FIVE

The limousine arrived at my home at 4:30, then drove to Shell Harbor Living to get Dorothy. She was expecting me, of course, and was seated with some other ladies on the front patio, chatting and laughing. Dorothy wore a calf length skirt patterned in a Seminole Indian inspired design of orange and turquoise, a white peasant blouse, and had accented it all with a necklace and bracelets of turquoise. She outshone me by a mile, as she always did, in my white pantsuit and coral-pink silk blouse.

Shell Harbor Living is an upscale residence for those retirees who are ready to give up the burden of maintaining their own homes, or who need a bit more assistance with day to day living. The place is posh and expensive, and the people living there are catered to and cared for by an excellent staff.

The place itself looked like a movie set, with elegant architecture, landscaping of tropical flowers and palms, and ponds with small geysers in their centers that, at cocktail hour, were part of an aquatic musical display. The limousine had arrived just in time to watch the fountains spout jets of water to the tune of The King and I's *Shall We Dance.*

Dinner was at The Turtle Club on Vanderbilt Beach. Tables set for fine dining are arranged on the sand, a few yards from the shore. Umbrellas provide shelter from direct sunlight, and guests are encouraged to remove their shoes while dining and enjoy wiggling their toes in the sand. This made my lack of pantyhose a stroke of luck, and the sand felt warm and soft under my feet. The sun was still golden and not due to set for another hour, so we would be able to enjoy the beauty of it all through dinner.

"Dorothy," I said after we'd ordered. "Have you ever heard of an actor by the name of Frank Preston?"

"No dear, should I?"

"He's one of the investors at Dan's and he's done some acting. Shakespeare for sure, but I don't know about anything else."

"He could have used a stage name. How old a man is he?"

"I'd put him somewhere around my age, late fifties, early sixties."

"Can't you just look him up with your computer? I thought you young people did that for everything."

"A, you know how I love when you refer to me as a young person, please continue to do so as often as you'd like."

Dorothy smiled and said, "I'm a generation ahead of you, which makes you young to me."

"Well thank you."

"What is B dear?"

"I beg your pardon?"

"You began your last sentence with A, I trust a B cannot be far behind."

"Oh, right, yes. Well, I did try looking him up online. You'd be surprised how many Frank Prestons there are that are not *this* Frank Preston. I cannot find this one. I'm embarrassed to tell you how many hours I've spent searching."

"That seems queer indeed."

Our server brought our bread, salads, and wine, and when she was gone Dorothy patted my hand and said, "Cupid really does seem to be at odds with you, doesn't he?"

I sighed and said, "I don't know what I did to piss him off, but yeah, he sure isn't making this easy."

Dinner was wonderful, and driving to, and getting out of, the limo in front of the theater made me feel like a movie star.

Our seats were so close to the stage I could hear Lady Macbeth's stomach rumble. I tried to enjoy the play, but around about the time Banquo's ghost began singing a blues number, I reached for the Playbill to read about the cast. I felt kind of bad for them. I imagined them at home, getting the call from their agents that they were selected for a great part in Macbeth, only to find out later that the murder scenes would be set to ragtime.

When the book fell automatically to the center page I let out an audible gasp, loud enough for the woman behind us to shush me.

"Maggie dear, are you alright?" asked Dorothy.

I couldn't speak so I held the book toward her and pointed to the actor playing Banquo, it was none other than Frank Preston.

"It's...it's...it's..."

"It's Hayden Reynolds, yes I know. I agree it came as a surprise to me too. I never would have recognized him behind all that makeup."

"Makeup," I said dumbly.

"I always thought he had a lovely voice, but it's not coming across that way with the intermittent ghostly moaning. I realize that the part calls for that at this time, but Hayden really should have been cast as Macbeth, such a waste."

"Dorothy, that's Frank Preston."

"No dear, it can't be, it really is Hayden Reynolds. Now that I know it's him, it's so clear to see."

"This," I pointed to the black and white head shot in the Playbill, "this may be five or ten years old, but *this* is the man I know as Frank Preston. And not just me, everyone thinks he's Frank Preston."

"I wonder then," said Dorothy, "if he's using a pseudonym for the theater, or if he's impersonating a real Frank Preston. Or, is Frank Preston really a person at all? In any case, it's a delicious plot, worthy of Shakespeare himself. Well, one of the comedies, anyway, those always had cases of mistaken identity. But I seriously doubt Hayden is a millionaire who likes to moonlight as a stage actor. I've known the man for years, and like most all stage actors, he scrapes by from play to play."

I wasn't paying attention, my eyes darted from the photo to the stage. I wasn't able to hear clearly, or even think clearly. This must be what happens to people when they go into shock, I thought.

"Maggie darling, are you alright? Listen to me rambling on about plots when clearly you've been set back on your heels. Would you like to leave?"

"Leave?" I repeated, barely aware of my surroundings, a buzz of white noise filling my head.

"Yes dear, we can go if you'd like."

"No," I said, shaking the stupor. "Dorothy, do you know the right people to get us backstage?"

I lagged several feet behind, once we'd reached the dressing rooms area. I purposely stood behind the rather beefy sized Macbeth, since it was my plan to surprise Frank-or-Hayden, at just the right moment.

Dorothy called to him as he signed an autograph from a young man who was gushing to the point of being annoying. Frank-or-Hayden seemed relieved to see Dorothy and waved her over, simultaneously dismissing his fan.

"Dorothy, I had no idea you were in the audience." Frank said, showing his movie star smile. "I'm delighted more than you to know to see you again."

"It's wonderful to see you too, Hayden. You played that role better than anyone I know could have."

"Alas, old friend, you and I are past our dancing days."

"If you're going to quote Romeo and Juliet, I'd prefer, *she doth teach the torches to burn bright*." Dorothy said the last line with that lilt to her voice that charms everyone she meets.

"Of course Dorothy, you are always the brightest light," he said squeezing her hand. "Tell me, did you come here alone? We could go for a..."

"Why no *Hayden,*" I said, "she did not come alone."

My entrance was made a bit less dramatic than I'd hoped, since at that moment a side door opened, nearly hitting me in the face. I regained my composure though, and stood before him wearing my most indignant expression.

"Maggie?" he asked, the color draining from behind his already powdery white makeup. He wavered a bit and I thought for a second he might actually pass out.

"I see you two have already met then," said Dorothy. "Splendid, I won't have to make introductions."

Dorothy suggested Frank-or-Hayden join us for drinks because, as she said, *one simply cannot be uncivil while holding a glass of Merlot.* I was not sure of that assessment, but I agreed because there were things I wanted to say, had to say. I just couldn't put the words in the right order without the chance to clear my head, or in the case of Dorothy's Merlot theory, to soothe it.

Sitting across the table from Frank-or-Hayden at the Piano Key lounge, I was struck by how much he didn't look at all like a millionaire with twinkly eyes, or even a super villain. He was a mere mortal, with his hand caught wrist deep in the proverbial cookie jar.

His head was bowed and mere inches from the rim of his wine glass. He was silent for a long time and then said, "How bitter a thing it is to look into happiness through another man's eyes."

"No," I said, "we're not quoting Shakespeare, not now, not tonight."

"I agree," Dorothy said, in her most soothing tone. "Maybe you should start somewhere near the beginning, like when you were asked to assume this identity."

Frank-or-Hayden raised his face to hers, eyes wide and asked, "How did you know?"

"Because it's obvious of course. I'm sure Maggie will agree," Dorothy said, turning to smile at me. "Don't you dear?"

"Oh yeah, sure," I said, "totally obvious. Saw it coming a mile awa…wait a minute. No, in fact, I didn't. Who the hell is Frank Preston if it's not you? And who are you by the way?"

Frank-or-Hayden opened his mouth to speak but I stepped in first and said, "And don't you dare quote Macbeth, or Hamlet or Doctor Seuss, just speak with your own words."

"Walter," he said.

"I beg your pardon?"

"Walter, my name is Walter. Walter Kojick. My stage name is Hayden Reynolds and Frank Preston is who I am paid to be right now."

"Well, who in hell is the real Frank Preston? Oh God, is he dead? Did you kill him? Oh Lord, you killed poor Frank Preston."

"No, no, hang on, I didn't kill anyone, I'm an actor. The only thing I murdered was that song tonight. I promise, someone is paying me to be this character, this Frank Preston."

"Who?"

"Now, that's the tricky part. I don't know."

"This is getting quite good, isn't it?" Dorothy said, beaming.

"Look at your grin," I said to her. "It's positively devilish. You're enjoying this way too much. Are you sure you didn't know anything about this?"

"Noooo," she said from somewhere deep in her throat, "but wouldn't that have been delicious?"

I turned back to Frank-or-Hayden-or-Walter and said, "You may want to start from the beginning, like Dorothy said."

"God, I've been wanting to tell someone for so long now, but after Alden died I was afraid for my own life."

"I think this calls for another bottle," said Dorothy, signaling to our server.

"That doesn't sound like a beginning to me," I said. "That sounds like someplace you need to back up from."

He sipped his wine, looked at me, then threw the glass back and downed the rest.

"I got a call from someone, someone calling themselves, and you're going to think this is really weird, this guy called himself Brassmonkey. *Mister* Brassmonkey, in fact."

"So far this is the only part of your story that doesn't surprise me," I said. "Go on."

"Mister B, and I'm going to call him that because I refuse to keep saying Brassmonkey."

"I don't blame you, continue."

"So, Mister B says he's got a great role for me, it's a long term gig, two to three years. Naturally I'm thinking I've landed a role in Le Mis or Phantom. I asked him why he didn't call my agent. That's when he explains what the job really is. He says he needs someone to play the role of a C.E.O., someone to go to board meetings and ribbon cuttings and, you know, stuff like that. He says the real C.E.O. is a recluse, hates to go out in public, but doesn't want the stockholders to get nervous so, he gets someone to play him, just in public. The rest of the time he handles stuff by phone, or emails or something."

Frank, (I had decided for the time being that was the name I was going with), poured himself another glass of wine, titled the bottle over my glass and raised his eyebrows. I nodded yes, he filled my glass, and continued his monologue.

"I wasn't sure about taking it, just, you know, it sounded too weird."

"Until he mentioned money?" I asked.

"Yeah, the offer he made, sorry to use a quote here but, it was one I couldn't refuse. I mean, literally, I couldn't refuse. It wasn't just the dollar figure, which was insanely high, but it was the way he did it. He said the money was already in my account. He just somehow, in the middle of talking to me, put the money in my account."

"He knew your banking info?"

"He knew *everything* about me including how maybe I didn't always report every single dollar I made to the IRS every year. I mean, the guy had dates, dollar amounts. Hell, I don't even keep those kind of records of my *own* finances."

"He threatened you?"

"Yes he threatened me. So when I say he made me an offer I couldn't refuse, well, I couldn't refuse."

"You mentioned Alden."

Frank looked smaller in that moment, his shoulders receded into his sport coat looking for all the world like a teenager in his father's suit. His eyes moved away, not fixed on anything in particular and he said, in an even more shrunken voice, "Alden came to me. He was worried about what he was being asked to do, told to do, to the dolphins."

"Like experiments?"

"He said they wanted him to tag them with something that acted on their echolocation system."

"What did you do?"

"I wanted to go to Dan first, or course, but I wasn't sure what his role was in any of it, or if he knew about me. That I wasn't, you know, really Frank Preston. I thought about it for a few hours, but before I said anything to him, I got a call from Mister B. Ironically, he was calling to tell me to keep an eye on Alden. I told him about the conversation I'd had with him. He said to leave it alone, he'd take care of it. The next day, well, you know what happened."

"God Frank, Alden really was murdered then."

"Yeah, it looks that way. I made a call to the cops. I didn't tell them my name, any of my names," he made a small chuckle here. "After that, well, I was hoping they would come in and investigate or something."

"They didn't?"

"If they did, I didn't know about."

"Have you talked to Mister B since then?"

"Yeah, but it's always just park business, and not even that. More or less just telling me to keep an eye on everyone. He's got me in a penthouse on Gulfshore Blvd in case anyone follows me, probably. I stay there when I'm not at the park or going to other meetings."

"Nice."

"You'd think so wouldn't you? But it feels like a prison to me. I'm afraid to go anywhere. I'm doing this play because, well frankly, I didn't think anyone would see it. It's a pretty bad production and besides, I'm only in one scene, and in makeup."

"You're picture's in the Playbill."

"Yeah, I didn't think that one through."

"So now what?" I asked.

"I don't know. I keep hoping the cops will come to my rescue because I gotta tell you, I don't see any way out of this for me."

"Ahem." Dorothy cleared her throat and we both turned to see her quietly grinning at the two of us.

"Don't you see Hayden dear, the play's the thing. To borrow from Hamlet, the play's the thing wherein we'll catch the conscience of the king. Or in this case, to simply catch the king."

After the three of us put together a tentative plan, Dorothy and I left in the limo. Since the night was warm, the driver opened the sunroof. The smells of fresh sea air mingled with Dorothy's jasmine scented perfume, and it soothed my senses and allowed me to relax for the first time in weeks. It was that, and all the wine, off course. The idea that I would be working with Frank, who felt far more approachable now that he was neither a hot shot billionaire nor super villain, may have also contributed to the headiness of the moment. I lay my head back and closed my eyes, willing myself to live in the moment. The wreaking havoc and letting slip the dogs of war would come tomorrow. This evening was itself, enough for now

ENTANGLED by Kathleen Cosgrove

TWENTY SIX

Although I had a late night, I was up hours before the alarm, too excited to keep my eyes closed. I was anxious to get to the park and see how Frank would go about implementing the plan we'd hatched the night before, but first I had some calls to make.

The last one on the list would be to my friend Shelby, on the west coast, since the time difference meant it was the middle of the night to her. However, at just barely 5:15 my time, she called me.

"I don't know who you're dealing with over there, but they must have your phone tapped," she said.

"Why, what's happened?"

"After spending the better part of two days tracking down anyone who might know something of those dead doctors, I go to my car tonight and found the passenger side window smashed and a note on the seat. Get this, the note reads, *next time it won't be just a window*."

"God Shelby, I'm so sorry, I never meant for..."

"Are you kidding me? That's the most exciting thing that's happened to me since the time we nearly got arrested at the Tennessee State House, remember that one?"

"Uh, yeah, of course I do. We had fake IDs and sat in on a sequestered vote. I still don't know how we avoided jail time on that."

"Maybe because they're a bunch of rat bastards, like whoever it is you're dealing with there."

"I'm really sorry though. I'm honestly shocked at how dangerous this guy is."

"Don't be, I think it means we're on to him. I didn't call the cops about the window, because I'm sure whoever did it was someone off the streets that got paid a few bucks to do it."

"You're probably right."

"Don't you wanna know what I found out?"

"Of course, yes, tell me."

"So, you may not know this, but 32nd street, that's the name of the naval base here, anyway, it's enormous. There's over twenty thousand personnel here, and that's not counting the civilians. Finding this someone was definitely a needle in a haystack proposition. Not counting the fact that military men can be such arses when it comes to telling women anything, most of them have such a Neanderthal mentality."

"That's your anger toward the ex talking, isn't it?"

"Could be—maybe—probably. OK, I'm still bitter. Anyway, I found someone at the Point Loma station, that's where the subs are. They train in anti-submarine warfare, clearing mines and lots of stuff I'd have to screw someone to find out. Anyway, this guy knew those three doctors you pulled out of the Gulf. They worked at Loma, and this guy was part of their team."

"What were they working on?"

"The guy couldn't tell me, most of the stuff here is classified, even the stuff you can find on Wikipedia. In any case, he wasn't free to say. Anyway," she continued. speaking quickly, "he says someone, and he didn't have a name, came here about a year, year and a half ago, looking for experts on sonar, anti-submarine warfare, and medicine."

"That's some specialized field, whoever it was must have already known there were men there who would be experts in all three," I said.

"Yeah, *were* being the operative word. Back in the day when they used to work with dolphins, they had a bunch of scientists who were trained in all three. That operation is no longer going on, so all those guys went to other departments or retired."

"Does your contact know who the guy was, that was trying to recruit them?"

"Not by name, guy called himself Brassmonkey. Funny, huh? But he did say the guy was a Brit, and that he was with a security firm looking to find new means to make ships less vulnerable to pirates, which by the way, is a huge problem on the open seas."

"Brassmonkey again, this fits in perfectly with some of the other stuff that's been going on here. Does your contact know if the three doctors took this guy up on his offer?"

"He had no doubt they did since all three left shortly after and my guy never heard from them again."

"And this guy wouldn't tell you exactly what they were working on?"

"No, he's still commissioned, I was lucky he told me as much as he did."

"You don't think he's the one who made a call about your snooping around?"

"Could be, but I talked to a lot of people down there, it could have been anyone."

"OK, well, now you're in danger until I can get this figured out. Can you go away for a while? I'd ask you to come here, but that's like jumping from the frying pan to the fire."

"Not to worry, the station is sending me to London. I'm doing a piece on George, the new heir to the throne. I'm scheduled to leave in a couple of days. Stay in touch with me though. I'll text you the number for my English phone."

"Will do, and of course if you hear anything more you'll call right away?"

"Of course, and be safe Maggie, I'd be pretty pissed off if anything happened to you."

When I hung up the phone, I was more convinced than ever that Big Kev was, if not Brassmonkey, at least an accomplice of his. That San Diego submarine connection was too much to be coincidence. But how, or why, all this was happening still had no common thread, at least none that I could see right now except Dan's place. Alden was murdered just days after those three divers died, and everything I'd seen since I'd come to Dan's, pointed to that place being ground zero for something. But what? And where was Dan? No one had seen him in days. I liked the big goof, and I was worried something bad, something very bad, had happened to him.

Gator showed up at seven next morning, and I was glad. Things were getting dicey, and I didn't want to be by myself. I invited him in for coffee since I wasn't ready to go to Dan's just yet.

"How's your leg?" I asked, pouring him a cup.

"Ahh, it's fine, just a couple of stitches, nothin' to talk about. So, what are we doin' today?"

"We? I asked, sitting next to him with my own cup.

"You don't think I'm gonna' leave you unprotected with all this happening around you, do ya'? No ma'am, I said I'd look after you, and that's what I'm doin'."

"You know, the most trouble I get into is when I'm with you, don't ya'?"

"Yeah," he admitted, a bit sheepishly. "But I figured you'd probably be getting in some kind of trouble with or without me, so best I'm around. I mean, if you think so too. To be honest, since I can't fly anymore, I don't know what to do with myself."

"You'll be flying again, and I'm sure it will be soon, too. How's the VA treating you by the way?"

"Oh, they're great, best group of guys in the world."

"Wonderful. And just so you know, we all need a little help. I don't admit it to anyone, probably don't have to, but I'm getting a little absent minded. It happens when you get to be sixty. I'm not bummed about it or anything, but, you know, we've all got something."

"Miss Margaret, you're as sharp as a tack. I won't let anyone say any different. You just have too much going on at one time, that's all. Don't you even think twice about it."

"Thanks, but in the meantime, I'll post sticky notes on my corn popper."

"Huh?"

"Long story. Anyway, we should probably head over to Dan's now for the big announcement. Have you ever seen Hamlet, Gator?"

"Nah, I tried one of them Shakespeares, but never could tell what anyone was sayin'."

"Doesn't matter, this will be better. Finish your coffee, we're going to a play."

Pam called while I was on my way to the park. She said it was compelling, which I took to mean urgent, so I told her to meet me there. She had her father with her and I arranged for them to be admitted to the park and to meet me at the Dolphateria. That was where Frank and I agreed to meet before his big announcement at 10 am.

When Gator and I got there, a little after 9:00, Frank was already there, minus his usual entourage. His blood shot eyes over puffy lids told me he'd had about as much sleep as I. I poured him a fresh cup of coffee when I fixed my own.

He stood and shook hands with Gator while I made the introductions.

"You've got a bodyguard?" Frank asked.

"I do today, where's yours?"

"Jorge? He's waiting outside. I'm surprised you didn't see him when you came in."

"Oh, we came in through the back, the employee entrance."

"Of course. Well, I asked him to wait outside. The last thing I need right now is my bodyguard finding out I'm a broke, part time actor."

"You're an actor?" asked Gator.

"Oh, yeah, I suppose I should fill you in," I told him, "but not now, I see Pam coming and the guy with her is no doubt her dad."

"Who's Pam?" asked Gator.

"Again, I'm afraid that'll have to wait." I turned to Frank and said, "And you better get into position. Have your people gotten the word out to the press?"

"Yes, and my fellow investors," and here he used little air quotes, "think my big announcement is that I'm franchising this place."

"Have you heard from you know who?"

"My phone's been ringing nonstop, a hundred emails, and I saw a car out front of my condo this morning. The guy inside had binoculars trained on my window. I took the service elevator to the back and got a cab. I had the condo's concierge get a note to my driver to pick up Jorge and meet me here."

"OK, well, nothing can happen to you here, there's the press, staff and us, oh and Jorge."

"I'm not worried," he said, the veins in his head bulging and his jaw clenched.

"No, I know you're not," I lied. "I'll be out there in a minute."

He left, and I watched Jorge walk with him to the area that had been set up for the press conference. As they were leaving, Pam and her father came in and I waved them over to where Gator and I sat.

I'm not sure why I expected Pam's father to be wearing a pith helmet and khaki vest, but I was surprised to see him looking well dressed and not carrying a spade. He was near my age with the same great smile as his daughter, deeply tanned, and as ruggedly built as you would expect someone who spent most of their time outdoors digging in the dirt.

After the introductions I said, "Bill, I'm pleased to see you looking so hale and hearty. Your daughter said you only left the hospital yesterday."

"The procedure was noninvasive, quite remarkable really. You see, they use sound waves, extracorporeal shock wave lithotripsy. It's quite fascinating, it was developed in Germany by a physician..."

"Can we skip ahead a little?" I asked. "We have a thing to get to."

"Oh, certainly, my apologies, of course. Well, you see the extracorporeal shock wave lithotripsy, and we can just call it ESWL to make things move ahead more quickly, uses focused, high intensity acoustic pulses that..."

"I'm sorry Bill, this sounds like it might take more time than we have right now. I wonder if we could reconnoiter after Frank gives his press conference. Would that work for you both?"

"Of course, of course, yes. You should handle the more pressing matter first," Bill said, and chuckled at his own pun.

"I've got to introduce Bill to Blowhole Bob," I told Gator.

"Blow what?" Gator asked and then said, "I know, you'll have to tell me later."

The four of us, myself, Gator, Pam, and her dad, Bill, walked to where the ad-hoc stage had been set up. We watched as two of the groundskeepers arranged folding chairs and a mic there.

There wasn't much press present, and we didn't think there would be with such a late announcement, but we had planned on that. We didn't need very many, even one would do. Frank's message would be broadcast, and that would legitimize it. There'd be no denying it, and no going back. Everyone knew that this man was Frank Preston, and the weight of all that that meant would be enough.

Less than the usual number of gray suits were there, and only three of the other investors. Again, it was irrelevant. Frank Preston's money controlled 86% of the operation. The others were there for window dressing, and to be able to call it a corporation. At least, that's what Frank had gleaned from the many conference calls and meetings he attended where he posed as the real deal.

The staff, which included myself, and my guests Pam and Bill, assembled with the press in front of the stage. Frank took the microphone and, looking very much the CEO and master of the moment, smiled at the assemblage and the half dozen flashing cameras. The weather was on our side as the baby blue cloudless sky created the perfect counterbalance to the storm that was about to blow through Dolphin Dan's.

"Ladies and Gentlemen of the press and valued members of the Dolphin Dan's family," he began. "May I extend a most sincere welcome and thank you to all of you for coming here on such short notice."

His performance was brilliant. He showed no signs of the fear and agitation I had witnessed earlier. He commanded the stage with the presence of a general speaking to his troops.

"First, I wish to congratulate every person who made this venture a reality. Speaking on behalf of myself and all the principals involved, I can honestly say it has exceeded our wildest expectations. You are to be congratulated on a job well done. Please join me in giving yourselves a hand."

ENTANGLED by Kathleen Cosgrove

He and the others on stage applauded as did the staff. It was at that moment I caught sight of Blowhole Bob and Frances coming at breakneck speed from the direction of the Dolphateria. I had the most horrid mental picture, for just a moment, of the two of them as a couple emerging from their clandestine, romantic rendezvous. I shuddered and put the thought as far from my mind as I could without the aid of alcohol or a lobotomy.

"Now, to the matter at hand," Frank continued. "After careful thought and some outside consultation, it is now my intention to steer the park onto a new course. Much will be the same, but even more will change."

The press made notes and the staff looked at one another and shrugged shoulders or whispered, except Frances who looked as though she wanted to murder someone, anyone, but probably Frank.

Frank went on, "Dolphin Dan's will no longer showcase Dolphins as performers, or even as swimming companions. We will be working closely with The Florida Fish and Wildlife Department, as well as with the folks at the Saint Petersburg Aquarium, on releasing the ones we have, in the most responsible and humane way possible."

"What?" Frances' guttural shriek was loud enough for the entire assemblage to turn and stare at her.

Frank ignored her and continued speaking, and all eyes turned back toward him.

"Going forward, Dolphin Dan's will be a rescue, rehabilitate, and release facility."

There was dead silence initially, but from somewhere behind me I heard the sound of one person applauding and turned to see Big Kev slowing clapping his hands. Soon, a few more of the staff applauded, while the press made notes, took photos, and spoke into microphones attached to video cameras.

The few gray suits on stage appeared shocked and bewildered, but when Frank turned to them, applauding, they followed suit, halfhearted though it was.

Just to put your minds at ease, let me state emphatically that no one will lose their jobs. In fact, I plan on hiring a staff of additional professionals to aid in rescuing and treating any injured marine life we can accommodate. There will still be areas of the park open to the public such as the indoor aquarium, and areas to view those animals we cannot safely return to the wild. I also plan to redesign the gift shop into an educational venue for school groups to come and learn about the wonders of the sea, with emphasis on our own Gulf of Mexico. So, as you can see, lots of exciting changes in store for Dolphin Dan's, and a renewed dedication to the Gulf, to the life that call it home, and to the people of Southwest Florida."

A few of the press shouted questions, but Frank advised them that completed press packets would be mailed out within the week. He left the stage, and I saw a reporter attempt to make her way to him but was thwarted by Jorge. In less than five minutes, Frank, Jorge, and their driver left in the car that had been parked next to the stage. I knew where he was going, but no one else did. It was going to be fairly easy for him to hide among the hundreds at Shell Harbor Assisted Living.

TWENTY SEVEN

Pam, Bill, Gator and I went back to the Dolphateria. I had Alden's notebooks with me and I wanted to go over them with her. We made casual conversation over coffee and pastries. Bill filled us in on his latest project in Turkey, and Gator asked him thoughtful and interesting questions.

"Gator," I said, "I had no idea you were so knowledgeable about archeology."

"Yeah," he said. "Once I flew some folks to a dig in Utah. While I was there I got bored and read a lot of the books they had. Since then, it's become a kind of a hobby."

"If you don't mind then, I think I'll let you and Bill have a chat. I want to go over something with Pam," I said, pulling Alden's notebooks from my bag.

"Hang on Maggie," Pam said. "First I want dad to tell you about his procedure."

"Now, seriously? Because, I don't want to sound rude, but I've got something pretty import…"

"Maggie, *this* is really important, trust me."

"OK, sure, go ahead."

"Dad, show her," she told her father.

Pam pulled a notepad from her purse and pushed it across the table toward her father. Bill opened it, and turned it at an angle so that I could see.

"Does that look at all familiar to you?" Pam asked.

"What am I looking at?" I asked Bill. "Because it has some of the same diagrams I saw on those napkins."

"Exactly," said Pam, "tell her dad."

"Well, Maggie, you remember earlier when I mentioned the ESWL. I said that was the abbreviation for Extracorporeal Shock…"

"That's OK dad, just tell her what the doctor said," Pam told him.

"Yes, of course, now, before the procedure to break up the kidney stones, the physician, hmmm, what was her name Pam?"

"Doctor Hunt dad, but that's not German to the conversation."

"I was going to tell her she meant germane but decided it wasn't worth it, so I said, "Please Bill, do go on.""

"Yes, now Doctor Hunt was very kind and drew these diagrams to show me a bit of the science behind the process. As soon as she began drawing these sketches, our Pam here recognized them as being similar to the ones those poor unfortunate men drew and left behind."

"Yeah dad, now tell her about what Doctor Hunt said about the modifications."

"Of course, yes, I was just coming to that. Now you see, Pam asked if there were other applications for this technology, if it could, in the wrong hands, be deadly. The Doctor admitted that, though she had never heard of any instances of such a thing happening, she couldn't completely rule out the possibility."

"Pam," I said, "look at these notebooks. They belonged to the veterinarian who died a couple weeks ago at Dan's. I just glanced through them, but I'm pretty sure I saw something that looked like the other sketches we saw."

While Pam read through some of the pages she found relevant, the rest of us sat silently. We stared at the top of her head as she read, as though answers would appear there. After nearly thirty minutes she looked up and stared at us, her face a mask of incredulity.

"Break out your aluminum foil hats people, they are actually trying to weaponize the dolphins here."

We left Dan's, with me blowing off my shift in favor of trying to prevent more murders. I figured that qualified as a legitimate excuse. The four of us agreed we'd reconvene at *3 Fisherman* in North Fort Myers. It's a restaurant situated on the Caloosahatchee River and has a spectacular view of both the water and the city skyline. Our thinking was, if we had to be somewhat covert, we may as well do it with a view. Besides, Bill remembered dining there previously and that they offered something called gator bites. He thought that might appeal to his new friend of the same name.

Once we'd been seated and placed our orders, Pam explained what she thought might be the answer to the drawings we'd seen. Although I couldn't follow all of it, and Pam wasn't even sure she understood half of what she'd read so far, I understood enough to know that was almost certainly how those Navy doctors, and probably Alden, died

I surmised that whoever Brassmonkey was, he'd found a way to use the dolphin's echolocation or sonar, combine it somehow with that shock wave that was used on Bill to break up his kidney stones, and operate it remotely to kill people by giving them heart attacks. Pam was also guessing that this thing worked underwater and may, in fact, *have* to be underwater for it to work.

"Do you think Professor Ballanchi figured this out too?" I asked Pam.

"I'm sure of it," Pam said. "It's probably why he was killed. Someone bugged your home, so they probably had your phone bugged too. We pretty much told the killer where to find him."

"So," I said aloud, just basically to put things in order in my own head. "This guy who calls himself Brassmonkey hires those three doctors to help him come up with this killer dolphin weapon thing. Then, once they'd done it, he uses their own device to kill them."

"Probably to keep from having to pay them too," added Bill, clearly wanting to help dissect the theory. "He may have promised them millions for all we know."

"That's true," added Gator. "And used the guy's car to tail you. He probably wanted to see if you'd lead him to anyone else who might be a threat."

"Yes," said Bill, "it's probably why he hasn't killed you yet."

We all stopped talking and looked at him. "Oh, sorry," he said. "But you had to know if he wanted you dead he'd have probably already done it. It's not like he's adverse to murder. No, he's most likely hoping you'll help uncover any other threats besides the professor."

"Dad," said Pam. "I think you might be scaring Maggie."

"No," I said, "he's right. It's not like I hadn't thought of that already. Plus, the dead fish on my door, and yours," I said to Pam, "is his way of telling us we're next."

We all sat there quietly to let that sink in.

Finally Gator spoke up. "What are we worried about? All we gotta' do is catch him first. Whoever it is, they'll have to make a move quick now that Frank, or Walter I guess his name is, said he's gonna let those dolphins go. I mean, the dude didn't spend all that money building a park and murder four people just to let it all swim away."

"I think Big Kev, he's head trainer at Dan's," I said, "may be an accomplice, but if he knows too much, then he's probably next on Brassmonkey's hit list."

"Do you think Dan is in on it?" asked Pam.

"If he is, or was, he may already be dead," I said. "No one has seen him for days. You know what guys? I'm going to try calling him again, and then I want to call Rose, tell her about the notebooks and Pam's read on them."

Our table was on the patio but I needed privacy, so I went outside to make the calls. I saw that, while my phone had been on vibrate in the bottom of my purse, I'd missed a call from Rose. I returned that one immediately.

"Why do you even have a phone if you're not going to answer it?" she asked, using her annoyed voice. "It's good I've got the ability to track it. What are you doing up on the river?"

"I'm at *3 Fisherman* with Gator and Pam and her…"

"Oh, I've heard about that place. Is it good?" Her voice changing to happy the way it always does when food is mentioned.

"I don't know, I haven't gotten my food yet. But listen, I've got something to tell you. It looks like someone's been tagging those Dolphins at Dan's to be, well, promise you won't laugh and think I'm crazy."

"Too late."

"Alright, well, here goes. I got hold of some of Alden's notebooks, they were hidden in Dan's office. Oh by the way, I took a gun from there too."

"I didn't hear that last part, but give it back to him."

"OK, but Dan's missing too, I think, and there's pot in there, but anyway, that's not the important part."

"Maggie, don't make me have to arrest you."

"Yeah, OK, forget all that. Anyway, in those notebooks, along with Pam's dad's kidney stone drawings, she figured out that they were tagging the dolphins with something that sends out some kind of sonar/shock wave pulse that can give people heart attacks. She's pretty sure she saw some notes about a remote controlled way to activate it too."

"Killer dolphins, with kidney stones. I'll quit before I have to take that to Mac."

"No, sorry, I was rambling. The dolphins don't have kidney stones, Pam's father does—did. That's how we knew about the ESWL or something like that. Anyway, it's how they cause heart attacks. That's how they killed those divers and Alden."

"Who is they?" Rose asked, sounding like she believed I was on to something.

"That's still something I'm trying to figure out, but I have a friend in San Diego who says someone who called himself Brassmonkey hired those divers."

"Him again. Mac got some help with the Feds Cyber-crime Unit to track that guy down. But there's more. The reason I was calling you, is to tell you we may have something on our old buddy Frank Preston."

"Really, what? Because I've got another story to go with that."

"If it doesn't involve kidney stones or killer dolphins I'm all ears."

"Well, first tell me what you were gonna say."

"All right, you know that company that I told you about that Preston used to own in England, the security firm? Well, turns out they were working on a program of using live operators for the GPS systems installed in cars. Want to know the cars that just had them installed this year?"

"Jags?"

"Since it's the same firm that made the bug we found in your house, it looks like someone at Preston's company, or Preston himself, could be our Brassmonkey. I guarantee he sent your professor off into the Glades to get ambushed. Now it sounds like we finally have a motive, although why Preston wants to rig up killer dolphins is something he's gonna have to tell us when I arrest his fancy ass."

"Well, you can't really arrest Frank Preston for anything."

"Why the hell not? I can and will bring him. Mac is getting a warrant from a judge now."

"Because Frank Preston, at least the man we think is Frank Preston, is really an actor by the name of Walter Kojick."

"That's it, I want all of you in here, now. I want that guy Walter, Pam, her father, and whoever else is with you."

"Gator."

"Not Gator. Shit, oh alright, Gator, and anyone at all who knows of anything related to this case to get themselves here and within the hour."

"OK, but we haven't gotten our food yet. I'll bring something to-go, you want anything?"

"Are you kidding me?" Rose asked, her tone rising to frantic level. "We're investigating murder, several murders, conspiracy, probably some kind of animal rights violations and God only knows what else before we're done."

"They have shrimp tacos and cheese grits."

"All right, bring me that. Be here in an hour and a half, no more."

Gator swung me by my house where I picked up my scooter since he had an appointment at the VA later that afternoon. He was in charge of carrying Rose's to-go order, and my bag that contained Alden's books, and Dan's gun. I reminded him, in the words of

Clemenza from the Godfather, "Leave the gun, take the cannoli, or in this case, leave the gun, take the books."

Our merry band of misfits arrived at the Fort Myers Police department en-masse with me on my scooter, Gator in Lucille, and Frank and Dorothy in a limo. Pam and Bill arrived in what looked like an oversized version of an eight year-old girl's toy car but was, in fact, a VW Bug with a rainbow colored paint job, hubcaps designed to look like fluffy white clouds, and a plastic unicorn hood ornament whose horn was the antennae. A sign on the back read, *Follow me to Fantasy Island Frozen Yogurt, Little Captiva.*

The rest of stood, slack jawed, no one wanting to be the first to speak.

Bill said, when he joined us, Interesting design for a car isn't it?"

"Interesting, yes, is that yours?" I asked.

"No, it belongs to a friend. He's got a date and he wasn't sure if the lady would be OK in this. It's a first date, so he's being overly careful I guess. He wants to make the right impression, so I let him borrow mine."

"Yeah, that was probably a good call," said Gator. "He never would have made it to date two in that thing."

The rest of us walked around the thing, admiring the audaciousness of it, until Rose came out to meet us in the parking lot.

"Everyone inside is asking if the circus came to town," she said. "That is until some smart ass says, *no it's just Shelton's usual gang.* Look at you all," she waved her hand around the area where we stood. "A bright orange scooter with a basket on the front, another car older than my daddy, a stretch limo, an oversized Barbie car, and I don't know what the hell that is," she nodded her head in the direction behind us. I turned and saw Sabina, of all people, in her modified German tank, parked in the space behind mine.

"It's good I follow you here," the old crone said, walking toward us on her toothpick legs. "You keep my Radu and not take him to the dolphins. That's a' what I tell the police here, you steal the dead and keep them in you house."

"Sabina," I told her, "this really isn't the best time to…"

"What's this about stealing bodies?" Rose asked. "I can't deal with stolen dead bodies, not today. I cannot go to Mac and say, oh, see that group out there, the ones that looked like they're setting up a carnival? Well, one of them stole a body and that old lady in the land yacht wants it back. And then he'll ask me, who are those people? And I'll have to say, those are the same people I asked to come here and help with the investigation."

She threw up her hands and shook her head. "I'm just going to quit now and go sell tacos out of one them trucks."

"I turned to Sabina and said, "I'm sorry, it's been really crazy for me the past week, but I promise, I really, really, really promise and cross my heart and everything, that I will take Radu to the dolphins tonight. Just, well, if you could just go home, and I'll call you tomorrow when I've done it, OK?"

She pointed her index and middle fingers at my eyes and said, "You do this tonight like you say, or the curse of Sabina will be with you for ten years. Ten years you will have this curse."

Then she turned and got into her car. We all silently and watched her as she backed up, again without looking, and drive onto the highway. Cars honked at, and swerved around, Sabina, a tiny bit of white fluff over the dashboard. Once she was out of sight, everyone turned to stare at me.

"Oh, don't mind her," I said. "She's just a little cranky because her husband is still in a box next to Captain Hornblower."

The stares continued so I said, "Well, are we going inside or what?"

TWENTY EIGHT

We were back in the Feng Shui conference room, most of us afraid to speak in case we were being watched through two way glass. As far as I knew, none of us had anything to hide, but despite the balanced ying and yang of the room, we were all on edge. Not everyone was nervous, though. Dorothy could have been waiting for a hair appointment for all the stress she exuded. She made small talk with Frank, who admittedly did have the most to be worried about.

When Detective Fergus McKenzie entered the room, the rest of us joined Frank in an overwhelming sense of fear and dread. The big Scot said nothing as he took a seat at the head of the table. He carried several folders under his arm and set them down firmly and deliberately, like maybe he was counting to ten and restraining himself.

"My people," he began, "the Scots, are very good at suspending disbelief. We've got a monster living in one of our lochs for nearly two thousand years. Then there's the ghosts, every castle, moor and petrol station's got at least three. Hell, we even consider there's sic' a thing as a decent Englishman, that's how good we are at believin' the impossible. So, I've been willing to accept this legend of an actor playing at being a hotshot CEO, and spending millions of dollars to build a park. And that in the park there are dolphins trained to give people heart attacks." He looked at me now, "And phantom cars that chase tour guides who dress up as sharks. Well, you see where the monsters and ghosts are easier to swallow."

I opened my mouth to protest but Rose, who was seated next to me, suggested I hold my thoughts for just a moment. She suggested this by kicking me in my shin really hard. I got the subtle message and closed my mouth, except to utter a small whimper of pain.

"And just so you don't think your tax dollars are *all* bein' flushed down the jacks, you should know that, hard as it is to believe, some of us who like to think of ourselves as *professional* detectives have been working on this too."

"You," he pointed to Frank. "We know you are not Frank Preston of Preston Securities Inc., and do you want to know how we know that? Because, and this may sound like science fiction to the rest of you, the police have ways of looking these things up. That particular Frank Preston died ten years ago at the age of sixty seven."

I opened my mouth to speak again, to say how I had tried to look that very thing up, but before I could say anything Mac pointed at me.

"And you, did you ever stop to think that a place with millions of dollars sunk into it, might have security cameras? That key card you've been usin', the one that dinna' belong to ya'. That every time you've used it, we can see it was not the assigned card holder, who, by the way, we have in custody for felony charges. No, turns out it was you, an undercover journalist determined to get herself and everyone she knows thrown into jail."

I whispered to Rose from the side of my mouth, "Oh, I didn't think of that."

"So now," continued Detective McKenzie, "you're all gonna be givin' statements to my officers. You're gonna be tellin' 'em everything you know, and I mean everything, even you my dear," and here he nodded to Dorothy. "But if you'd be more comfortable at home, I can send officer Shelton to take your statement there."

"That would be lovely," said Dorothy, "but I believe I'll wait for Walter." She squeezed Frank's arm. "We arrived together."

"We'll make sure he gets home," Mac told her. He turned to Rose and said, "Please follow Mrs. Callahan home, take her statement there."

"Yes sir," Rose answered. Then to Dorothy she said, "Whenever you're ready ma'am."

It took Pam, Gator, and I nearly three hours to give our statements to the police. Bill was only questioned briefly, and was waiting for the rest of us when we emerged from the station.

"Looks like the police will be taking it from here," Pam said.

"I don't like it," Bill said. "That Brassmonkey villain is sure to know he's got to act soon, and getting rid of witnesses will be his top priority. You do know that your life is in imminent peril, correct?" he asked me.

"Sorry," Pam said. "Dad's used to dealing with corrupt officials and shadow governments. He doesn't realize not everyone," and here she emphasized the last word looking directly at her father, "enjoys hearing such a blunt presentation of facts."

"Oh dear," said Bill. "I apologize. Pam is correct, my manners have become reprehensible."

"He's right though," said Gator, pushing his ball cap back and wiping the sweat from the back of his neck with it. "I mean, he could be right, probably is, you know, right."

"Well," I said, "We'll just have to get him before he gets us—me."

"How?" all three asked at once.

"Gator, is Foxy Lady seaworthy enough for a short voyage tonight?"

"Yes," he said. "As a matter of fact, I was just picking her up from the marina after my V.A. appointment. She's not reliable enough for the open water, but here and there along the coast, bays, inland waterways, she'll be fine."

"Don't take her out of the marina, we'll just board her there, is that ok?"

"Uhmm, yeah, sure, but where we goin'?"

"The lagoon at Dan's of course. You remember I told you I saw someone working with the dolphins, letting them in and out of the lagoon through a gate?"

"Yeah."

"I'll bet he's using them to bring smuggled goods into Dan's. I saw someone take a small boat behind the waterfall and not come out, there has to be a way to get into Dan's from there."

"That's ingenious," said Bill. "He can use dolphins to find whatever contraband he's unloaded, probably dropped in moderately shallow water by a larger vessel. Or, no, that's not good, a low flying plane. They would fly under the radar over open water."

"Then they bring it to Dan's," I said. "Through that gate, and the Coast Guard or Marine Police would never see a thing."

"And, of course, he'd want an undetectable way to kill his disloyal partners, witnesses, law enforcement, anyone really," said Bill. "The whole thing is genius."

"Dad," Pam said, "you're doing it again."

"Oh yes, sorry, terrible business," said Bill, trying to sound apologetic. "But really, you have to admire the ingenuity of it."

"No, I don't really think I do," I said.

"But the concept is brilliant, he went on. "Why you could bring drugs, guns, if they were light enough, all sorts of contraband, and it's all done with dolphins. And then, the technology that went into the shock wave, well, that was pure inspiration."

"Bill," I said, "not now."

"Of course, I won't say another word."

"What time should we meet?" asked Gator.

"How about seven tonight," I said. "Pam, you know more about dolphins than any of us. Bill, you know more about guns, if that's what they're bringing in. It would help to have you there too."

"Wouldn't miss it for the world," said Bill.

"Of course I'll come," said Pam.

Gator gave us the address for the marina where Foxy Lady was docked, and Bill and Pam agreed to pick me up so I could help navigate them there.

"Will you still have the dream car?" I asked Bill.

"Yes, I'll have it till tomorrow morning. I'm afraid we'll have to take it on this evening's clandestine operation."

"Fabulous," I mumbled under my breath. "We'll be just like James Bond, but if he were gay."

"What?" asked Bill.

"Oh, I said, I hope we don't get asked for ice cream on the way."

TWENTY NINE

What Gator referred to as a marina, turned out to be a half dozen slips behind a tackle shop on Bonita Beach Road, the colorfully named Master Bait and Tackle. The dock was missing several planks so I was glad we had just enough daylight to avoid me falling into the waterway.

The smells of bait mixed with diesel fumes and the aroma of fried food coming from the Fish House restaurant a few yards away. The sun was turning dark orange, and seagulls dove for the small fish that swam near the waters of the dock. It was summer, but I pulled on my sweater against the slightly cooler evening air.

"Hello," said Gator, "and waved his arms at us from his position in a smaller than I expected boat. "Did you make sure you weren't followed?"

"Gator," I said. "We drove here in a car that people took pictures of when we stopped at traffic lights."

"Oh yeah, I see your…"

"There's a sign on the back that asks people to follow us."

"Yeah, I forgot about…"

"Children lowered their windows and begged us to stop and give them ice cream."

"Gee, that must have been…"

"The driver in a pickup truck in the next lane was distracted looking at us and rear ended a cop car."

"It's a miracle you made it here at all with all of…"

"And Bill had promised his friend we'd stop and pick up his wacky, wavy, inflatable, twirling arm thing, look." I said and pointed to the thing poking out of the backseat. "It was on a pole and we couldn't remove it, so it just sat next to me with its arms waving out the window at everyone."

Gator had nothing more to say, or try to say, so we just stared at the ridiculous car in silence until I got a good look at the boat we were about to sail off in.

Foxy Lady's seaworthiness seemed questionable at best, and it looked a bit small to my untrained eye for all of us. I questioned Gator about this.

"So, how many people can this thing hold?"

"Oh, not to worry, I've carried as many as five people on her before. She'll be fine."

"OK, but I want a life vest."

"Sure," he said, digging around under seat cushions and pulling out the bright orange vests. "Oh, damn, looks like I've only got three. We won't be legal."

"I'll go inside the tackle shop and see if they have any for sale," I said. "I'll be right back."

I did not find a life vest but got something I thought would suffice.

"Are those arm floaties?" Gator asked.

"Yes, but they'll fit me if I don't have to push them past my elbows," I said.

"I don't know," he said, "not sure it's legal."

"I'm not sure anything we're doing tonight is legal," I said.

"She's right," added Bill. "I'd wager that if we don't get ourselves killed or sunk, we could face some kind of jail time if caught."

Everyone stopped what they were doing to look at him.

"Sorry again," added Pam, "he's used to looking at worse case sceneries."

We turned to stare at *her* this time, but only for a moment when I said, "Come on Gator, let's crank up this old girl and get going, I don't want to miss anything."

Gator backed out of the slip as Bill untethered the restraining rope and hopped in. We tugged along slowly out of the waterway, and by the time we were in open water, the sun had set.

It is truly remarkable the number of stars one can see when light pollution from the city fades. They appear to multiply before your eyes exponentially until there appears to be no distance between them. If the ancients thought the stars were gods looking down on them, the sheer number must have felt both comforting and intimidating.

Besides staring at the heavens, I kept a constant vigil on the deck of Foxy Lady. It's not as though I didn't trust Gator, but based on our previous adventures, I was at least cautious. We were nearing the outer edges of Dan's lagoon, and I was happy to note that Foxy Lady was not taking on water, which in itself, felt like a small victory.

We instinctively became quiet, speaking to each other in loudish whispers. For me, this would normally be troublesome because of my less than perfect hearing, but because of the way sound travels on water, I was able to hear everyone pretty well.

"Now what?" asked Gator.

"Now we wait," I said.

"For what?" asked Pam.

"She doesn't know," said Bill.

"I don't know," I concurred.

Gator cut the engine and we watched the lagoon in silence. Only the waves slapping the side of the boat, and the growling of my empty stomach, broke the stillness.

"I hear something," said Pam.

I held my breath. Gator had already cut all lights on the boat, but I ducked my head in a kind of reflex movement and noticed everyone else had done the same.

A pinpoint of light on the far off horizon could have been anything. A lot of boats sail the Gulf of Mexico, and at the distance we were from the light, it was impossible to tell if it was a dingy or a cruise ship. The sound, however, was much closer. A slow and rhythmic splashing and rolling of water that I knew to be the familiar sound of swimming dolphins.

Pam leaned to the side and gently slapped the side of the boat. Nothing happened. She waited a couple of minutes and did it again. A few moments after the third attempt, we saw a fin near the boat, then two. The dolphins swam close to us, intermittently raising their heads from the water. One made a trilling noise, which startled Gator who was standing, and he lost his balance. I grabbed him by the shirt tail to steady him.

"Look here," said Pam. "Dad, get your phone and give me some light over here."

Bill used his phone as flashlight, and while this sent one of the dolphins away, Pam had a firm hold onto a rope that was attached to the dolphin nearest her.

Bill followed the rope line with the light, and we could see a small buoy, about the side of a cereal bowl, at the end. When he moved the light at an angle, we were able to see three more of the small buoys.

"Keep the light back there dad," Pam said, "I'm going in. Gator, you hold the rope here," she motioned to a metal ring that was attached, at the other end, around the dolphin's snout.

"Pam, no, are you crazy?" I asked. "There could be sharks in there."

"No, the dolphins would have behaved in a far more agitated fashion. I'm not going to go far."

She went over the side, her father following her with the light. The dolphin dove and swam out of sight, despite Gator's hold on the rope. I used my own phone to try and track it. The buoys didn't sink though, and we could follow the animal's path by watching them. It was headed to the lagoon.

Bill's light was still trained on Pam, who was pulling on rope as she swam back to the boat. Gator grabbed the rope while Bill helped Pam up the ladder.

"I was able," she said, panting and catching her breath, "to get one of the ropes loose. She's still pulling about three more."

Pam was shivering and Gator found a towel and some blue tarp to wrap around her.

"There's a box or something attached to the rope, hard to tell. Can you pull it in?"

The rope was tied around a container the size of a shoe box. It was wrapped in some kind of silicone, and the rope not only went around but through the container. There were no markings on the outside except a small button sized object that flashed red.

"What's that light?" asked Gator, "you think it's a bomb?"

"It could be," said Bill, picking the thing up and holding it to his ear. "But I don't think so. The distribution of weight indicates something densely packed and even, like papers. I would guess money. Although this," he pointed to little flashing red light, "could very well be a homing beacon, in case it were lost or dropped."

"You can get all that from just holding it?" I asked.

"It's kind of what I do," he answered. "Now, I hesitate to say this knowing my propensity for being the voice of doom, but I'm almost certain someone has noticed this missing and will be able to track it to…ahhh, yes, I believe they are coming now."

No sooner had the words left his mouth, when the noise of an approaching boat engine grew louder, coming from the direction of the lagoon. In the next moment, a searchlight moved across the water until it stopped directly on us.

"Gator," I said, "now would be a good time to get the hell out of here."

Foxy Lady's engine took longer than I would have liked to turn over, but when it did, Gator accelerated so quickly the rest of us were thrown back onto our seats, or in my case, onto the deck.

The boat slammed heavily onto the water, and with each pounding I became slightly airborne, clutching at the railing to keep from flying out. Bill and Pam were closer to the center, but in the narrow space of the small boat, I was forced onto the port side, holding on for dear life. My hips, back, and head alternately hitting the deck over every wave.

"Their speed is outmatching our own," said Bill. "It seems inevitable they will eventually close the gap."

"Seriously Bill," I said, "you've really got to work on that." To Gator I said, "Hurry Gator, they're gaining on us!"

"I'm going to try for Master Bait," shouted Gator, "but if I can't get there in time, I've got a plan."

"Really?"

"No. Wait. Maybe, hang on tight," he said, and swung Foxy Lady around sharply, the boat leaning almost completely on its side. Water came over the rail in a gush, and the spray knocked me down, sending me onto my knees.

"I told you to hang on," Gator shouted.

When he got closer to the approaching boat, he made another sharp turn, but this time I was still on my knees on the deck and instead of falling, I slid to the center where Pam and Bill caught me.

"What's he doing?" I yelled to them.

"I think he's trying to capsize them in our wake," answered Bill, "but I'm confident that plan will fail. There isn't enough…"

Bill's prediction of doom was cut off by the sound of a gun firing.

"Hit the deck," screamed Gator, and he turned Foxy Lady back to our original direction, away from the pursuing boat.

Still on my knees, I was thrown onto my back and slid to the opposite side of the boat. My mouth, open in a scream, filled with a gush of sea water. When I hit the side I bounced back onto my stomach, choking and spitting, and grabbed for the rail. I pulled myself up just in time to hear gunshots, and to see Gator turn Foxy Lady in a near ninety degree angle. My hand slipped with the hard crash of the boat going over its own wake. I landed onto the deck and slid across it again, this time though, in the direction of the boat's twin engines. I was helpless to stop the momentum, and groped helplessly for something to grab onto. I was seconds from sliding overboard and into the whirling blades when hands grabbed my wrists and pulled me away. Pam had my arms, her father had her waist, and together they yanked me away from what would have most likely been a very ugly death.

More gunshots, and this time I heard one hit the boat. Where it landed I didn't know until we decelerated so quickly it was as though Gator had applied the brakes. Another shot, and I was certain I heard the sound of the bullet rush past my ears. I covered my head.

Foxy Lady was now dead in the water and the pursuer's boat came along side. A voice over a bull horn said, "You've got something of mine and I want it back."

I picked up my head and squinted past the other boat's searchlight.

"Frances?" I asked, "Is that you?"

"You have to be kidding me," Frances said. "It cannot be that idiot woman."

"Frances?" I asked again.

I was astonished at what her being there meant.

"You can't be—no—it's impossible—you're not—are you Brassmonkey?"

She looked at her companion, who nearly glowed in the moonlight, and said, "Listen to her, how can anyone that stupid cause me so much trouble?"

The giant albino, who held his rifle military style across his chest said, "Can I shoot her?"

"What?" I said. "No, no, you can't shoot me. Tell him he can't shoot me Frances."

"No Bobby, I don't want you to shoot her, not yet."

"Yeah Bobby, see?" I said. "Frances doesn't want you to shoot me, put your gun down."

I turned to Pam and Bill, and whispered, "Her sniper's name is Bobby. Bobby, what kind of name is that for an assassin?"

"I doubt his mother knew he'd grow up to be a hired killer when she named him." Pam whispered back.

"Well, you'd have thought he changed it when he went into the henchman business"

Then to Frances I said, "What do you want me to do Frances? Because if it's the bundle of money you want, I can toss it over, well not me, because I don't toss well, but Gator or Pam..."

"God, for the love of God, please stop talking. It's all I can do to stop from shooting you myself," she said. "First, shut up, second, you're gonna help me get the rest of my bundles ashore. Since that no talent actor sent for Fish and Wildlife to get my dolphins, I have to get it all in tonight."

"Well, technically they're not really your dolphins. You're Frances the Dolphateria lady, and he's Frank Preston as far as everyone else is concerned. And besides, dolphins aren't slaves, you can't own them, they're..."

The hammer on Bobby's gun clicked, and I dove for the deck, covering my head.

"Wait," Pam shouted. "I'm a marine biologist, I know dolphins. Since you seem to have already killed off most of your associates in that field, you could probably use my help with getting the rest of your cash ashore."

"True, don't shoot that one Bobby. The rest you can kill and dump like usual."

"No, that's not how this is going to play on," said Pam.

"Out," I whispered to her, "play out."

"Right, this is not how it's going to play out," said Pam. First you let my father and my friends go, then I will help you."

"Fine," said Frances. "We'll take you back to the lagoon. The rest of you can wait there while your friend helps us get the remaining bundles in. I've got a couple million in cash, heroin, coke and, well, it's not your business, just follow me to the lagoon."

"Foxy Lady is dead," said Gator, "you killed her."

"All right, come aboard."

"In there, with you?" I asked.

Then I turned to Gator and said, "Are you sure Foxy's dead? Maybe we could row in, do you have oars?"

"Get in the damned boat or I honestly will shoot you myself," said Frances.

Gator climbed in first and helped the rest of us onto the cramped boat. Bill held the package of cash and I had my bag with the notebooks and phone. I wanted to slip my hand in and dial 911, or Rose, but Frances never took her eyes off of me.

Once we were aboard, I noted how the boat dipped significantly. Gator, Pam, and Bill were still wearing life vests, and I had my arm floaties. Since Frances and Bobby were not wearing any, I thought sinking might be to our advantage. I looked around for something to make a hole in the bottom with, then realized that I was not in an 18th century wooden ship and considered other ways we could take on water.

"So, while we have some time," I shouted to Frances over the noise of the engine. "Tell me something, why Brassmonkey?"

"It was my nickname in the service, the guys said I had more balls than any of them, and I did. But even so the brass, those pricks, didn't allow women in anything I was qualified for. No subs, no seals, nothing, just because I was a woman."

"You were Navy?" I asked.

"Naval intelligence, sixteen years. No matter how smart, how qualified, how much better you were than a man at anything, those bastards would never let you get past your lack of testicles. I finally had enough, left the Navy, left the whole damned country. Started my own intelligence firm in England, the best in the world."

"Well, that's really something. So, you proved that a woman could be as good, if not better than, a man."

"God, you are even more stupid than I thought. Why do you think I hire actors to be me, to be Frank Preston? Because the world still won't take women seriously."

"I hear ya'." said Pam.

"Not now, Pambo," said her father.

I kept my eye on the sea level which was only a foot or less than the boat railing. Every time Bobby slammed us over a wave, we took on more water. Frances had the gun trained on me and although she swayed slightly on the jolts, she remained steady. She may have had a bullet with my name on it, but I had to admire her sea legs.

My hopes of sinking before we reached shore were, in fact, sunk. Bobby idled the boat through the gate and behind the waterfall.

Behind it was a twenty or thirty foot wide beach of hard packed sand in a relatively large cavernous area. The area was horseshoe shaped, with a rock type wall on three sides, and the waterfall concealing it from the lagoon. Though I was surprised at what I saw, I was even more surprised to see who was there.

Dan, Big Kev, and a woman who may have been Miss GiGi, but since her eyes and mouth were covered in duct tape, I couldn't be sure. They were seated on the ground, backs against a metal door, and from what I could see, tied together.

Both Dan's and Big Kev's mouths were also covered in duct tape, though not their eyes. The closer we got, the surer I was that the woman was Miss GiGi. I was more scared for her than for myself. She appeared unconscious, slumped against Dan, who wore a terror filled expression. Big Kev stared at Frances and I could see the rage in his eyes.

So, I thought, Big Kev was not in cahoots with Brassmonkey. I was glad, I liked him.

"What's this about?" I asked. "What are they doing here?"

"Insurance. After that half-baked actor pulled his little stunt today, I had to move things forward quickly. Letting go of these dolphins would set me back a year or more, and I've got people who are not willing to wait. I get my bundles, these guys go free. If

I don't get my bundles—well, see that door back there? It opens and the whole place floods."

"Oh, the pools," I said, "and that's like a dam. You open it for the dolphins to get in and out?"

"Right. You're still and idiot, but yeah, you're right."

"And the dolphins, they killed your doctors and Alden?"

"Ah, and here we are, back to moron," she said.

I looked at Dan who was shaking his head and nodding it toward France, his eyes bulging and wild.

"Now you two," Frances waved her pistol at Bill and Gator, "you stay here. Bobby, tie them up, then wait for my signal."

"Bobby threw a rifle over his shoulder, stepped out of the boat, and was waist deep in water. He used his thumb to motion Bill and Gator to do the same. I watched as they joined Dan, Big Kev, and GiGi.

"You're staying with me," Frances said, her hand on my shoulder as she pushed me down onto to the seat. "I need to make sure this one," her head tilted toward Pam, "does exactly what I tell her."

When my butt hit the seat, I landed on my bag and noticed that it felt less like notebooks were in there, and more like there was a gun in the bag. Gator obviously misinterpreted my earlier Godfather reference and I wanted to hug him for it.

"Good," I told her in my new found confident tone. "I had no intention of leaving Pam alone with you anyway."

"God, if I do get to shoot you," said Frances, "it'll be the highpoint of my life."

I watched Gator and Bill join the others on shore. Bobby yelled at them to sit. The noise seemed to startle GiGi and with her head raised she looked at Gator and made a muffled scream. Gator lunged at her and yelled, "Jackie!"

Bobby hit Gator in the stomach with the butt of his rifle, and I watched my friend double over and fall. GiGi screamed again, this time trying to cover Gator with her body.

"Wait," I said to no one in particular, "Miss GiGi is Gator's ex-wife, Jackie?"

With that, Frances moved the engine's throttle, throwing me once again onto my bag. I didn't mind though, the thought of my butt covering my gun which would be soon covering my butt, gave me hope.

As the three of us, Pam, Frances and I, made our way back out of the lagoon I moved close to Frances and said, "What did you mean I was an idiot when I asked if the dolphins killed those men? I saw Alden's notes."

"Because you can't get a dolphin to cooperate, can you miss scientist?" she said to Pam.

"That's right," said Pam. "There've been all kinds of attempts to use dolphins as weapons but they are too independent to be reliable. Those doctors came as close as I'd seen anyone before though. My father was right, it was genius."

"But the sonar weapons exist right? I mean that's how they died?"

"Of course, but it wasn't the pea brain dolphins, it was me. It's still a good weapon if used properly, so it wasn't a total waste."

A light flashed briefly in front of us on the horizon and Frances accelerated.

"I can still get rid of anyone who gets too close," she said. "I'll just do it my way. In the meantime, the dolphins still bring in the cash, literally and figuratively and drugs. Tonight's score is more than enough to pay for that park, everything after that is all profit."

We were moving fast and the six dolphins traveled with us, jumping in the boat's wake or swimming alongside.

"Throwing dead fish at our doors wasn't very high tech," I said. "It doesn't sound like anything some fancy super villain would do."

"Again, stupid woman, that wasn't me. That was the other idiot, Dan. It's why I had to get him out of the way. He was making too many reckless moves, him and the Iranian, Kevin. That one got too nosey."

Something green and fluorescent glowed in the water just ahead of us, and Frances slowed the engine to an idle.

"There's the marker," she said, then stood and blew the whistle suspended from her neck.

Several dolphins approached. It was hard for me to tell how many but I guessed at four, and I watched as they jumped and dove.

"You," Frances said to Pam. but pointing the revolver at me, "make sure they get the bundles."

Pam slapped the side of the boat as she had done previously, and two of the dolphins swam toward her. They poked their heads from the water expectantly, and Pam took fish from a well in the side of the boat and threw them to the animals who squeaked, moved their heads in a nodding motion and dove again.

While Pam repeated this process, I plotted how to either get the gun from my bag, flood the boat, or somehow send Frances over the side. It was while I was contemplating all that, that I saw the familiar dorsal fin of my old friend Kate approach the boat on the side where I was being held by the point of a gun.

"What are you doing out here?" I asked her. "You're not supposed to be a part of this right now."

"Who are you talking to?" asked Frances, who then spotted Kate. "That one's useless," she said, took aim and fired twice at the dolphin.

"Stop," I yelled and grabbed for my bag.

Just as I had my right hand on the gun in the bag, I heard a crack, saw a blur of movement as Pam lunged for Frances, and felt a searing pain go through my left arm. Then a feeling more powerful than pain overcame me, the fear of seeing Frances taking aim at my head, blinded me to anything else. Instinctively, I raised my own gun, and without much of an aim, fired in her direction.

The force of the gun was unexpected and I lost balance, falling backwards and over the side, into the deep blackness of the Gulf. I fell hard onto my back, and it felt more like hitting pavement than water. The wound in my left arm would have made staying above water impossible had I not been wearing the arm floaties.

The pain in my arm, surprisingly, subsided a little and I feared I knew why. I was probably going into shock. I dipped my face in the cool water in an effort to stay alert.

There were more gunshots, this time hitting the water. One came close enough to send a splash of water into my face. Frances was hurt, she was doubled over, but she wasn't dead, she was much worse, she was enraged.

I realized then that the fluorescent pink of the arm floaties made me an easy target. I pulled them off, gently sliding the one over my bleeding wound, opened the air valves with my teeth and let some of the air escape. The effort it took to do this had the effect of time moving in slow motion. I managed to reseal them, and held them under water with my right arm. My head slipped under, I gulped in salt water, and choked it out

I watched helplessly as Pam wrestled Frances, but the image was distant and out of focus. I forced myself to stay conscious by moving my uninjured arm in a swimming motion, whispering to myself, *don't black out, don't black out*.

I saw Frances hit Pam with the butt of her now emptied gun. Pam fell and didn't move and I watched in horror as Frances reloaded her pistol and took aim at my friend.

In a matter of seconds, a rush off water and dorsal fins moved past me and toward the boat, hitting it with a force so hard that it nearly capsized. It sent Frances overboard. She fell on the side opposite of where I was. I tried paddling toward where I saw her fall. I felt like I should try to rescue her, but I was unable to anything but bob up and down helplessly.

I moved in and out of a dreamlike state. Blackness, water, and then a sensation of something hitting my head jolted me awake. A rope was within my grasp, and the distant sound of a voice urged me to grab hold of it. I didn't want to turn loose of the floaties in my hand, they were keeping me alive, but my left arm wouldn't move.

"Grab the rope, grab it," Pam urged.

I couldn't lift my head enough to see anything but the snake-like rope, and in a moment of blind faith, I opened my hand, let the floaties, slip away and reached for it. I gripped it with a strength I thought I'd lost and let it pull me through the water. I was alongside the boat when her hand grabbed at the back of my shirt and pulled me up and over. I fell on my face and turned to see Pam, her head bleeding, fall onto her back.

"I couldn't risk it," she said, panting, and out of breath. "Going in after you. If I passed out in there, we'd have both drowned."

"Frances?" I asked.

"Shot, bleeding, overboard, lost her from view."

"Pam, are you going to black out?"

"I think I might, what about you?"

"No, I'm OK. Hang on, you're going to be fine. I think…"

"I'm pretty sure one of us has to…" Pam started, then her voice trailed off.

I put my fingers to her neck and her pulse was there, weak, but beating. I pulled my t-shirt off to make a bandage for her head and used its long sleeves to tie it tight enough to keep it in place. I elevated her feet using the bundles of money and drugs she had pulled over board. I was dizzy and losing my balance. I knew I had to stop my own bleeding. I pulled the laces from Pam's sneaker and made a kind of tourniquet for myself. It was only barely effective since I was using one hand to tie it. I crawled to the front of the boat, unable to walk, the darkness overtaking me. I prayed I could hold on long enough to start the boat's engine. I turned the key, the engines sputtered, then stopped. I lay my head across the wheel, the pain in it, and my arm, so excruciating that I told myself, if I could only close my eyes for a moment, just to sleep for a moment, I could get some relief. Just a little relief, that was all I wanted. It was then I remembered Frances telling Bobby to kill the hostages if he didn't hear from her.

Stay awake, get to them or they'll all die, I thought, and then everything went black.

A far off sound of static woke me, and it took me a moment to recall where I was. I began to cry when I heard what was, to me at that moment, the most beautiful voice in the world.

"This radio is as old as a hemorrhoid on a dinosaur, how do you expect to…OK, OK, I'll use the bastard."

After a loud tapping noise he said, "Frances Preston, this is detective Fergus McKenzie of the Fort Myers Police. Bring your boat in now. The marine patrol is on its way to your location to escort you in."

"Mac? It's me, Maggie, I'm about two miles west of the lagoon at Dan's. Send help and hurry please, my friend is badly injured."

"We're on our way. Turn the lights on, there should be a wee switch near to the radio."

I found it, flipped it up, and red and green lights shone on the front of the boat. I flipped the switch next to it, and white light illuminated the interior. I turned to look at Pam, who was still unconscious but breathing, the bleeding had stopped. I remembered Dan and the rest of the hostages, and felt a sense of panic.

I shouted, "And get some people to the lagoon too, there are people in danger there and…"

"Maggie, chill out," I heard Rose's voice say through the speaker. "That's where we are right now, they're safe, they're all safe."

I began to sob uncontrollably.

"Rose, Rose, I'm so happy to hear your voice. You saved them, us, you—uhmm." The lights appeared to dim, I felt dizzy, and slipped to the floor.

"Rose? I think possibly I'm bleeding to death"

THIRTY

Dave's band, dressed in sarongs of wild floral patterns, was finishing the last chords of their cover of John Denver's Calypso, when Frank moved to the stage. The crowd applauded and cheered, even me with my arm in a sling. The day was straight out of a Chamber of Commerce brochure, with deep-blue cloudless skies and enough of a breeze to keep everyone comfortable. The print-press gathered in front of the stage, their photographers on the ground, gear bags strewn around them like shells on the beach. The broadcast media were stationed behind the rest of us, their video cameras trained on the stage, after their return from wandering the newly renovated park, shooting B-roll footage.

I leaned into Rose who was seated next to me and asked, "So, how was dinner? Where did Mac take you?"

"I'm not going to gossip with you about this," she said.

I remained quiet, waiting for her to change her mind, like she always did.

"We went to Harpoon Harry's. He remembered me sayin' I liked it."

"That's so sweet. But what's going to happen now that the permanent detective has come out of his undercover status? Is Mac going back to Brooklyn?"

"No, he's staying. Howard decided not to take the job after all, he's going to customs. After he busted Marty on possession and helped uncover the operation here, they made him an offer he couldn't refuse."

"Are you going to fill me on any romantic details?" I asked.

She gave me the same look Frances did just before she shot me. That reminded me to ask Rose about her.

"How's Frances doing?"

"She's still recovering, but prison hospitals are notoriously under budget, so they'll probably put her in with the general population soon. Good thing you're a horrible shot, you just got her in the shoulder. Still, if that dolphin hadn't alerted our guys to her, she'd have gotten away. She managed to get herself to Gator's boat you know."

"Yeah, that's what I heard. Good old Kate, she's the one who found her. I'm glad she's going free, Kate that is, not Frances. I hope that witch stays locked up forever. You know she had Alden chip all six dolphins with something that shocked them if they went past some perimeter the divers set up. That's what they're doing this week, removing the chips, then they'll be released. What about the giant albino assassin?" I asked.

"Tried swimming away, rip tide got him. He's either drowned, shark food, or on his way to Mississippi via the gulfstream. He's not the kind of guy who blends in, if he's alive, they'll pick him up."

"Did you know that Miss GiGi was actually Gator's ex-wife? Isn't that wild? What are the odds? I love it that they're togeth…"

I stopped talking when I saw Frank step up to the center of the stage to speak.

When the applause died down, Frank took to the microphone and introduced Charlie from the Saint Petersburg aquarium.

"On behalf of all the staff at Saint Pete Aquarium," Charlie began. "I want to thank everyone who made this possible. We never imagined, in our wildest dreams, that we would ever have a facility like this to operate from. Our promise to you, the citizens of Florida, is that we will always do our best to uphold our mission of, rescue, rehabilitate and return all the marine wildlife in our care. And we promise to provide the best in education and prevention, through the generosity of the Florida Fish and Wildlife who will coordinate those activates here."

Frank took the microphone again and introduced Gator.

"Gary Brooks, or as most of us know him, Gator, will be volunteering his services as helicopter pilot to bring injured animals here from all over the state."

A loud round of applause put an embarrassed smile on Gator's face. I saw Miss GiGi, or as we now knew her, Jackie, beaming at him with pride. He left the stage and she greeted him with an embrace. They took their seats down the row from me, holding hands. Their daughter Terri smiled so broadly I thought her face probably hurt.

When the ceremonies were over the guests were treated to a tour of the facility, which was now more a hospital than a park. Pam and Kevin were speaking to the group in front of the manatee rehab center, and I thought they looked a little cozy. I smiled at her and she winked back, confirming my take on their relationship status. I gave her a thumbs up and moved to where I saw Blowhole Bob creating balloon animals at the turtle exhibit.

"Glad you decided to help out today Bob, you're right, the folks love you."

"Thanks Sharkey, gotta say I've missed your tail."

"Thanks for being so predictable Bob, catch ya' later." I said and waved to Rose who was watching the people coming and going from the gift shop.

"Give it a rest," I told her. "I know it's your hobby, but the cashiers can spot the shoplifters. Come on, let's go to the Dolphateria, I want some froyo."

The tables inside were full so we took our deserts to one outside.

"How's it looking for Dan?" I asked her, stirring the hot fudge in my Dutch-chocolate and coconut mixture.

"He's getting probation and time served. He really was mostly clueless, he's only copping to possession."

"Good," I said. "I know the aquarium will be as glad to have him back as much as he will be to get here. He's goofy as hell, I'll grant you that, but he loves these animals."

"Did you know the confiscated money is going to the city who's using it to pay to keep this place open?" Rose asked.

"Yeah, Frank told me," I said. "He said it belonged to drug cartels. They were moving it into the U.S., and going through some other thing Frances set up to hide it from the IRS."

"Yep, there's literally billions sitting in offshore banks.

"Do you know how much they recovered?" I asked.

"Nope, that's confidential, but you saw enough to realize it's in the millions, right?" said Rose, tossing her empty cup. "Not sure of the street value of the drugs, that stuff gets destroyed pretty quick, but I'm sure it was in the millions too. Some Columbian drug lord is gonna have a bad night's sleep."

"So, the dolphin release is next week, are you coming to it? It's private you know."

"I know, and yeah, I'm coming."

"Are you bringing Mac?" I asked, smiling too big I guess, because she gave me that homicidal look. I took a different tact.

"Did you notice Pam and Kevin are a couple, and then there's Gator and Miss GiGi, and you and Mac and me and..."

"It's a little like one of them Shakespeare comedies, isn't it?" she said. "Where everyone pretends to be someone else, and the most unlikely people pair up at the end."

I looked at her, stunned. The woman never, ever ceased to amaze me. I guess she read my mind because she said, "What, you think just because I'm a cop I don't appreciate good literature?"

I wanted to say something but wasn't sure what, so I hugged her, wondering how I could have missed noticing her sentimental, sensitive side. She was an enigma and I had failed to see it. I hugged her again.

"If you tell anyone else though," she said. "I'll cuff you and leave you by a canal full of gators."

It was release day for the dolphins and I had arranged for Gator to take me out to the Gulf in Foxy Lady to watch from there. I needed some privacy, I had Radu with me and I was, at last, going to keep my promise to send him off to his great reward. Once we were in position, a hundred yards or so from the mouth of the lagoon, Gator cut the engines and we waited.

"Sure feels a lot different now than it did when we were in this same spot last month," Gator said. Nothing in Nam came close to what I was feeling that night. I was so worried about you—well, and the others of course. And then finding Jackie and afraid I was gonna lose her again. So much for my brain to process that..."

"But you held it together. You were brave and strong and smart and...I don't think we'd all be here today if it weren't for you."

Before he could answer, a cheer rose from the crowd at Dan's and we turned to see the amazing spectacle behind us.

Dozens of dolphins were headed our way, toward the lagoon. Once they reached an area just beyond where Gator and I were anchored, they leapt, splashed, and as far as I could tell, were there to greet their brothers and sisters waiting to be released from the lagoon. They reminded me of the crowds you see at airports, families waiting for returning soldiers.

I cried with joy when I watched the six in the lagoon do the same. They were going home. Somehow they knew they were going home and somehow they communicated that across the ocean miles.

"There's never going to be a better time than now Radu," I said as I took the box from my bag. "It's time for you to go home too. I must say, though, that I've kind of enjoyed our little chats, one sided though they were. I'll make your goodbyes to Captain Hornblower."

I waited until I spotted a dolphin swim about five feet from out boat, then dropped the box into the water.

"Hope one of you guys knows the way to the Blest Land," I hollered to the spot I'd last seen a dolphin fin.

When I turned to speak to Gator, I saw his eyes widen as he pointed to the sea and yelled. "He's got it, one of them dolphins. I swear I saw it dive for the box."

"What, really? I strained my eyes to catch a glimpse of the falling gilded box but it was too late. What I did see, however, was one of the dolphins with, and I would never swear to it in a court of law, but I was pretty sure I caught a glimpse of shining beads on its back.

"Gator, you don't really think that..."

"Today, I'll believe anything."

"Yeah, me too Gator, me too."

Another cheer went up from the crowd and we saw the six dolphins from the lagoon make their way to the open sea.

The celebration of the family of dolphins, of their loved ones returning home, was breathtaking. The joy was evident in their leaps and squeals. We stood there for a long time, watching them swim, literally, off into the sunset.

I looked at Gator, tears rolled down his face. I grabbed his hand and said, "Freedom Gator, you fought for freedom again, and look, you won."

EPILOGUE

"You sure you don't mind if I stop calling you Frank?" I asked, snuggling into the crook of his arm. "Walter is nice, and less super- villainy sounding to me."

"I like being Walter again," he said. "No more gray suits following me everywhere I go."

He stretched out his long legs to rest on the coffee table, wiggling his toes still covered in the black formal socks of the day.

"Speaking of going," I said, untangling myself from his arm. "I'm heading to the kitchen for that pie I picked up today. You want some?"

"Has it got whipped cream?" he asked.

"Of course, it's coconut."

He grinned and I watched his cat's eyes crinkle when he said, "Then may I suggest bringing it with us in there?" he motioned to the bedroom.

"That depends, are you going to say something romantic to me by Shakespeare?"

He took my hand and, leading me to the soft light of the open door said, "Of the very instant that I saw you, did my heart fly at your service."

But here's the joy, my friend and I are one.
William Shakespeare, A Midsummer Night's Dream

ENTANGLED by Kathleen Cosgrove

ABOUT THE AUTHOR

Kathleen is a native of Miami, Florida and currently lives in Nashville, Tennessee. Visiting Southwest Florida often to visit family, helps her to reconnect with her beach roots and spurs her creative spirit.

Entangled is her second Maggie Finn novel. Her short stories are published in several anthologies. She also performs as a comedic storyteller in venues around Nashville.

She is currently working on the third Maggie Finn novel, Entrapped, as well as a collection of her humorous essays.

ENTANGLED by Kathleen Cosgrove